The Quiet Ang Moh

For and in memory of my father, Edmondo Guler 1929-2014. Det här är bara början på en ännu större resa.

For my sister Bianca, and her family—you were there when the story began.

For the Ang Moh crew (they know who they are).

For the common people of the little red dot on the map—the red dot also known as Singapore. The little red dot that for many years was my home.

For all who have stepped out of their comfort zone into the light, and followed their dreams.

Last but not least….for all who dare to speak their mind.

There is no such thing as an end, only the fear of the end itself.

To be honest is easy
To be honest to yourself is harder
To be yourself, sometimes, is even harder
So throw away those mental chains that bind you
Ask for help, if in need. True friends will be there for you
To be a little afraid is good—it keeps you alert. However, a life spent in fear is never good
So open that door, tear down the walls. Step into the light, be true to yourself, be you, and live!
—The author

"Careful, my friend. There is a story here. A story worth telling...my story—come darkness, come light, we all have one "

– A man in a bar on Boat Quay, Singapore. Still standing strong—long after the last call, and long after lights out. A story not too late to be told, and not too late to be heard—come darkness, come light. The man is gone now, yet the story remains.

Prologue

June 30, 2013
Marseille, France

Mustafa al Taqwa and Joseph Salwa sat down and leaned their backs against the wall of the hot metal cargo container. Another twenty African men were with them inside the container. The battle for the walls was long over; the strongest among them had soon realized that the chance for survival was higher next to the air holes in the container's metal walls. The high temperature and smell of sweat, urine, and vomit created an odor that penetrated their bones and souls.

Now, after twenty days of journey at sea, twenty days of hunger, thirst, misery, and death, they would finally arrive at their destination, Marseille, and the promised land of France. Mustafa and Joseph each had twenty dollars in their pocket, having used the remaining part of their life savings—US$2,000—to pay the agent in the Congo. That was the price of the ticket, the price for a seat in the container that would take them to the land of milk and honey. They had sailed from the Congo in Africa via the Cape Verde Islands on to the Canary Islands, and finally now they would arrive in Marseille. There had been 125 African men in five containers when the journey had started, and now they were much fewer, as many had died along the way. For the whole journey, they had been forced to remain in the container below deck. Only once a day, for five minutes, would one of the boat's crew members open the door to let in fresh air, throw in some PET bottles of water, empty the shit bucket, and remove the dead. The smugglers had abandoned the use of small open boats for their human cargo, they were too easy for the authorities to detect. The new traffic was on commercial ships—the human cargo well concealed below deck.

Mustafa and Joseph knew that their container had now left the cargo hold and deck of their ship, the SS *Botaki Star*, and was somewhere in transit in the harbor and customs zone of Marseille. They heard voices speaking French outside, voices they did not recognize. Suddenly, the doors opened and bright sunlight filled up the container's dark interior, blinding Mustafa and Joseph, who had not seen any sunlight in three weeks. Against the bright sunlight, all they could see were the shadows of uniformed men who seemed to stare at them. "*Mon dieu—Ils sont tous noirs, noirs comme la nuit!*" ("My God, they are all black, black like the night!") one of the officers exclaimed, his partner nodding his head in agreement.

CHAPTER 1

Friday, 4 January, 2014
Singapore

His e-mail inbox signaled an incoming message, but Richard Lardelli ignored it. He continued to look over the past month's revenue statistics, his bank revenue performance, and the assets under management. The performance report came weekly, but the monthly report from the bank's finance department was more reliable. It had been a good month for Richard so far; his revenues were up, and his assets under management (client funds deposited in the bank) were constant. He had $388,000 in revenue booked for the past month, most of it from his Hong Kong client who had been particularly active on the trading side during the past month.

This particular client was one of Richard's favorites, not only because the client helped provide the bank with favorable revenue, but also because he liked the client on a personal level. The client was an older woman from Hong Kong who traded stocks on the Hong Kong market, and over the years she had become one of Richard's largest clients. She had made millions upon millions thanks to her shrewd and timely trading strategies. She was a high-maintenance client, but it was worth every effort to service her account and to maintain the profitable relationship. She had for many years run a small restaurant in downtown Hong Kong, and over the years as her financial power increased, she had diversified into real estate and other business ventures—most notably, she owned and operated a casino in Macau. Her youngest daughter still ran the family restaurant downtown, and the oldest daughter ran the other business ventures of the family. Richard would always eat at the restaurant when he was visiting Hong Kong, although he never received a discount. In the bank in Singapore, the lady was only known as the Tiger Lady. She never asked for any investment advice or bank research because there was no need. The few times Richard had tried to tell her about some of the bank's in-house investment funds, she had simply hung up the phone. After that, Richard realized that it was best to let her be to do what she did best: make money.

Over the years, a strong relationship had developed between them. The Tiger Lady was money, and money was the Tiger Lady—"My life, my money," or "My money, my profit," as she always said in her broken English. The Tiger Lady did not speak much English, but she made up for it in her knowledge and understanding of numbers. She could count faster than any Shanghai-educated Generation Y whiz kid. She had a large house in one of the most exclusive parts of Hong Kong, high up on the slopes of Victoria Peak. She had made enough money to last her and her family several lifetimes, yet she still spent most afternoons in the family restaurant to check on her daughter, and at closing she still counted the money—"My restaurant, my money," she explained. The Tiger Lady spent most of her evenings at her other favorite place: inside the special glass observation cubicle high above the gaming floor of her casino, accompanied by her young suitors. Despite being an older woman, her appetite for men, particularly younger men, had never vanished—it was as if she were ageless. She was a tiger, and to see but not be seen was her game. The large glass cubicle suspended high over her casino floor, where she would spend hours overseeing her investment, was the throne from which she reigned.

Richard had worked for the renowned Swiss private bank Rossi & von Horstenbrik Compagnie Bank (Rossi & von Horstenbrik Cie

Bank) for the last seven years, the first two years of which he worked in the bank's head office in Zurich. The last five years he had been stationed in Singapore as a private banker at the bank's branch there.

Rossi & von Horstenbrik Cie Bank was a small private bank that had been formed in 1888 by business partners Sergio Rossi and Wolfgang von Horstenbrik. Sergio and Wolfgang had been active traders in the textile trade. Sergio Rossi had been a silk merchant from Genova who came from an old merchant family that ran an international shipping line. The Rossi family shipping line also had trading outposts in Hong Kong, Shanghai, Singapore, and Jakarta. Wolfgang von Horstenbrik had been a textile trader from Zurich who had supplied many of the royal and noble families of Europe with the finest silk and porcelain from the Far East and China for decades. The two trading partners had decided it was a good idea to start a bank; this way they could control all their finances under one roof. It would also give them the ability to issue letters of credit to all their suppliers and clients, facilitating their trades. Having the bank was also convenient for their international clients, giving them a bank to do business with in Switzerland.

Over the years and decades, as the silk trade diminished, the bank had developed into a more traditional private bank that catered to the old European aristocracy wealth. The funds deposited in Zurich were far away from foreign governments that constantly called on their nobility and well-to-do to finance their wars. The bank in Zurich kept the money of these few very wealthy families safe. The families were few, but they were the ones that counted, and the sum of wealth deposited at Rossi & von Horstenbrik Cie Bank was enough to buy nations. The bank had branches in several financial centers of the world. They were especially well represented in Asia, thanks to their historical trade ties there. With the coming of World War II in 1939, most of the international trade houses and banks had closed their representative offices in Asia. This was in line with the fall of most colonies to the Japanese occupation. As a result, Rossi & von Horstenbrik Cie Bank had closed their offices in Singapore, Hong Kong, and Shanghai. They reopened them in 1947 and kept a small staff of a half dozen employees both in Singapore and Hong Kong. These were purely representative offices that had no formal banking activity.

In 1995, then CEO and director of Rossi & von Horstenbrik Cie Bank in Zurich, Mr. Maximillian von Horstenbrik, decided it was time to take the opportunity to "ripen the fruits of the Asian wonder," as he said. In other words, it was time to expand in Asia. Few of the bank's controlling board members in Zurich had much to oppose. Mr. Massimo Rossi, the deputy CEO in Zurich, had little to say in the matter, as the Rossi family only controlled 15 percent of the bank's ownership.

The small ownership of the bank by the Rossi family traced back to Massimo's grandfather, Mario Rossi. Mario Rossi had been an avid supporter of Mussolini and Fascist Italy during World War II, and as a result, the bank had lent money to the Italian state during the first years of the war. The von Horstenbrik family went along as silent supporters for as long as the war was going the way of Mussolini and the Fascists, and as long as the bank was making money. When the Italians' luck changed, so did the fortunes of the Rossi family. When the war ended, it was inevitable that a family feud between the two families erupted, and the bank's existence was in danger. At the time, the Rossi family made up the majority of the bank's shareholders, and Mario Rossi was the chairman and chief executive officer of the bank. Mario Rossi was killed in an avalanche accident in the Swiss Alps in 1947. The accident had occurred under the most mysterious conditions. Five members of the six-man Alpine expedition were swept away by the avalanche and killed. Only Kurt von Horstenbrik, then deputy CEO of the bank, survived. He had timely sought refuge in a mountain cabin "to warm my frostbitten feet," as he later explained to the police. It was reported by newspapers that a large explosion had been detonated near the location of the incident. At the time of the explosion and avalanche, Kurt von Horstenbrik was already in the cabin. The origin of the explosion was never found, nor the people who had set it off. It was under these circumstances that the von Horstenbrik took control of the bank, while the Rossi family was deprived of Mario and their control of the bank. The Rossi family was also short of liquid means and was in debt, and as a result, they sold their controlling stake to the von Horstenbriks. Today the von Horstenbrik family controlled 36 percent of the ownership of the bank, the Rossi family 15 percent, and the remaining 49 percent was owned by common shareholders with limited voting rights.

In 1995, Maximillian von Horstenbrik, great-grandson of Kurt von Horstenbrik, made a trip to Asia to visit the various Rossi & von Horstenbrik Cie Bank offices in the region. He also developed a taste for young Asian women. In Singapore, he spent most of his time in the many bars on Boat Quay by the Singapore River, close to the financial district. He also became a connoisseur of the red-light district of Geylang. Maximillian had only one objective after these nocturnal experiences: to move to Singapore permanently. He was not interested in local food or culture, nor was he very interested in expanding the bank's activities; his objective was purely to bed Asian girls, the younger the better. Maximillian reasoned in numbers: age is a number, number of girls bedded is a number, money is a number. Beauty was of less importance because beauty is not a number.

After his two-week tour of Singapore, he returned to Zurich, his mind set that he would go back to Singapore permanently. Maximillian's decision had been largely influenced by one girl, a young Singaporean beauty whom Maximillian had met in one of the bars along the river on Boat Quay. Her name was Shirley, and she was a twenty-two-year-old Singaporean girl of Chinese origin. Shirley had swept Maximillian off his feet, and forty-year-old Maximillian had fallen like a rock for her. She had said and done all the right things: she had taken great interest in the life and history of Maximillian and the bank, and she had even asked Maximillian how much he paid in rent for his Zurich penthouse. When he explained that he owned the building, she had replied, "I think you a very happy man lah." What a delightful girl, Maximillian had thought. Miss Shirley was an SPG, a *sarong* party girl. Sarong party girl abbreviated SPG, was an expression sometimes used to describe local Singaporean and Asian girls who preferred white men to local Singaporean or Asian men; the size of a man's wallet was sometimes also an exponential variable part of the SPG equation. Maximillian was in love, however, and asked no questions, such as why a beautiful young local girl almost half his age would be interested in him. Maximillian had always gotten what he wanted in life, and he had learned long ago that if you want something there is always a price—and love was no exception.

When Maximillian returned to Switzerland, he divorced his wife in Zurich in a costly divorce. His ex-wife got the penthouse, and he moved to Singapore the following month. Soon afterward, he started his grand Asian marketing and development program; Rossi & von Horstenbrik Cie Bank was going to be big in Asia, and Maximillian was going to be even bigger. He had already planted the first seeds of his plan in Shirley, and soon the harvest would follow. He married Shirley two months after his arrival back in Singapore; she was four months pregnant at the time.

Maximillian had found a niche in the Singaporean and Asian banking sectors. He was going to develop the private banking side of the business in Asia. In the next years, Rossi & von Horstenbrik Cie Bank in Singapore went from ten employees to over eighty in the Singapore office. The market niche he had found proved to be a good one. At the time only the large Swiss banks had offices in Singapore and Hong Kong, and they were largely concentrated on investment banking and trade finance. Wealth management and private banking in foreign banks was underdeveloped. Maximillian made no effort of acquiring a local client base, and to compete with the local banks, he was going to sell his banking platform to the clients at the head office in Zurich. At this time many clients were ready to diversify and spread their deposits and assets to other financial centers outside of Switzerland. The more funds Maximillian could attract to the bank in Singapore, the more staying power he would acquire in Asia. He would regularly organize and invite key clients from Europe to Singapore and the bank there. At night he would, of course, invite select clients to come with him on his "nightly tours" to see the places he loved and enjoyed the most in Singapore.

Business was good, and in the following years the bank's client base doubled year after year, along with the revenues and client deposits. A few years later, only after securing his permanent resident status, Maximillian divorced Shirley and left her with two daughters. He was now free to dedicate even more time to pursuing young Asian girls, the younger the better. He made a name for himself as "Five-hundred-plus Max," the number making reference to the number of girls he had bedded, prostitutes not included. To many of his like-minded key European clients, all selected by him, he was a master: the King of Singapore by night, the player of players. "He owns the night. Everybody else pays the rent. He's the man!" one of his Swiss clients enthusiastically said to his friends upon his return to Switzerland. In the eyes of most of the local Singaporean employees in the bank, however, Maximillian was a man they feared, but not respected. As a result of Maximillian's character and lack of management of the banking business, the effective running of the bank was left much to Massimo Rossi, the deputy CEO. Massimo Rossi had been transferred to Singapore a year after Maximillian and had done a good job running the bank. In fact, much of the success of the bank in Singapore could be directly or indirectly attributed to Massimo's hard work and commitment to the bank, the business, and to the employees. He despised Maximillian and the von Horstenbriks, as had his family for the last two generations—since 1947 to be exact—since the death of his grandfather Mario Rossi in that fateful avalanche.

Chapter 2

Friday, 4 January
Singapore

Richard was thirty-five years old upon arriving in Singapore; he was now forty. He was of average height with an average build. He liked to think of himself as in his prime, although some of his local Singaporean colleagues called him "Uncle," the Singlish expression for older man. Singlish was the delightful local Singaporean dialect of English, and it was really its own language: an English with many Chinese and Malay words and expressions incorporated into it. The dialect also had its own melody and beat; it was like no other language or dialect in the world and learning it was indeed difficult. Richard had once been told by a local friend that "*Ang moh cannot learn Singlish cannot lah, you can understand OK lah, never to speak lah, it's in da genes lah.*" The expression *ang moh* (also written *ang mo*) is a racial epithet for white people. It is used mainly in Singapore and Malaysia. The expression derives from the Chinese Hokkien dialect. Traditionally it was often used in a racist or derogatory context, or as a racial slur; however, in modern times, the expression has been reclaimed and it is often used just to describe a white Caucasian person—no malice intended. Many considerer it acceptable in everyday use as long as it is not used in a derogatory context. Richard heard it all the time, and his Singaporean friends called him ang moh frequently, and he took no offense. It is also up to the person on the receiving end to decide whether a word is offensive or not, at least this was Richard's opinion. What an ang moh could learn, however, was to understand some basics, and it was really helpful to pick these basics up quickly. In Singlish many sentences and expressions always seemed to be abbreviated to their essential meaning, and often an adjective, superlative, or even a few words with similar meanings were added to a sentence or expression to stress its meaning and importance. Sentences often ended with the word *lah*. "I'm going home now" became "I go home lah." "Can I pay in cash?" became "I pay cash OK lah?" "This one is much better than that one" became "This one much more better lah." It was brilliant—a language that removed all unnecessary words, got to the point, and mostly eliminated all grammatical use of present tense and past tense; it was just "so good lah."

Richard had grown up in Asia, primarily in Hong Kong and Macau. His father was Swiss, and his mother was Italian of Swedish origin. His father had been a businessman in Asia working in importing and exporting, and his mother was a missionary. His father and mother had met in Tsingtao, China, where his father had been working with a local Tsingtao beer producer at the time. Richard had attended boarding school in Macau, which was at the time a Portuguese territory, and he then attended secondary school in Hong Kong. He then attended Bocconi University in Milan, Italy, where he acquired a degree in economics. Thanks to his international upbringing, he was fluent in English, Italian, German, Swedish, Portuguese, and French, with a partial knowledge of Singlish. He had two brothers and two sisters who lived in Sweden, Switzerland, and Cyprus. His parents were now retired and lived in Rome.

Richard had been single for the last six months. Richard never involved himself in pointless gossip—"Why so quiet lah?" his local Singaporean friends used to say to him. He knew how to get what he wanted through action and spoke as little as he could. Some of his friends jokingly referred to him as "the safe" in reference to a bank safety box—what he heard and saw usually stayed with him. This sometimes led to problems for Richard, as friends, colleagues and even clients often used this attribute to ask for his advice on personal issues, and sometimes just to cleanse themselves of their sins and other undesirable experiences. Despite his quiet nature, he had come to realize that he had an astute sense of humor that often won the day at parties. Richard's big interests in life were music, film, history, and food; in fact, he was a food junkie. Almost any local Asian food was a passion of his. Richard's other big passion in life was beer—beer in all shapes and forms, dark or blond, light or thick.

Over the years, Richard had built up a respectable book of private banking clients. The strengths of his bank client book were the Tiger Lady and the Lawrence account. Lawrence was the nickname for an eccentric German billionaire who was rumored to live in a long house together with a native headhunting tribe deep in the jungles of Sarawak, on the island of Borneo. It was also rumored that he believed he was Lawrence of Arabia. In addition to these two large accounts, Richard had built up a good-size client book of local Asian clients. His strength lay in his ability to adapt to new people and situations. In Asia, he had found that food was an excellent deal maker when doing business with clients and prospects. First, he would find out what food they liked and then surprise the hell out of them. Richard would often take these clients to a local restaurant. In Asia, the best food is often served in the simplest establishments. When in Rome, do as the Romans do, and when in Asia, eat like an Asian.

It was 7:00 p.m. on a Friday, and time to leave the office. Richard took a last look at his Reuters and Bloomberg computer screen to see the latest market prices. Due to the time difference, it was still lunchtime in Europe; Asian stock markets were now closed for the day, and the New York markets were not open. If he was going to leave the office, now was the time. He reread the e-mail from CEO Maximillian von Horstenbrik, stating that he wanted to see Richard on Monday morning as he had some big important news he wanted to communicate.

Richard left his office, and by the elevator he ran into Eric Wong, the night foreign exchange dealer. Eric was just going on the night shift. Rossi & von Horstenbrik Cie Bank had market coverage twenty-four hours a day, like most of the major banks in Singapore. The clients of the bank could transact in share dealing or foreign exchange around the clock in all the different time zones; money truly never sleeps. Eric was a quirky Singaporean who looked more like a doctor than a trader. The night trading room staffers in most banks were a breed unto themselves; like the doctors and staff of an emergency unit in a hospital they worked when others slept. They sometimes had to face chaotic situations when market events occurred and too many clients called at once, and as a result, they had a very special sense of humor. Eric was dressed as usual in casual clothes. Richard noted that Eric was wearing a green wind jacket that had SAVE THE BORNEO RAIN FOREST printed on the front; it was always freezing in the air-conditioned trading room.

"Hello, Eric. You go to work lah."

"Yeah, you go home lah," Eric said before the elevator doors closed. "Save the forest lah!" he shouted.

What a truly original character, Richard thought. He took the elevator down to the main lobby and said good-bye to the Indian night guard. He stepped out into the hot and humid Singaporean night. He walked in the hot tropical air through the middle of the financial district, known as Raffles Place. Being after 7:00 p.m., the area was still full of pedestrians and commuters walking toward the MRT underground station to head home. But Richard was going out.

As he stepped outside, the Ghandi twins cycled by on the street. The Ghandi twins were Indian Singaporean lawyers. They were regulars at Richard's favorite bar, and they also did Richard's taxes. They were called the Ghandi twins because they always wore traditional white Indian linens like Ghandi, drove no car, always traveled by bicycle, practiced law just like Ghandi had, and always carried umbrellas with them.

"Coming down to the pub, Richard?"

Richard nodded his head in agreement. Tonight was going to be fun, he thought. Fridays always were.

CHAPTER 3

Friday, 4 January
Singapore

After leaving the office, Richard walked down toward Boat Quay, and entered the narrow walkway next to the Singapore River. Along the small walkway, facing the river, stood the small old shop houses. These traditional houses and low-rise buildings—most were no higher than two floors—had been at the heart of Singapore's rich history. Boat Quay was the traditional inlet to the Singapore River. It was here that the center of commerce had developed. It was called Boat Quay because of all the small boats that used to be anchored on the river here. Many people had lived on the boats as well. Rumor had it that the traditional inlet was shaped like a carp, a fish that was considered auspicious (lucky) by Chinese mythology, hence the traders had set up shop here. Nowadays there were only tourist boats that went up and down the inlet and along the quay. Today Boat Quay was largely an entertainment area, with bars and restaurants that mainly catered to the people working in the nearby financial district and tourists. Mondays to Fridays, 5:00 p.m. till late, Boat Quay lived; on the weekends it was quiet.

Richard passed the busy Harry's Bar, supposedly where the trader Nick Leeson, the man who brought down Barings Bank, used to drink. He passed the busy BQ Bar and arrived at his destination—his second home, Midnight Oil. It was a small pub run by Jonas Booth, a forty-five-year-old Caucasian. Jonas came from a wealthy farming family from the island nation of Vanuatu, the New Hebrides island group as it was once called. When his older brother had inherited the family farm and all the land, Jonas had called it quits and opened up a pub on Boat Quay in Singapore instead. The pub was a simple institution that catered to everything and everyone between heaven and hell. All sorts of people had made this their second home, and for some it was practically their home, come rain or shine. Here there were expat bankers, washed-out rock stars, Singaporean office girls, tourists, traders, salesmen, sad people, butterflies of the night, rich people, poor people, and of course SPGs. No matter their social background, race, sex, income, or motive for being there, all Midnight Oilers loved to listen to live music, drink from the well-stocked bar, and have a good time. Anyone looking for something different than the average Boat Quay bar, where the after-work finance people talked about how much money they made and who they were, found it at Midnight Oil. Most bars on Boat Quay had air conditioning and nice interiors; however, almost everybody stood outside with their drinks in the hot, humid temperatures to be seen. At the Midnight Oil, however, everyone stayed inside, and when the place was full, it was rocking. Here people did not speak about money or careers; they spoke of rock 'n' roll. Richard had a theory that if people talked about money within the first five minutes of conversation, when meeting someone they did not know, they were either selling something or they wanted something. The Midnight Oil had been around for twenty years, so it was more like an institution by now. The owner, Jonas, knew how to run a bar and how to keep his guests happy. Jonas was one of those characters who made an impression on people, but when asked people could not put their finger on what that impression was. But it must have been OK, because people kept coming back. The bar had a faithful group of regulars, and when the Midnight Oil was, on rare occasions, closed, some regulars had serious withdrawal and stress symptoms.

Richard was one of the regulars. Richard had made the Midnight Oil his main watering hole and place of social interaction. Everybody needs a family, and when you don't have a family and you are far away from home, you choose your own family. When you find your family, you stick with it. The Midnight Oil crowd was Richard's family. He had only to step inside the bar, and the barmaid would pour him a pint of his favorite beer and his space next to the bar would be vacated.

Jonas, the owner, appeared sweaty and stressed out when Richard walked into the bar. He had a large beer case in his hands and a smile on his face, and he shouted to Richard, "Shit, they're drinking all the pale-ale cheap stuff. You mark it down one dollar a pint and they all go crazy." Richard laughed. Same old Jonas, he thought. Two minutes later Jonas appeared with more beer cases, shouting, "Premium beer regular price now. Come and get it, you big spenders. Come on, you cheapskates." The bar was full now, and the live band was playing. Richard was soon joined by his two friends, Matt Jones and Giorgio de Matti. Matt and Giorgio were both bankers. They were like Richard, all now part of the furniture of Midnight Oil. Between the three of them, they knew every in and out of the bar: the secrets of the staff, the barmaids, the customers, and the live bands, and of course they knew the drinks menu by heart.

Matt Jones was in his forties, an old punk rocker from Newcastle, who twenty years ago had left his job as a vegetable market stand worker in his hometown to go to London to find fame and glory. Somewhere along the way, Matt had ended up in Singapore working for an investment bank. How he ended up in Singapore was a mystery to all, a tale not told, a story surely lost in translation along the way. Matt had lived in Singapore for the last eight years.

Giorgio was an Italian banker from a noble background: he came from a notable noble Roman banking family. He dressed impeccably, like he had walked out of the latest Armani fashion show. He was in his late thirties, considered notably handsome, and had no problems with the opposite sex. Giorgio had a nose for girls, a Roman nose. Richard and Matt never knew what Giorgio did in his bank, and most likely Giorgio did not know either.

On this particular night, Giorgio was depressed. His Chinese Singaporean tailor had decided to raise the price of the custom-made shirts that Giorgio ordered on a monthly basis, twenty shirts every month, one for each working day. Giorgio had no clue that the significant price hike had been caused by his friend Matt. A few weeks prior Giorgio had sent Matt to his tailor because, in the eyes of Giorgio, Matt looked like a bum. Matt had taken the advice and gone to Giorgio's tailor, where he had ordered ten shirts. The tailor asked Matt what he was doing in Singapore, and Matt replied that he was a banker just like Giorgio. The Chinese Singaporean tailor replied, "Good for you lah." The result was, of course, that the tailor raised his prices, much to the disappointment of Giorgio, who was the main recipient of this sudden price adjustment to accommodate Singapore's inflation.

It was 10:00 p.m., and the live music was starting. It was crowded and hot, but the drinks flowed and the good times rolled, and it was a good night. Georgie "the Elvis" Fernandes was on stage. Georgie "the Elvis" was a regular at the bar and a friend of Richard's. Georgie "the Elvis's" one ambition in life was to be like Elvis Presley—to sing like him, dress like him, look like him, and drink like him. Georgie was from the Philippines, but his accent was American, just like Elvis. The Midnight Oilers all loved Georgie "the Elvis," and Georgie "the Elvis" loved them back—and he loved the bar even more.

By 1:00 a.m., closing time, Matt was sleeping in the bathroom. Jonas closed the entrance door to the bar, pulled down the shades, and put the "We're Closed" sign up in the window. Now the real party, a private function now, would begin, involving Richard, Jonas, and another bloke from Australia, along with three girls from New Zealand. The drinks flowed, everybody requested music and their favorite songs, and they all danced and forgot who and where they were. As night turned into day outside, they all slowly drank themselves into oblivion. The bar always lived up to its name during the after-hours sessions; after all, the bar was called Midnight Oil. It was a "fantastic performance evening" as Giorgio called these nights. But the day after one of these nights was never fantastic. At some point during the early hours, Richard caught a cab and went home alone. He was in no shape for any further activities, and besides that, he already had one girl on his mind.

CHAPTER 4

Saturday, 5 January
Singapore

The next day, Saturday, Richard awoke with a pounding headache and a dry mouth. He felt like a truck had passed over him. He got out of bed, put on his clothes, and made a light breakfast, despite it being past noon. Richard lived in one of the bank's houses, a black-and-white bungalow on a small road off Tanjong Katong Road on the east coast of Singapore. It was a three-bedroom house with a garden. The bungalow was an old colonial wooden house, or black-and-white as they were often called, because of the traditional black and white colors they were painted in. These traditional wooden houses, built by the British during the colonial days for employees of the colonial administration and civil servants, can still be found from India to Malaysia. The house Richard lived in had been purchased in the 1970s by the bank, when the properties were relatively inexpensive. Nowadays the houses were hot on the Singapore real estate market. There were a few hundred of these unique houses spread out over Singapore. Most were classified as heritage buildings and were protected, while some commanded rents up to SGD$25,000 (Singaporean dollars) a month, or more. To some foreign expatriates with big expat employment contracts who wanted to live the colonial dream with maid, gardener, and driver, these houses were the hot ticket. Some of the larger ones were on sale in the market for over SGD$50 million. Richard had been lucky when he moved into the house upon his arrival in Singapore five years prior. The previous Rossi & von Horstenbrik director who had lived there with his family was going back to Switzerland. Richard paid no rent; it was paid by the bank. Richard knew he was extremely lucky to be able to live in the beautiful black-and-white bungalow. The majority of Singapore's population lived in public-housing apartments, or HDBs as they were called—apartments subsidized by the housing development board, hence the name HDBs.

After a cup of coffee, he left the house and walked down to the Katong swimming complex. Richard was a swimmer and went swimming at least three times a week. He paid the one-dollar entrance fee and changed in the locker room. Two minutes later, he was in the large fifty-meter Olympic-size pool; his normal thirty laps would be harder with a hangover. An hour later, he was walking back to his house, the sun shining and the air force jets flying low above him; there was an air base not far away. After arriving home, he parked himself on the patio veranda in the garden and read the newspaper, *Singapore Straits Times*. There was nothing new in Singapore, he soon realized, so he put the paper down. He then went online to the website of the French newspaper *Le Figaro* to check the European news. Nothing of interest seemed to have happened. He started reading an article about human trafficking: a Paris court case involving the trafficking of 101 African men on a ship from the Congo in Africa to Marseille in France, who were now being held in Marseille. The ship had been seized in June, the preceding year. He skimmed through the article, and after reading it he shook his head and thought to himself what a waste of time—the guilty organizers of the trafficking would get off, and some low-ranking crew member would be charged. It was always like this. The police could claim that justice had been served; someone did, after all, go to prison. Some poor sod would go to jail, and the real culprits would go free; the Africans would be sent back to Africa as illegal immigrants. Justice in the twenty-first century had been served—right. It was all a show, Richard thought, and then he fell asleep on the rattan couch.

At 5:00 p.m. the phone rang. It was Prosper, Richard's best friend. Prosper was Belgian and of French origin. Richard had meet Prosper the first year he was in Singapore. They had met through his ex-girlfriend Anna, who was a friend of Prosper's wife. Even though Anna was long gone, Richard still had a friend worth gold in Prosper. Prosper's real name was Sylvain de Rouge, but Richard called him Prosper because one time, years ago, Prosper had tipped Richard off about a small Singapore electronics company that traded on the Singapore Stock Exchange. Prosper had said, "Buy it and prosper," and Richard had done so and had made good money on the investment. After that Sylvain became "Prosper," and the rest was history.

Prosper was forty years old and married to Marie, who was French. Both Catholic, Prosper and Marie had six children. Prosper was also a banker and worked for a British bank. He was calling to invite Richard to his house for a dinner party. It was a bit short notice, but Richard accepted the invitation for 7:00 p.m. that same evening. He made his way to Prosper's condominium on Lady Hill in Singapore, not far from the Shangri-La Hotel.

The dinner went well, and the roast lamb that was served was outstanding. The apartment was relatively small, and there were children everywhere; however, what the apartment lacked in space, Prosper and Marie made up for with their generosity and their hearts. Another French couple had been invited as well, and they were nice. What was it about the French expats in Singapore? Nothing against the French, Richard thought, but lately there seemed to be a French invasion of Singapore; they seemed to be coming out of the ground like mushrooms.

Richard had recently gone to the nearby island of Pulau Ubin, a small island adjacent to Singapore that was part of Singapore. The small island, which was composed of jungle and plenty of trails and small roads, was a popular destination for hiking and biking trips.

Richard had gone there to escape into the countryside, and to get away from Singapore proper for a day. He had brought with him a picnic lunch along with his mountain bike. At one point, he left his mountain bike and wandered down one of the trails that led through the mangrove forest by the shore. He saw the old wooden view tower and climbed the four stories up the staircase that led to the top. This was the place, he decided, where he would take his picnic lunch and marvel at the fantastic view of Singapore and the ocean. When he arrived at the platform on top of the tower, there were six bare-chested Frenchmen wearing small Adidas shorts and sneakers sitting in a circle on the wooden floor listening to a portable CD player that was placed in the middle of them. The song playing was, of course, by a French band, Daft Punk. "*Bonjour*," they greeted him as he came up the stairs, but Richard turned around quickly and walked down the stairs again. So much for solitude, he thought. These French were everywhere.

After the dinner at Prosper's, Richard excused himself and took a taxi down to Boat Quay and Midnight Oil. He met up with Giorgio, and after a few beers they took another taxi to Club Street on An Siang Hill. They checked out the rooftop bar, the Screening Room, and later walked over to another rooftop bar, the Yin Yang. While Richard was ordering his gin and tonic at the Yin Yang, he was approached by a Filipina girl who asked him, "Hi, how are you?" followed by "Are you a banker?" She was fishing; she was of course interested to find out if it was worth her while to spend some time with Richard. Richard did not fancy her, and he had already been approached by several SPGs already, so he replied, "No, I am a white slave trader." This statement, which he had used before, always produced one of two outcomes: the girl would laugh, or she would turn around and leave. This girl was obviously not into white slave traders, so she left. Richard and Giorgio recognized some friends at the outside open rooftop bar, so they moved outside and worked up a healthy bar tab, and created a happy bartender. Toward the end of the evening, a drunk Italian girl wanted to take Richard home, telling him she was ready to show him the stars. "*Ti faccio vedere le stelle*," ("I will show you the stars") she whispered in Italian in his ear. The poor girl could hardly stand on her feet. Richard left her with her twin sister, who could barely stand on her two feet, as well. The night wore on, and the DJ played some European music by Swedish House Mafia. At closing time Richard left, but before he caught a taxi, he stopped by the B29, the whiskey bar in the basement, for one last drink—one for the road—which soon became five for the road. He went home alone, however. Tomorrow he would meet the object of his desire, Louise.

In another part of town in a dimly lit room, Maximillian von Horstenbrik had just finished. He put on his trousers. He sat on the side of the bed, catching his breath.

"You want shower?" the young Vietnamese girl asked.

"No, baby, it's OK," he responded.

"You so good, so strong man. You come OK? You want again?" she continued.

Maximillian did not have time to answer the girl because his phone rang and he answered.

The voice on the other end spoke, "Hello, Max. It's me. Ten boxes of red wine have been ordered." It was the phone call that he had been dreading to receive—the one he knew would come.

"I told you not to order any more wine. No way. And half a box was enough. You promised," Maximillian replied. He pleaded and begged with the voice on the other end of the line to no avail.

"We had a deal, remember? Remember that, Max?" was the only answer he got to his plea. "You know what will happen if you don't accept the order, Max? Try me, I'm serious," the man at the other end said and then hung up.

This was not good, not good at all. It was a disaster. But there was no way to say no now. But maybe there was something he could do for himself—yes, maybe he could improve his situation and better the odds a little, Maximillian thought to himself. "Red wine" was the agreed-upon code for US dollars. One case equaled $1 million; each case had ten bottles, so one bottle, the smallest unit, equaled $100,000. He used this code for some of his most paranoid bank clients—the ones who were convinced that someone or some authority was listening in on their phones, or the ones who just preferred to deal in the dark, the ones who had a tendency to avoid daylight. The caller was one of the latter, and would of course go through with the transaction. When the client said he had ordered the boxes of wine, this meant he had wire transferred money to his bank account at Rossi & von Horstenbrik Cie Bank in Singapore. The clients who spoke in alcohol code never sent less than $100,000 because Maximillian had convinced them that real men don't drink or order half bottles and certainly never transfer less than $100,000—at least this was Maximillian's theory. It was quite simple; $1.5 million meant a case and a half, and ten cases meant $10 million, and so on. They had a different type of alcoholic beverage as code for each kind of currency; "lager" meant the British pound, and "white wine" meant the euro, etc. To cover up this code, Maximillian, of course, had backup in the form of an uncle who ran an import-export outfit in Zurich, importing and exporting alcohol. When bank clients signaled that they were sending money to their bank account in Singapore, Maximillian sent the corresponding amount of physical boxes of alcohol to the client just to back up the funds transfer transaction with a real alcohol import-export deal in an effort to confuse any potential eavesdropping financial authorities or ensuing investigations. So now $10 million was on its way. He had to find a way out of this mess. He took out four fifty Singaporean dollar bills, threw them on the bed next to the girl, and walked out the door.

"You come back soon, OK?" the Vietnamese girl shouted to him as he closed the door.

He opened another door in the long, dark corridor, the door that led to his nocturnal temple where he found his sanctuary, his bliss. The room was no larger than eight square meters, just big enough for a simple bed and night table. This particular room Maximillian rented on a monthly basis from the pimp who ran the noble establishment. No girls or patrons were allowed here; it was his and only his. Maximillian would retreat to this room after each visit with a prostitute to relax and think. The room was situated between two frequently used bedrooms. Once inside he got undressed, put on the tight, black, full-body latex suit, hooded mask included, and lay down on the bed. Here he would lie in the dark and listen to the sounds of the house—the grunts, the moving beds, the fake screams and orgasms of the girls, the discrete knocks on the doors (the ones you only hear in a whorehouse), the sounds of pleasure, pain, misery, money, and ultimately, the lonely cries of help from lost souls. To hear and not be heard, to imagine but not see or touch, to get excited, but not too excited. The bodysuit prevented him from getting too excited; any increase in muscle size on any part of his body would cause shortness of breath, which could be potentially fatal. It was all part of the game, his game, his release. This was his bliss, his temple of control, the ultimate sex game. Maximillian had realized a long time ago that sex is all in the mind—control the mind and you control the body. Here he would lie in the dark and fantasize about all the bodies he had touched and felt, the sounds of sex in the neighboring rooms adding another dimension to his private experience. Thoughts of the past combined with the noises from the joining rooms made his memories come alive. Maximillian was not so interested in the sexual act itself—all the girls he had slept with were just a number and an act. Maximillian was a collector—a collector of sexual memories and ecstasies. It all helped him to think, to plot, and to feel secure and in control—oh, yes, so in control.

Later, on the way out down the stairs, the pimp appeared out of nowhere, the way pimps do after a complete transaction. "You like? She good lah?"

"She OK lah, but you know I like them younger than that. Get me some new triangles!"

CHAPTER 5

Sunday, 6 January, Morning
Singapore

Richard walked into the church and sat down in his regular seat, close to the door. The church was Wesley Methodist Church on Fort Canning Road, situated adjacent to Fort Canning Park and located in the civic district next to the Singapore National Museum. The Sunday morning service was full as usual. Besides the minister who would conduct the service, there was a choir and musicians. Richard had felt uncomfortable the first time he participated in the service, especially during the part when all new members and participants were supposed to stand up and be recognized. Richard had participated in the exercise, and in hindsight he was happy he had done so. Richard was not particularly religious, but he felt good when he was in the church—he felt safe. Maybe he would even meet some nice Singaporean girl there and settle down. He preferred Singaporean girls to Western girls—when in Rome do as the Romans do.

It was after that first service he had attended three months ago that she approached him. Her name was Louise, a beautiful thirty-something Singaporean girl of Chinese ethnicity. She had long black hair tied up behind her head, large eyes, and a lovely smile, and Richard fell for her straightaway. She had boldly approached him and asked him where he was from. Many Singaporeans were, in Richard's view, quite shy, but Louise was not shy at all. They had spoken for a few minutes that first day, and when they said good-bye, Louise had left him with the words, "See you next Sunday." What a brilliant example of missionary work, Richard thought. If that phrase could be used by attractive religious women on single men globally after a church visit, most churches worldwide would have more visitors than seats available.

Richard was no exception; he went back the next week, and the week after that. After that first "See you next Sunday," they had met and talked every Sunday since. Richard learned that Louise was divorced and had a three-year-old daughter. Her Singaporean husband had left her soon after the birth of their daughter. They had been together since they were teens and when Mary, their daughter, was born there was just not enough love left in the relationship. The split had been mutual, and they were still friends and shared custody of little Mary. These first innocent meetings between Richard and Louise led to meetings for dinner a few times. They were still not romantically involved, but Richard knew that all the ingredients were there. Louise was funny, intelligent, and beautiful. Louise, in Richard's eyes, was perfect, and he contemplated whether she was the one—if there was such a thing as the one.

Today, when the service was finished, Louise introduced Richard to her father, her uncle, and her daughter Mary. Her father, Edwin, was a retired police officer, and her uncle, Arnold, was the proprietor of a food stall in a food court or Hawker Center, as they were called locally. The whole family, including Louise and Mary, lived in a large HDB public housing apartment in Bedok South, a district on the east coast of Singapore. Her father had an iron-fist handshake and a stare that saw straight through Richard—at least that was what Richard felt. They talked about the weather and the recent heat wave that had hit Singapore, always a good, safe, neutral conversation topic when meeting new people. Louise's father, all of a sudden, burst out, "Join us for lunch, Richard," but it came out more like a command than a question—the man was a retired police officer, after all. Richard accepted the invitation, and from the corner of his eye he saw, for a fraction of a second, a smile on Louise's face and possibly a quick blush as well. The uncle hailed a taxi outside the church, and they all got in. Thirty minutes later they all were sitting in a food court on the ground floor deck of a public housing complex.

Being Sunday afternoon the food court was full of people, and the air there smelled of fried chicken, sesame, curry, and coco. These particular apartment blocks mainly had many Singaporeans of Malay and Indian descent as their tenants, hence the coco and curry. On Sundays many of the families who lived in these housing blocks ate their Sunday lunch here. The food courts were a sort of social institution in Singapore. People ate, socialized, read papers, drank, and just hung out there. On Sundays, the food courts were particularly busy. Sometimes when Richard visited the food court close to his house during the week, people were all stressed out and ate in high-speed mode, but today he found the opposite to be true; people seemed to relax and take all the time in the world to finish their food. There were many food stalls in the food court: Indian, Malay, Chinese, and even a stall serving English toast with eggs and bacon—what a culinary legacy the former colonials had left behind.

Louise's uncle was the proprietor of food stall number seven, and his specialty was chicken and rice. The food stalls had always fascinated Richard. They were small, simple, kiosk-like stalls, most no larger than a few square meters inside. These few precious square meters contained a full kitchen, fresh produce, refrigerators, a cooking area, and a cash register. Inside the temperature was surely twice that of outside the stalls. Many Singaporeans ate their daily meals in these food stalls. The food was also relatively inexpensive. For the price of a pint of beer down by Boat Quay by the financial district, here one could buy a whole lunch of several dishes, including a main course, sides, and dessert, even squeezing in a bottle of beer. The food was mostly outstanding and well prepared. This was light years away from the downtown fancy restaurants. Arnold, Louise's uncle, proudly showed off his stall and its menu and the *A* marking on the signboard, the highest rating on the grade scale. The food stalls were regularly inspected by health authorities and had to meet strict criteria in cleanliness of cooking facilities, quality of produce etc. The scale went from *A* to *D*; however, *D*-rated food stall owners rarely visibly displayed their signs. Arnold had every reason to show his sign.

Their table was soon filled with local steaming-hot delicacies: chicken and garlic rice, fried rice, duck, etc.; there were countless dishes Richard had never seen or tried before that just kept coming. The dishes were accompanied by local Tiger Beer for the gentlemen and lime juice for Louise and little Mary. No Indian or Malay dishes were allowed on the table, nor any other dishes from any other food stall. Only food from the uncle's stall was allowed.

After a good and hearty lunch, where the conversation had mainly been between Richard and Louise, Arnold stated that it was time for a little whiskey. Louise's father soon explained to the disappointed uncle that it was Sunday afternoon and not the time nor the place. Much to the disappointment of Arnold, he declined and suggested some local coffee, or *kopi* as it was called, instead. After the coffee, Richard offered to pay for the whole feast, but he was refused by Louise's father. "You are our guest," he said to Richard. Richard thanked him for the great lunch; he understood that Edwin was not a man one argued with. Louise had suggested she and Richard go for a walk. As Richard stood up and said good-bye, Louise's father said, "See you next Sunday, Richard." So much for next Sunday's program, Richard thought. "See you next Sunday" must be a family thing, he noted.

Louise and Richard, accompanied by little Mary, walked down toward the small park adjacent to the large housing block. There was a small playground there where some children were playing. Louise approached two of the Singaporean Malay mothers sitting on a bench next to the playground. She asked them if they could watch little Mary for a couple of minutes, and they agreed. Little Mary started playing with the Malay children in their colorful batik Malay clothes. Louise did not know any of the woman or the other children, it was not a problem, she was not worried that anything would happen to little Mary. Some Singaporeans called it the *kampong* spirit, which, loosely translated, means village spirit. The housing blocks were like this; people took care of and watched out for each other, and in many ways it was still like a village, a kampong. Singapore was a large multicultural metropolis, but in so many ways it was still like a village. Richard and Louise walked for a few minutes on the small trail that led into the small park. Out of sight from others they sat down on a bench next to a large palm tree. Richard felt extremely good after the long lunch and beers. Louise looked at him and said, "Richard, I like you. You make me feel safe."

Richard was caught off guard and managed to utter the words, "Me too."

The moment he had said them, he thought, fantastic performance; he had been waiting for this moment for such a long time, and now all he could say was "Me too." This was surely not one of his best performances; he felt like a schoolboy. He had always been shy with girls he was really interested in—it was a good indicator of his feelings—but he was often a disaster when striking up a conversation with them. There was nothing he wanted more than to take Louise home and make love to her—forget words. Louise took control then and took his hand, and then leaned in and kissed him. They kissed, and afterward they looked into each other's eyes but said nothing; there was no need for words—what was happening between them was beyond words, the start of something new and big. They stood up and walked back toward the playground holding hands.

Little Mary saw them and smiled, and they quickly let go of their hands. She ran toward them, saying, "Look, look, Mommy! I found a rock, a special rock. Look, look!" Before Louise had time to answer, Mary grabbed Richard's leg, putting her arms around it like it was a tree trunk, and squeezed. Then she let go and looked up at Richard. "Here, it's for you. It's a special rock. It's for you!" she said as she took his hand, opened it, and placed the small round rock inside his palm. "Now you are special too!" she said, then she ran back toward the playground. Richard was again caught off guard; he did not know what to say. There he stood with a small round rock in his open hand. It was just a small rock, but he just could not find any words to say.

"I think she likes you," Louise said and laughed. "It's OK. You don't have to say anything. Just remember it's a special rock," she said as she took his open hand and closed it. "Now it's really yours."

Louise followed Richard to the taxi stand. They kissed again and said good-bye. Richard got into the taxi, and as it pulled away, he looked back, where he saw Louise smiling and waving at him. He told the taxi driver to take him down to Boat Quay.

He arrived at Midnight Oil and sat down outside in the beer garden. On a Sunday at 5:00 p.m., few guests were there. He was soon joined by Jonas, the owner, who greeted him with a feisty, "Hello, lover boy."

Richard looked at him questioningly and replied, "Lover boy?"

Jonas just smiled at him, tapped Richard on his shoulder, and laughed. "It is written all over your face, mate."

CHAPTER 6

Monday, 7 January
Singapore

Richard hailed a cab down at the crossing of Tanjong Katong Road and Mountbatten Road in the direction of the city. The time was 7.10 a.m. He passed all the millionaire's homes on Mountbatten Road; many roads had English names, all remnants of the British colonial rule. They passed the peculiar Sing Hoe Hotel on the right. They passed by the Tanjong Katong Heritage sign close to the Katong swimming complex. Their journey continued, eventually arriving at Nicoll Highway and, passing by the MRT station with the same name, the Suntec Towers on the left. They passed the Stanford Road crossing, over the bridge, finally arriving at his destination, the Fullerton Bay Hotel. Richard always alighted at the Fullerton Bay Hotel. The uniformed doormen of the hotel opened the door of the taxi as he got out, just as if he were a guest of the hotel. After all the years, Richard was well-known to the hotel staff, and he had developed a particular relationship with these doormen. He had found out that a few of them were keen investors on the Singapore Stock Exchange with some of their spare pennies. Richard would sometimes mention to these men a stock he was interested in and liked, or one he had bought or followed for his personal share portfolio. A typical conversation might go something like this:

Hotel staff: "Good morning, sir."
Richard: "Good morning to you."
Hotel staff: Good day today, sir?"
Richard: "Nineteen twenty-eight HK."
Hotel staff: "Have a good day, sir."

From this conversation Richard had mentioned the name of Sands China Ltd, a common stock traded on the Hong Kong Stock Exchange, with the stock identity code nineteen twenty-eight HK. This was neither a buy nor a sell recommendation, but merely an indication that Richard liked the stock. It was up to the door staff at the hotel to have a look and decide what to do. They had been playing the little game for years. The whole idea had developed after one of the staff had asked Richard if he worked in a bank and what stocks he liked. Richard had told of a stock he had recently bought for himself that he thought had good potential. After that exchange, the rest was history; the staff continued to open the door for him, and Richard shared his knowledge and thoughts of rising stars in the stock market. He must be doing something right, he thought, because they continued to open the taxi door for him. He knew that it was their job to do so, but he also knew that a few of them had made a buck or two in the market thanks to his tips. After speaking to the hotel staff, Richard walked over the walking bridge over Collyer Quay, a busy avenue. He arrived at the heart of the financial district and Raffles Place.

Three minutes later Richard was sitting down at his desk at Rossi & von Horstenbrik Cie Bank on the twenty-first floor in one of the financial district's skyscrapers. Brenda, his assistant, briefed him on the day's schedule and handed him some phone messages, one of which was that his boss wished to see him.

He walked over to Maximillian's office. His secretary, who sat outside the glass cubicle that was his office, greeted Richard and said, "You can go straight in."

Maximillian was wearing his usual red suspenders, just like Gordon Gekko had worn in the classic movie *Wall Street*. No one had dared to tell Maximillian that suspenders had been out of fashion in financial circles for the last twenty years or so. Maximillian thought he looked hip and virile. The real reason he wore them, however, was that he was a believer in the peacock theory. The peacock theory stated that girls were attracted to men who stood out from the crowd and wore bright colors. All this Maximillian had learned after reading the book *The Game* by Neil Strauss. The book was the ultimate pick-up Bible and introduction to the game—the game of picking up women. He was finishing a phone conversation Richard assumed with one of his little girlfriends. He heard him whisper, "Wear that black top tonight," before he hung up the phone. Maximillian then greeted Richard in his strong Swiss-German accent that he had when he spoke English: "Hallo, Richard. Won't you have a seat?"

Maximillian was in his late fifties, rather chubby, and had a receding hairline. He always wore his hair greased back, again just like Gordon Gekko. Richard took a seat in the visitor's chair opposite Maximillian's desk. Maximillian then explained to Richard the reason he had called him in for this meeting was that his nephew, Yann von Horstenbrik, who worked in the Singapore office as a junior private banker, apparently had a French client who he needed some help with. The client was a twenty-eight-year-old student named Bernard Strydsteen, He was currently residing in Phnom Penh, Cambodia, and the account had been opened four years ago by Maximillian himself.

Yann von Horstenbrik had been sent over from Zurich for a two-year stationing at the Singapore office of the bank, because he was the protégé of Maximillian von Horstenbrik. As a von Horstenbrik, Yann would surely be sitting in as a member of the bank's board of directors in a few years. Richard had run into Yann several times at different night spots and bars over the last year. Yann was always with his blue-blooded friends from the Zurich and Geneva banking elite. He was rarely in the office, instead always out on business or at client meetings, although he had only one client who had never deposited any funds in the account. After one year in Singapore at Rossi & von Horstenbrik Bank, Yann had contributed little to the bank's revenue bottom line. No one ever said anything because he was the protégé of Maximillian and from Zurich. Yann was not a bad person, he just happened to have been born on the right side of the fence in life. He was arrogant, sure, but he knew nothing else; it was the way he had been brought up. Richard suspected that Yann would go far in the business, not because of his feats or qualifications, but because of his last name. When Yann had first come to Singapore, Richard and Yann had gone out for drinks several times. They had many common interests, in particular they were both interested in history and art. At a certain point they had stopped to socialize with each other, Yann had suddenly seemed to have no interest in continuing the friendship. Richard had not pursued the friendship after Yann did not seem to have any interest in continuing the friendship. It was only later that Richard was told by another person who had overheard a conversation between Yann and his uncle Maximillian, where Yann had been told not to socialize with Richard or other employees of the bank, the reason being that; Yann was a member of the von Horstenbrik family and it was important to keep a certain distance from the "common employees". Richard had never questioned Yann if this was true or not. If this was what Yann wanted, so be it.

Maximillian explained that Yann had received the first funds deposited in the only account under his management. A small deposit of $500,000 had been wired to the account a few days ago, and more funds were supposed to arrive soon. Maximillian wanted Richard to take over the account while Yann was away on a trip to Monte Carlo. It was important that someone with experience monitor the account, someone with Richard's expertise, to make sure that everything was handled correctly, Maximillian explained. It was important to see that the client file was in order, and to do some background checks on the client as well. Richard knew what this meant: if lots of money came into the account, Maximillian and Yann would receive all the glory, but if something went wrong it would be Richard's fault. Maximillian then played his ace when he told Richard that he would consider it a personal favor, and that it was important for the bank to secure this account. Richard hated when Maximillian used the term personal favor; Richard worked for the bank, not for Maximillian. It was the bank's name on his paycheck, not Maximillian's. Richard agreed, however—why not? He had been asked to help the bank, and it was his job. Maximillian ended the short meeting by saying, "Great, Richard. I will see to it that you get the file and that you get the account sign-over documents delivered to your desk. From now until further notice, the account is yours." The meeting was over.

Richard returned to his desk and started his normal working day of speaking to clients, following the markets, and placing client orders. He ate an in-house lunch at his desk and continued working nonstop. At 5:00 p.m. he opened Yann's client's file and started his review of this important client who was now his client, at least temporarily.

The account holder was a Curaçao Netherlands Antilles company. The beneficial owner was named Bernard Strydsteen. This meant that the Curaçao company was the account holder and name that appeared on bank statements, and Bernard was the owner. Bernard's name appeared on no bank correspondence. Opening an offshore company was relatively easy. The client could approach any of the many company service providers, either in Singapore or anywhere else in the world, to have a company created. The offshore company could be created in a few days, depending on the jurisdiction chosen by the client: the British Virgin Islands, Panama, Belize, Bermuda, Cayman Islands, Gibraltar,

Netherlands Antilles, or the Channel Islands. For some individual bank clients, the main objective of using a corporate bank account structure, was that of adding a layer of confidentiality. No one outside the bank, and in some cases not even the commercial registrar of the company in its offshore jurisdiction, knows the identities of the shareholders or the real owner of the account and funds. Many international jurisdictions are slowly adapting new rules to combat money laundering, and as a result, some banks have been reluctant to accept corporate account structures for private individuals.

The data in Yann's client file left much to be desired. Besides the basic data—name of the client (beneficial owner), nationality, passport number, and address—most other data was missing. Under occupation, Richard read "Student." What was young Bernie Strydsteen studying in Phnom Penh, Cambodia? Under origin of incoming funds, it said "Savings." Family background was marked as "Wealthy Family," but that was all. Richard quickly skimmed through the information provided and then decided to do his own research. He went on the Internet and searched the name Bernard Strydsteen, and there was one hit, a newspaper article from an English-speaking newspaper in Cambodia. The article stated that Bernard had been involved in a pub brawl in Phnom Penh together with other expatriates. He had supposedly beaten up two American tourists in a bar called The Heart of Darkness. The article referred to him as the son of Mr. Alain Jean Sebastian Strydsteen. Richard decided to refer to him as Alain from now on. Richard typed the name of the father into an internet search engine and received over twenty hits. After doing some reading, he learned that the Strydsteen family was a notable family of South African Boer origin. The family had emigrated to France at the end of the Boer War in 1902. They had built up from scratch a global shipping business, which today was a global force in the shipping industry. Richard discovered that Bernard's father was under investigation for money laundering and human trafficking, suspected involvement in the sponsoring and financing of illegal rain forest depletion, along with several other charges, in a Paris court. The fact that the son was receiving a half-million dollars from another offshore company heightened Richard's attention. Yann had marked the incoming funds as savings. OK, so what brilliant savings scheme did young Bernie have in Gibraltar? Maybe Bernie was a financial guru, or maybe he had inherited the funds from some childless auntie, passing over his father in the process; stranger things had happened. Richard had learned over the years that things are not always what they seem, and that went for banking as well as the rest of life. However, Richard had the feeling that something was not all hunky-dory here—not a great start to a fact-finding mission.

Richard decided to close the file and look at it again with fresh eyes the next day; it was already past 7:00 p.m. He closed his workstation and walked out of the office and then out of the bank doors. He ran into Eric the night trader again by the elevator. "Hello, Richard. You go home lah?"

"Hello, Eric. You go work lah?" It was their usual procedure and exchange of comments. Before the elevator doors closed behind Richard, Eric screamed out, "Hey, Richard, you join Greenpeace yet?" Eric felt very strongly about the theme printed on his jacket. Richard had had countless five-second elevator conversations with him about the subject each time they took the elevator together. Adding together all their brief common elevator ride times from the eighteenth floor to the twenty-second floor, they had spoken a lot about environmental issues. Richard had studied the topic extensively in university, a time that seemed a lifetime ago.

Richard blocked the elevator door open, smiled at Eric, and said, "You know, I once had a soul and conscience, but then I started working here, and look at me now."

Eric smiled back, pushed the close-door button, and as the doors closed, he replied, "Yeah, look at you now. Such a shame!"

As Richard left the building, he decided to take the bus home, bus number ten. After he arrived at home, he went to bed straightaway, but even though he was tired, he slept uneasily.

CHAPTER 7

Tuesday, 8 January
Singapore

Richard awoke at 6:15 a.m. the next day, more tired than usual. He jumped into the shower, got dressed, and left the house. He arrived at the office at 8:00 a.m. and discovered he was the first one there. The cleaning lady was still vacuuming the floors. He checked the overnight market movements and spoke briefly on the phone to the night trader, who was about to hand things over to the day shift. He wanted to check if some of his clients' foreign exchange orders had been executed overnight, but no orders had been done. He called a client in Europe. It was 1:00 a.m. in Europe, but this particular client always wanted to be called, whether the order was done or not. The client was one of those sleepless trading junkies who believed money truly never sleeps. The client thanked Richard for the call and asked him about the weather in Singapore. What was it about the weather, Richard thought. He could have replied, "Yes, we have a storm and flooding, and today I went to the office in my kayak," and the client would reply, "Great. Speak to you soon."

After ending the conversation with his client, Richard continued his research on the Bernie account. He read a newspaper article from a newspaper in Paris, dated one month ago. The article described the court case Bernie's father was involved in. It was then that Richard remembered the article he had read on the Internet over the weekend.

Six months ago the freighter SS *Botaki Star* had been seized in the port of Marseille, France. The shipment seized was composed of electronic equipment worth over $20 million, mainly radios, DVD players, and TVs, all of Asian origin. The boat had come from Borneo, Indonesia, via the Congo, Africa. The products were all counterfeit and falsely declared to customs. The whole ordeal did not improve with the fact that in the cargo hold of the boat, custom officials found 101 African men from the Congo with no passports or identification papers. They were all dressed in rags and in terrible physical states, all carrying their earthly possessions in single plastic bags. "We thought we were traveling to a better life in the land of milk and honey. Instead these ungrateful men in uniform and speaking French greeted us and placed us in prison," one of the detained men had told the newspaper. The 101 surviving men had paid their life savings to reach the "promised land", and now they were behind bars. The seizure was surely a tip-off from some competing shipping line, the paper stated. In fact, a competing shipping line from Borneo had its warehouse in Marseille burnt down to the ground a few weeks after the incident, and police suspected it was a payback. It had never been proven, so far, that Bernie's father, Alain, was aware of the shipment, yet he was the owner of the shipping line. In Alain Strydsteen's words, it was the action of the ship's captain alone, and the case was still in the courts. Reading other articles, Richard gathered that Bernie's father had been involved with several incidents and disputes with the law over the years, in particular incidents involving human trafficking and illegal lumber logging; however, nothing had ever been proven. Richard also found out from his research that Bernie was registered as a law student at a Paris university—so much for studying in Cambodia, and so much for Yann's KYC: know-your-customer work. The client file also read that the client was recommended from the Rossi & von Horstenbrik head office in Zurich. Surely all this information had not been available to the local compliance officers in the bank in Singapore when the account had been opened a few years ago. All the newspaper articles were dated after the account opening, so there was no chance the local in-house Singaporean compliance officer could have known. It was the responsibility of the banker handling the account to inform the bank compliance department of any irregularities regarding the account or background of the client along the way. The bomb hit when Richard, just out of curiosity, went into the online directory of the Curaçao Registrar of Companies, which he had access to online. He checked the company that was sending money from the Gibraltar bank to the Curaçao-registered company account in Singapore—the account of Bernie Strydsteen at Rossi & von Horstenenbrik Cie Bank in Singapore. The company sending the funds, Parbal Bry N.V., happened to also be registered in Curaçao Netherlands Antilles, as well. Richard could not believe his eyes. Although he could not see who the owner was, he could see who the directors were, and he saw that Maximillian von Horstenbrik was one them.

What did this mean? This was big. What did Maximillian von Horstenbrik do as a director there? What was Maximillian von Horstenbrik, CEO of Rossi & von Horstenbrik Cie Bank in Singapore, doing as a director for the company that was sending money to Bernie Strydsteen at Rossi & von Horstenbrik in Singapore? There must be some explanation, Richard thought. He started thinking about how he would write his report. Even if there was a logical explanation to all he had found, it was, in his eyes, a considerable reputation risk for the bank. Bad publicity in the paper was not good, especially not for a small bank like Rossi & von Horstenbrik. The newspapers were hot on writing about banks, especially after the recent financial crisis. He decided to start writing his report as soon as he had finished his normal day-to-day work; after all, he had his own clients to look after as well. More than one thing was not right here, however, and Richard sensed that it was very wrong indeed. Why had Maximillian given him an account that was potentially a ticking time bomb?

After lunch Richard received a call from his biggest client, who was also the biggest client of the bank in Singapore. The combined portfolio and deposits of the Lawrence account at Rossi & von von Horstenbrik Cie Bank in Singapore surpassed over $5 billion. Naturally, this account was the center of Richard's attention. The account was known in the bank as the "Lawrence account ". The client was an old German trade and shipping family, the Holzstam family. The family operated their vast business empire out of Sarawak on the large island of Borneo, the state of Sarawak, was a part of Malaysia. The family business traced its roots back to the early twentieth century and Tsingtao, China. Tsingtao, the then German trading outpost on the Chinese coast, was a trading outpost and German territory. Tsingtao was much like the other colonial enclaves and trading outposts along the Chinese coast, including Hong Kong, Canton, among others. These ports and cities had been the center of intercontinental trade between China and Europe and the rest of the world. The shipping dynasty had been founded by Mr. Otto Holzstam, who had started with one small freighter that shipped goods from China to Germany and Europe, and up the Pearl River into the Chinese mainland.

In the fall of 1914, shortly before the fall of Tsingtao to the Allied powers in World War I, when Germany was at war with England, France, Russia, and Japan, Otto made his move. In the last weeks before the fall of Tsingtao to the Allied powers, he completed his coup, later to be known as "The Great Otto Coup." Otto had gathered all his savings and bought up the majority of the other German ships and freighters that were docked in the then encircled and besieged harbor. Many of the German residents owned and controlled trade houses with their headquarters in Tsingtao, and they had not foreseen the possibility that Germany could lose the war and Tsingtao. Blindly they had all believed that the German emperor, the *kaiser*, was unbeatable. These shipping magnates and families were desperate, and the port and town were encircled, soon to fall to the Allies. They were all short of cash, desperate to save what could be saved, and frantic to buy themselves and their families a ticket out of Tsingtao to safety. Many ships were sold to Otto for cheap prices. The brilliance of the move was that Otto realized that most of the ships he had bought that were docked in the harbor of Tsingtao would be lost to the Allies. However, the vast amount of ships that were out on the oceans all over Southeast Asia could be saved. The deal with the ship owners was that for every ship he bought in the harbor of Tsingtao, he would acquire one more ship that was out on the high seas, including those carrying cargo, at a very favorable rate indeed. Also, Otto had paid off a local German colonial administrator, and without the deal there were to be no legal exit residence permits issued. For this second ship out on the high seas, he offered to pay double the amount he had paid for the ship anchored in the harbor. It was a bargain indeed, of course, because the sellers were desperate and wanted out. For Otto, it was a huge risk and gamble; the high seas of the Pacific and South China Sea were controlled by the Allies. Otto managed to salvage most of the fleet on the high seas, and even managed to orchestrate a brilliant escape of some of the freighters in Tsingtao Harbor. After that, the whole fleet of his various ships around the world set their course for South America, where they docked in a neutral port and remained there for the rest of the war.At the end of the war in 1918, Otto Holzstam and his family had made their new home in the country of Sarawak on the northern shores of the giant Borneo Island. Sarawak was, at the time, a nation, yet a British protectorate. The Holzstam family made the capital of Sarawak, Kuching their new home. The shipping fleet was registered and operated mainly out of other countries and ports in Southeast Asia.

The Holzstam family remained in Sarawak, where they became citizens, until the start of World War II. At this time their shipping dynasty was a notable force and a powerful trade house in Southeast Asia. When the Japanese started beating the war drum, Otto again realized that it was time to make a move; he had to save his shipping dynasty from the onslaught of the invading Japanese forces. The Holzstam family left for Australia before the Japanese occupation in 1941. Otto's shipping dynasty once again rode out the storm in the neutral ports of South America.

The family returned to Sarawak after the end of World War II and the capitulation of the Japanese in 1945. The Holzstam business empire was intact, and business flourished in the years after the war. A large part of the British, Dutch, and Japanese merchant navies and shipping industry had been crippled by the war, but Otto Holzstam was there to fill in the gaps. Business expanded and the family became one of the wealthiest families in Southeast Asia. Their interests were no longer just in shipping, however. The Holzstam business empire expanded into mining, exporting spices, raw materials, and rubber, and investing in the gaming and casino industry in the Portuguese enclave of Macau, close to Hong Kong.

Today, in the twenty-first century, the Holzstam business empire was officially run by the grandson of founder Otto Holzstam, Thomas Holzstam. However, it was common knowledge that the business empire was still mainly run by Thomas's eccentric father, Andreas Holzstam. Andreas Holzstam was known as "Lawrence," and at Rossi & von Horstenbrik Cie Bank in Singapore; he was known just as Lawrence. Andreas the old eccentric, and effective ruler of the business empire, believed he was Lawrence of Arabia, hence the account was called the Lawrence account. The Lawrence account was the largest account by far at the bank in Singapore. In fact, it was the bank's largest client globally. The portion of the Holzstam wealth deposited in Rossi & von Horstenbrik was only a fraction of the whole family's wealth. Richard knew that the family had bank accounts all over the world, including at competing banks in Singapore and Hong Kong.

Richard had inherited the Lawrence relationship from a previous Swiss banker who had returned to the head office in Switzerland. The Lawrence account was always managed by a banker sent out from the head office in Zurich. The account was too large and important to be managed by a local Singaporean banker—although a local Singaporean banker probably would have been better at serving the account from an Asian perspective, this never happened. The bank's head office in Zurich considered it too much of a risk; the chance of the Singaporean banker jumping ship to go to a competing bank was considered too large, and judging by the turnover of Singaporean bankers at Rossi & von Horstenbrik Cie Bank in Singapore, they surely had a point. The most important and deciding factor was the simple fact that the Holzstam family had always wanted and demanded a German-speaking banker from the head office to be the banker in charge of their account. They wanted an outsider, someone not Asian, to manage their account. The philosophy of old Otto Holzstam had always been "keep your neighbor close, drink beer with him, and learn his secrets and weaknesses, but never let him know the ingredients of your daily soup." What a wise and charming character Otto must have been.

Richard received a text message from Louise: "I miss you" it read. He replied "Me too." Jonas from Midnight Oil called and asked if Richard was coming down for beers that day, but Richard replied that he was busy and would catch up with the Midnight Oil crew over the weekend. Richard was going home tonight. He needed to think.

CHAPTER 8

Wednesday, 9 January
Singapore

Richard awoke as usual just after 6:00 a.m. and felt miserable. He had had a weird dream that he was on a boat on a river that was surrounded by jungle, and the boat was surrounded by Africans and Arabs, with the captain of the ship wearing a green wind jacket. The dream ended with Richard falling from a high tree. The dream was some weird combination of Joseph Conrad's book *Heart of Darkness* and the epic 1962 film *Lawrence of Arabia.* Richard left the house and took bus number fourteen straight to the financial district and to work. He alighted at Collyer Quay, close to the Fullerton Bay Hotel. When he arrived at the bank, he checked the overnight client orders and called one of the clients in Europe.

"Hello," Richard said. "The order was not executed."

"Great," the client said. "Have a nice day, and by the way, how is the weather in Singapore?"

"Hot and humid."

"Great. We have snow here."

"Good for you," Richard said.

Richard sometimes missed the four seasons and the climate in Europe, especially those splendid sunny days in the mountains and the snow. He missed having a glass of red wine with friends in some *osteria* or bar in Milan, warm inside and cold outside.

Suddenly Richard's phone rang. It was Maximillian saying that he wanted to see him immediately. When Richard stepped into Maximillian's office, he saw that the deputy CEO, Massimo Rossi, was present as well. Richard took his seat in the other vacant visitor's seat.

"Good of you to come by, Richard, on such a short notice," Maximillian said.

"Sure, no problem."

"Massimo will join us today so that he is up-to-date and in the loop as well."

"OK."

"So what have you found out about the Strydsteen account? Hope it's all good news."

Richard thought, there goes Maximillian again with his self-good psychology. Richard knew this game. By anticipating good news Maximillian was trying to make his opponent feel inferior. If that person had to deliver bad news, he or she was in a weak position. Some people would prepare themselves with some good news that could be delivered along with the bad news to soften its impact Richard did not have this issue; he always responded by stating the way things were. Maximillian might run the office under his personal reign, but he did not control Richard. Richard leaned back and prepared himself for a long session of Maximillian's verbal masturbation—the man loved to hear his own voice—hell, the man was in love with himself. Both Maximillian and Massimo were quiet, so Richard started his presentation.

"I have looked into the account and its background and have come to the conclusion that there are several inconsistencies in the client's background. Inconsistencies that could damage the bank's reputation. Something does not add up here, and as a result, I really think we should close the account. Also, well, I really don't understand, Maximillian...What are you doing as director of the Curaçao company, Parbal Bry N.V. that is sending money to the Strydsteen account here?"

"What? Are you crazy?"

Richard took out a printout of the company's registered details from the Curaçao Chamber of Commerce and Industry internet site. He handed it to Maximillian, and there it was in black and white—Maximillian von Horstenbrik, director, and then the name of the company, Parbal Bry N.V., and its location, Curaçao.

"It's a mistake," Maximillian assured him. "I have recommended a company formation specialist in Curaçao to many clients, hundreds of them, on behalf of our bank. One of the lawyers in Curaçao must have mixed my name up with someone else's—a mistake, that's all.

"OK," Richard replied. "But it sounds very weird, though. I mean—"

Maximillian interrupted him. He slammed the desk with his fist then proceeded to shout at Richard, his face all red just like his suspenders. This was obviously not the news he had anticipated.

"How dare you question my integrity or the integrity of the client? This client, who, by the way, comes highly recommended from the head office in Zurich!"

"This is what I believe, and what my research and background checks have led me to think. Have you seen the file?"

Massimo Rossi interrupted the heated conversation between Richard and Maximillian. "OK, let's take a step back here. Why did you come to this conclusion, Richard?"

Massimo was the bridge builder in the office. As deputy CEO, he had repaired countless bridges between Maximillian and the local staff at the bank. Massimo had seen a number of talented bankers leave the bank simply because they could not get along with Maximillian, and some of these bankers had been very profitable as well. Richard again repeated what he had come up with, stating all his findings and his conclusion. Maximillian stared at Richard, and his face said it all—he was furious. Massimo Rossi again saved the day.

"OK, Richard, can you put all the facts in a brief report and send it to us?"

"There is no need for any damn written report here," Maximillian said. "What we need here is someone who asks the right questions, not the wrong ones. Come on, Richard. I know you dislike young Yann and the fact that he will probably be sitting in one of the director's seats in Zurich very soon—all this while you will still be talking to clients and locals about what stocks they should buy and sell. Yes, yes, I know, Richard. I know of all of your little share-trading schemes with the Hong Kong lady and others, and how you take your clients to cheap local restaurants instead of…well, instead of treating them like our clients should be treated, not as buddies of yours, but with finesse and exclusiveness. We are a bank, not a bar!"

Richard realized that it was useless to argue with Maximillian; arguing was what Maximillian was good at. Richard saw that the whole office outside was watching their exchange. Any normal CEO and head of a bank would be pleased if one of the bankers brought a case with a suspected reputation risk to his or her attention. It's called thinking ahead or damage control—but obviously not to Maximillian von Horstenbrik.

"OK, I am sure we can solve this problem," Massimo said, "if we think."

"*He* is the problem—Richard is the problem, and he does not sit in our boat," Maximillian said. "He follows his own interests and agenda. Look at him. He is happy now. It's all to get at Yann. He's jealous."

"OK, can I leave now? I think we're done here. I have done the job you asked me to do, and this has nothing to do with Yann."

"Yes, sure, you can go now. Go wherever you want. Yes, you are done here."

Richard left the small office and walked back to his desk. As he walked by the other bankers and assistants in the open office space, they all picked up their phones and pretended to be having conversations, the way people always do when an uncomfortable situation occurs in an open-landscape office. Richard sat down at his desk and stared into the air. Brenda, his assistant, asked him, "Everything OK, boss?"

"No, but it will be all right"

Richard took a long lunch and thought about what had happened during the meeting. Maximillian was surely not all well in his head.

When Richard returned to the office later that afternoon, Massimo came by his office and looked at him. He then lowered his head and spoke to Richard in Italian.

"*Tutto bene*?" ("All well?")

"OK."

"Remember to send that e-mail with your report to all, do you understand?"

"*Si, capo*." ("Yes, boss.")

Richard did as he was told and sent the e-mail with return receipt. *Voilà*, *finito*, *kaputt*, *schluss*, *färdigt*, *fin*, finished, time to leave for the day. *Les jeux sont fait* (The bets are placed), he thought, and he closed his computer terminal.

Richard left the office early, just after 5:00 p.m. Outside, the sun was shining and the temperature on the billboard marked thirty-two degrees Celcius. He decided to go down to Midnight Oil and have a few beers—what else was he going to do? He needed to think. He reached the bar on Boat Quay and sat down at one of the tables outside, his back toward the bar entrance, facing the walkway along the river; he was alone. Soon people would start to arrive at the various bars, as most offices closed down after 6:00 p.m.

Being Wednesday, it was ladies' night in Singapore. The bars along Boat Quay would soon be filled with single and not-so-single girls. Sometimes some girls would get lonely and bored with their all-female company. And just maybe some of these girls, after over-consumption of alcohol, were open to other suggestions and activities. For a male at the right place and at the right time, anything was possible. Groups of girls had already started arriving at various bars, and the noise level was getting louder by the hour. Richard drank his beer and watched the world pass by in front of his eyes on the walkway in front of him. He liked to come here by himself sometimes and just sit and watch people; it helped him think.

At the table next to him there were two British guys in pinstripe business suits a la 1980s London mode. The guys were obviously visiting Singapore; one could tell by their suits. They were wearing their suit jackets in the hot, humid Singaporean weather, and they were sweating rivers. Nobody wore a suit jacket in Singapore; it was standard and acceptable to just wear the shirt and tie as it was just too hot for jackets. When Richard and his friends saw these poor, uninformed visitors, they usually called them "head office," meaning that these people were obviously in Singapore on business, sent out from their head office, and no one had ever told them not to wear jackets. One time Richard had even seen a British banker wearing a winter coat. Maybe the air conditioning was uncontrollable in his office. In Hong Kong, on the other hand, people wore suit jackets year-round, even in the hot Hong Kong summer; every region had its customs.

Richard watched the people passing by: two Western girls in miniskirts with tennis rackets in their hands, a tattooed Cajun Louisiana rocker in a T-shirt and torn jeans holding a guitar, a group of girls who probably just came from the office, stopping at the various bars and looking at the drinks menus; they were surely looking for the place where they could get the most bang for their buck. A lady of the night, probably Thai or Cambodian, wearing a short miniskirt that demonstrated much of what she was marketing, walked by for the third time and smiled at Richard. Then she walked toward the go-go bar further down the road. Richard could hear the calls from the lightly dressed bar girls sitting outside that go-go bar, calling out to potential customers: "Hello, sir, won't you come in for a drink?" Any man who looked their way for more than a split second was game. The traffic of people passing by was getting busier and busier. At 7:00 p.m. Prosper arrived out of nowhere and without notice.

"*Bonjour*, *mon ami*."
"*Bonjour*, my French friend."
"Thought I'd find you here."
"Eureka! You're a genius."
"What's wrong, man?" Prosper asked. "You look like shit."
"Yes, had a fight with the master of the universe in the office."
"That's not good, man. You know he is not all good in his head."
"Yes, but it was inevitable."
"Shit, you have a problem, man. I can see it in your face."
"You want to talk about it...or just drink beer?" Prosper asked.
"Let's just drink beer." Richard replied.

They continued talking about other things and drowned their sorrows in beer.

Sometimes when you've had a bad day in the office, lost money, broken up with your girlfriend, or had a fight with your boss, it is better to get drunk with a friend, much better, at least, than sitting at home watching the walls around you.

Richard and Prosper left the bar around 9:30 p.m., just as the first glasses started to break on various bar tables on Boat Quay. These were the first signs that people were getting royally tanked up, when that magic line between after-work drinks slowly wandered into skipping dinner, continuing drinking, and hitting the town in full immersion. They stopped at McDonald's for a burger or two—a burger always increased the feel-good factor after a drinking session. Then they said their good-byes, and Prosper walked in a different direction.

Chapter 9

Wednesday, 9 January
Circular Road Taxi Stand, Singapore

After leaving Prosper, Richard walked over to one of the taxi points on Circular Road. When he saw her, it was too late; she had already seen him. Her porno-blond hair was blonder than ever, Richard thought. She shouted to him, "Richard! *Ciao*, Richard!" It was Anna, his ex-girlfriend, and running into her was not what he needed right now. She was about twenty meters ahead of him, walking toward him on the other side of the road. Then he saw it—the rumor was true—she was pregnant, her stomach shooting out from her well-trimmed, aerobics, yoga/marathon-running/model/bunny-shaped body, making it look like an upside-down ice-cream cone. He felt his anxiety level rise, the way it always did before an anxiety attack, first from his stomach, then to his chest, resulting in shortness of breath and the inevitable increase in body temperature, before hitting him in the face. It was too late to run away now, he knew. He had been avoiding her for months now, skipping her calls, avoiding the places they used to go, and avoiding her friends. He had not seen her since the breakup, and now of all nights to see this oversexed, soon-in-full-bloom flower was not his ideal scenario.

Anna, whom Richard had met upon arrival in Singapore, was a blond Swedish estate agent, ten years younger than him. She had left him for an older Swedish banker in his fifties living in Singapore.

The older man did not have more money than Richard, but he had a desire for children and a noble-sounding last name. His original name had been Magnus Svensson. Svensson was a very ordinary Swedish last name, much like Smith in England, Rouge in France, Torres in Spain, Tan in Singapore, and so on. Magnus had come from some not-so-glorious suburb of Stockholm, and in his younger years, he had been fascinated by the posh people of the well-to-do district of Östemalm in Stockholm. Magnus wanted all that they had, and to have that he needed to change. He had gone into banking and taken a job in a foreign bank in Stockholm. He had cut out all his old friends from his new life, stopped speaking to his family, started speaking in a posh city accent, and finally, the ultimate step, changed his name. In Sweden and Europe, in certain circles, it was sometimes more important where you came from than who you were or what you had accomplished in life. Magnus had not let his humble beginnings stop him; he had invented a new past, one that fit his new lifestyle, and a name that matched. Magnus was no longer a Svensson; he was now Mr. Mälarstål, taken from *Mälaren*, which was the name of the lake close to where Magnus had grown up, and *Stål*, which was the Swedish word for "steel." The name was supposed to sound noble, but Richard thought it was just stupid. Richard despised Magnus and all that he stood for. In Richard's eyes Magnus was a big fake.

Magnus and Anna and their circle of friends in Singapore, were like a few other white foreigners in Singapore and Asia: people from simple beginnings who had invented pasts for themselves that fit their new lives in Asia, pasts, in their minds, which could excuse their behavior toward some Asians. It had probably been the same one hundred years ago—behavioral patterns of certain people always seemed to stand the test of time. After a few months in Asia, they started acting like colonial masters of a long bygone era. Anna and her friends wanted to live a life like in the film *Out of Africa*, the only problems being that they were not in Africa, and they were at least fifty years too late. The ang moh-zation process could start: first the maid, then the colonial furniture, then the champagne brunches, high tea for the ladies and etc. It was ridiculous, and the sad part, of course, that they thought that the local Singaporeans looked up to them, Richard thought. The only reason any local Singaporean or Asian sucked up to these ang mohs, if they did, was because these ang mohs had something they wanted—their money—and why not? If it made these ang mohs happy, live and let live, Richard thought.

The name change had worked for Magnus, and it had worked for Anna too; she came from a simple beginning as well. The fact that Anna had dumped Richard for this older, arrogant, wannabe, "noble banker" did not help to raise Magnus Mälarstål on Richard's personal list of favorite persons. The breakup had been painful for Richard, because despite her faults, he had loved Anna deeply, but for Anna their relationship had merely been a change of scenery.

Looking back, Richard was happy that he and Anna were no longer an item. Anna had wanted to constantly be out and about, to be seen with the right people in the right places. After countless numbers of champagne brunches and various cocktail parties, Richard was fed up. After their breakup, he came to know that he had merely been a tool in Anna's vast toolbox. And he was not the only tool, unfortunately. Anna had had several other affairs during their time together; in fact, Magnus had been in the picture all along. Today Richard was single and happy with that. But now here she was again. What did she want?

Anna crossed the road and approached Richard, who was waiting at the taxi stand line. "*Ciao*, Enigma," she greeted him. That was what she used to call him. Anna had always tried to speak Italian to Richard when they had been together. She only knew a few words, but she had always done so, especially in public, because she thought speaking Italian sounded chic and cool.

"I'm fine. How are you?"

"I'm great. I'm pregnant."

"Yes, I see…How far along are you?"

"Almost six months now."

Richard did the math in his head. No, the baby could not be his.

"Don't worry, it's not yours!" Anna said just then.

A feeling of relief passed over Richard, and the tension that had built up in his body was released. First his body temperature dropped, then his shortness of breath evaporated, and lastly his feet again felt light, light like those of…a free man. They spoke for a few minutes until a taxi arrived. Richard offered the taxi to Anna and opened the door for her. Anna kissed him on his cheek and said good-bye with a "*Ciao*."

At one time he had loved her, at one time he had thought she was the one, but now she was the past, a memory on the shelf. He had dreaded meeting her again, but now he realized that it had felt good. Anna was definitely in the past now. Richard caught the next taxi and went home. Better to go home, he thought, as he was in no mood for any more surprises this day.

CHAPTER 10

Thursday, 10 January
Rossi & von Horstenbrik Cie Bank, Singapore.

It was 9:30 .a.m. as Richard sat down by his desk in the bank, the bank's transfer department called him, advising him that $10 million had just been transferred into the Strydsteen account, sender Parbal Bry N.V., from a bank in Gibraltar. One moment later, Maximillian's secretary called him, and requested his presence for a meeting with Maximillian on the double.

"The head office and I have come to the conclusion that it's time for you to go back to Zurich, Richard, to take up that position as head of the Asian team" Maximillian said. "Ulrich von Hoffstetter unexpectedly resigned yesterday as team head there, and the position needs to be filled urgently. You have been here for five years now, so it's high time to go back. I know this comes as a little surprise to you. Just let me say that this decision has nothing to do with the conversation we had yesterday. It's just a coincidence, Richard. Really, we have been discussing this for a while with the human resources department and the board of directors in Zurich, and now, well, it's just time to go home, Richard."

Richard was in shock. He could not believe what he was hearing. His whole body felt numb and dead. He could not believe that this was happening to him, not now. He knew that someday the day would come, but not now, not after the meeting they had yesterday.

"You have done a good job here, so you have every reason to be proud and to go back with your head held high. You have taken good care of Lawrence and the Tiger Lady. For this I am grateful, and so are they. It's time to go home, though, Richard. It's just the way it is."

"I don't want to go back home, though, not now," Richard said emphatically.

"This is business, Richard, and it has to be this way."

The angry and aggressive Maximillian from yesterday was gone. Now he was the understanding father like figure. The only problem was he would never be Richard's father. This was surely the role he played when he broke up with his little girlfriends after he got tired of them, after they had done everything he had asked them to do, and when they had started to ask him about the future and commitments. He would leave them like that, by being nice and understanding, and at the same time delivering the bad news. The young girls would, of course, for the rest of their lives, ask themselves, was it me? Was it something I said?

"I have already booked you a flight back to Zurich Saturday night. The movers will come to your house tomorrow. We will take care of everything, Richard. Zurich will call you this afternoon and confirm all the details. You will be expected to report to work in ten days. Call human resources at the bank in Zurich when you arrive, and they will set you up in one of the bank's flats. They are really nice flats, you know. I stayed there for three months a few years after my first divorce. I also have the pleasure of telling you that you will be receiving a 20 percent raise effective upon starting in your new position in Zurich. There. See it's not all bad news, is it…my dear Richard?"

"What about all the accounts? Who will take them over? What about Brenda, my assistant?"

"We're still working on the account split, but it will most likely be Yann. Brenda will continue working here and will be Yann's new assistant."

Of course it would be Yann, Richard thought. Yann had no client book, and he was a von Horstenbrik —how convenient. Richard felt the anger and frustration rising in him and it showed.

"So you are saying this has nothing to do with the facts that we discussed yesterday and the e-mail report I sent out? Nothing to do with the $10 million that was just transferred into the account?"

"Richard, please do not make this any harder than it is already. Accept it and move on."

Richard saw that Maximillian was getting upset and angry. He was not used to someone questioning him. The ones who had in the past were no longer working in the bank, and it looked like Richard would soon join them. During the previous conversation, Massimo Rossi had been quiet. Now he spoke.

"This is good for you, Richard," Massimo broke in and assured him. "Accept it and move on."

So Massimo was in on it as well, Richard thought. Of course he was. He had too much to lose.

"So, do you have any questions?"

"No, again. I believe you are sending me away because I know that you are involved with the Strydsteen account. I know too much and will be a thorn in your side if I stay here in Singapore. I know that you are up to something."

There. He had said it. He had lost control for a few seconds. Not a very diplomatic move, but it had to be said. He had cleared his mind. Maximillian's reaction was swift and predictable. He stood up and started his theater act; everybody in the office had to see who was in control here. He ruled like some Machiavellian prince, and his subjects had to fear him. He started shouting obscenities in German, such that the local Singaporean staff would surely have hid under their desks had they understood what he was saying. After his performance, Maximillian sat down again and calmed himself.

"Are you done?" Richard asked. "Can I go now?"

"Get out of my sight," Maximillian replied.

Richard stood up and walked out the door and slammed it behind him. He saw Maximillian stand up again and continue his show. The whole office was quiet as Richard walked toward the exit and left. None of the other bank staff picked up their phones this time; this was prime-time entertainment live, a real soap opera. One elderly Singaporean banker shook his head and said, "These stupid ang mohs, always so theatrical lah."

When Richard reached the street, he called his assistant Brenda, who picked up the phone instantly. He told her he would be out of the office the rest of the day, that he had been asked to go back to Zurich to start a new job there. It would happen quickly, and he would be in tomorrow to make some calls and say good-bye. He also told her that she would of course keep her job. "It's a bit short notice," he said, "but as you realize by now, I was just told myself." He could hear that Brenda was close to tears. "Don't worry, Brenda. You will be OK."

Richard took a taxi home. As the taxi was traveling on the ECP Highway toward the east coast and his home, he felt numb. He felt like he was part of some bizarre movie or news clip. He felt his world as he knew it, had been turned upside down.

After he came home, Richard quickly changed into shorts and a T-shirt and walked toward East Coast Park and Beach. He walked out on the sandy beach and sat down. The park and beach were full of people during the weekend, but today on a weekday it was deserted. He looked out on all the ships that had dropped anchor there in the bay. He knew there were thousands of ships out there, all waiting to dock at the busy Singapore port. A Singaporean friend had once told him that when there were a lot of ships anchored times were not so good. Richard had replied, "What do you mean 'not so good'? Lots of ships mean business, no?" The wise friend had explained to him the opposite: "When you see lots of boats anchored for days, it means that they are waiting for shipping orders and business. When times are good, boats never remain anchored for long; they just queue to get into the harbor." It made sense, Richard thought. Singapore was one of the busiest ports in the world, and if this brilliant theory was true, one could measure the world's economy by just looking at the boats—what a brilliant economic thermometer. Thousands of overpaid economists around the world, who could not predict the economic cycles even with their advanced rocket science and algorithmic models, would be out of a job in a moment.

Richard went for a long swim. He felt like his life had just ended. He looked out on the boats in the distance and started swimming toward them. He swam for an hour, at least, although he did not know why; he just swam. His brain was in a trance, in some sort of psychotic in-between land. He felt like what had happened this morning was not real, that it was not happening to him, not now. He found a good spot and started treading water; then a cramp in his leg set in, intense and painful, anxiety and fear followed. He floated there in the water and looked up into the sky. Had his luck run out? Was this the end? Was this his destiny? The cramps intensified, and he tried to find a position in the water that made the cramps go away—it didn't work. He was at least two kilometers from the shore line. The large container vessels out on the Singapore Strait were far away as well. A small fishing boat approached him. Richard started moving his hands, waving, trying to catch attention. The man on the boat saw him, and began shouting and gesturing frenetically. As the boat came closer, an elderly fisherman offered his hand, and Richard grabbed it, feeling safe. The man helped him into the boat and gave him a dry towel and a blanket.

The old fisherman said nothing, and neither did Richard. They looked at each other for a few minutes, but said nothing. Then the old man spoke in broken English with a Malay accent, "Bad day lah?"

Richard responded after a while, "Yes, you could say that."

The old fisherman continued smiling while he cut open a fish with a knife and cleaned out the interior organs, throwing them into the water. "Sometimes in life, we have to throw away what's inside us, good and bad, and move ahead in life, my friend." He spoke now with a perfect Oxford English accent.

Obviously there was more to this man than what met the eyes, Richard thought.

"Look, now the fish is clean—bad things gone, and good things gone as well," he said in a friendly voice.

Richard tried to figure out who this New Age, sea-born, philosophical, fishing guru was, but of course he found no answer. The old man never introduced himself, nor did Richard; there was no need. Sometimes in life you meet someone, if only for an instant, and you have the feeling that they see straight through you, that they know it all. On that small fishing boat, Richard and the fisherman talked for hours, about things that Richard had kept bottled up inside himself for years. It was as if the floodgates had been released, and he no longer felt like a bank safe; there were things that needed to be said. Richard helped the old man to clean and fillet the fish, and they talked and talked. The old fisherman then took Richard back to shore and left him there. Richard never learned the man's name or identity; all he knew was that his life had been saved.

After having left Richard at the shore, the old man picked up his large old Motorola mobile phone from 1990 and dialed a number. "He is on his way now. He will be OK now."

Richard went back to his place on the beach and sat down again. He contemplated what had just happened. He had almost lost his life out there on the ocean, and had it not been for the old man he would have been crab feed by now. He tried to focus on what had happened in the office earlier in the day. He had been told by Maximillian that he had days to leave the country. He had a new job in Zurich waiting for him, and it was a good one too. The reassignment was so quick, faster than usual procedure, and came only one day after he had confronted Maximillian with the findings of his research. One day after asking him his part with the account and his role with the company funding the account. Oh, dear old Max was in deep, Richard thought, and his reactions had been additional proof of that. If Richard's imminent transfer date had been set already, why had it not been mentioned to him before? Why had Maximillian asked Richard to look over that account if he was potentially involved? The risks would be too high that Richard would find something. The whole matter did not make sense. He summed up in his mind the reasons he thought were most logical:

1. Richard had discovered something Maximillian had not anticipated that he would find.
2. Maximillian had served him a hot potato that he did not want to handle himself. Richard was the responsible banker in charge of the account. He had accepted to take over the account from Yann. If anything went wrong, Richard would take the fall.
3. Maximillian was protecting Yann, his protégé. With Yann managing the Lawrence account, Maximillian's staying power in Singapore was secured.
4. Maximillian was involved in some scheme with the client and needed Richard out of the way, far away.
5. Maximillian was securing Richard's loyalty to the bank. He would keep quiet and take up the position in Zurich.
6. Maximillian was just a bastard who needed no reason for anything he did.
7. Maximillian disliked Richard.
8. A combination of all of the above.

Richard was not worried about any wrongdoing on his part; he had sent the e-mail to the compliance department as well. It was the compliance department that would decide whether the matter warranted further investigation and action. He had recommended the account be closed and raised the issue of reputation risk as well. However, the question remained: Why would Maximillian go through all of these steps and potential risks to his own position? He had a great job in Zurich waiting for him—maybe it was time to move on. What about Louise, though, and his friends? Could he leave them all behind with a "Thank you very much lah. It was nice." Singapore was home now. The sun was setting over the horizon, setting on his future, his past, and his dreams.

Richard walked home and parked himself on his couch, put on a DVD, and pressed play. *Lawrence of Arabia*—"Just the man for me," he said as the movie started.

CHAPTER 11

Friday, 11 January
Singapore

Richard spent the morning in the office making phone calls to all of his Asian clients; he had called all of his European clients the night before. He informed them as briefly as possible that he was going back to Zurich to take up a new position at the bank there, thanking them for their support during the last five years. Some of the clients already knew—news travels fast. When speaking to each client, memories of each one flashed before his eyes, the good times and the difficult moments as well. He had some difficult customers, but today no one gave him any problems. He called all of his clients other than the Tiger Lady and Lawrence — they had already called him.

He passed by the human resources department, signed all the necessary forms, and gave back his security entry pass. He had a meeting with Brenda in a closed client reception room. He felt like a robot by now—no emotions left at all. It wasn't easy saying good-bye to five years' work in one day. Brenda told him that the Strydsteen account had been blocked by compliance. *Voilà*! At least that is something, he thought. He had a meeting with Massimo Rossi in another client reception room as well. Massimo told him that he was sorry that Richard was going, but that he was sure they would see each other again soon. Massimo ended the meeting with the cryptic Italian words, "*Non disperare Richard. C'è sempre la giunglia,*" ("Don't give up Richard. There's always the jungle") and he smiled at Richard. Massimo often spoke to Richard in Italian, especially for important communications—they both shared Italian as their mother tongue. A common language is so much more than just a means of communications—it's a bond that goes beyond words.

Richard responded, "What the hell do you mean by this? I don't understand."

"In time you will understand. You will understand everything," Massimo said.

Richard thought Massimo was probably on some prescription drug. The guy was weird. He had definitely run too many mental marathons, but this took the prize. They shook hands, and the meeting was over.

Later Richard walked over toward Maximillian's office. He saw Maximillian stand up, getting ready to greet him. The whole office was watching Richard's every move. A few meters in front of Maximillian's office, Richard turned around and walked the other way. The last thing he heard before he walked out the security door that functioned as the entry and exit to the bank office was Maximillian shouting obscenities. Richard's move and exit had obviously caused Maximillian serious loss of face, something that happened rarely in the office.

He arrived home at the house just as the movers arrived. There were ten movers accompanied by their leader, Clarence. "Hi, I'm Clarence, your moving manager today." The ten effective movers packed all Richard's things in two hours. Most of the furniture belonged to the house and stayed on for the new occupant. Richard knew it would be Yann von Horstenbrik.

At 7:00 p.m. he was going to make the hardest call of them all, to Louise. He decided to wing it and took a taxi down to her uncle's food court in Bedok South because he knew she worked evenings there sometimes. He had to see her and tell her his news in person.

Twenty minutes later he arrived at the food court in Bedok. He was greeted by a Tiger Beer girl in her blue and white miniskirt and top; blue and white were the colors of the local Singapore beer, Tiger Beer. The Tiger Beer girls were sales personnel from the beer company who worked the tables in the food courts and sold beer. She greeted him, "Some beer for you, sir?" But Richard told her not now, but maybe later. He saw that Louise was standing next to her uncle's food stall talking to some customers. She saw Richard and excused herself from the customers and walked toward him, her whole face smiling.

"Richard, what a surprise to see you here!"

"Yes, well. I wanted to see you."

"Had dinner yet?"

"No, I thought we could eat together."

"Great. I'll get us some food."

She walked off and started ordering some food from her uncle. Arnold, the uncle, looked over at Richard and waved at him. Richard sat down by an empty table. Two seconds later the beer girl arrived again. "Some beer for you, sir? "Richard again declined.

He looked over at Louise. How do you tell someone that you love them and at the same time tell them that you are leaving? How do you do that without making it emotional? Well, you cannot; that's the simple answer. He knew now that he did love her. They had not even had sex yet, but he was so sure about what he felt. Although maybe she did not feel the same way about him. Maybe he was just an interesting distraction to her daily life. If that was the case, it would probably be the best-case scenario and the easiest situation for both of them. Louise arrived with the food and sat down.

"So what *really* brings you here, Richard? You know I dreamt of you yesterday. It was kind of weird. You were on a plane and…I was with you."

"I have to tell you something, something that is not very easy."

"You are leaving," Louise said.

"Yes, but how did you know?"

"I just knew...I felt it."

Of course. She was a woman. Her intuition had told her so. She saw straight through him, and she probably always had.

"I have received a transfer back to Zurich, and I am leaving tomorrow night. I just found out. They need me back in Zurich to take up a position that has been vacated. It's urgent, they say."

"It always is. Well, how do you feel about it?"

Richard saw that tears had started to form in her eyes.

"Maybe its better this way," Louise told him. "You would leave one day anyway. Maybe it's better sooner rather than later."

"I don't know. My life has just been turned upside down in the last forty-eight hours."

Louise was a grown woman and a mother. She was a realist, but she had to ask. She just had to ask. "Will you come back and see me?"

She was crying now, and the Tiger Beer girl approached and gave her a paper napkin. The Tiger Beer girl gave Richard a nasty look. She even walked away without asking if they wanted any beer this time.

"Yes, of course I will."

"OK. Let's not talk about it anymore now."

"But I want to tell you that I—"

Louise interrupted him by putting her hand on his mouth. "Sometimes it's better not to say anything at all."

They ate in silence and talked a little about church and her uncle's food. Her uncle had burnt the fried rice due to the healthy beer consumption that had taken place in the food stall before Richard s arrival. The cause of the celebration had been that her uncle had found a new chicken supplier that sold him chickens for a bargain price. Richard and Louise both laughed; it felt good to laugh again. After dinner Louise walked Richard to the taxi stand, where they said good-bye and kissed one last time. He could see her standing there from the taxi's rear window as the taxi pulled away. Then he saw her uncle come over and embrace her; she was crying. As the taxi rounded the corner, she was gone. Their love story had ended before it had even started—a building without a roof. It was not over, because it had never started, so why was it so heartbreaking?

CHAPTER 12

Friday, 11 January, 10:00 p.m.
Midnight Oil, Boat Quay, Singapore

They all sat down at one of the tables outside the bar. It was Friday night and Boat Quay was busy.

"Thanks, guys, for coming here on such short notice," Richard said to his friends.

"Hey, what is happening?" Giorgio asked. "Somebody die, or what? When you called this meeting of the Three Musketeers—sorry, Prosper, Four Musketeers—I got a bad feeling."

"I called you here because I have something to tell you," Richard said.

"Oh no," Matt said. "Here it comes—the gay confession."

They all laughed.

"Piss off," Richard said.

"Just joking, man," Matt replied. "OK, so it was you who got Anna pregnant, you sly bastard."

The whole table erupted in laughter again.

"You're a wanker, Matt!"

"So are you going to tell us, or what?" Giorgio asked.

"I am leaving," Richard stated. "I am going back to Zurich."

"No way. Get out of here," Matt said. "You have to do better than that for another vodka shot."

"It's true," Richard explained. "I am leaving tomorrow. Found out yesterday. Have to take up a position that has been vacated in the head office. It's urgent."

Silence set in. Nobody said anything. Matt finally looked at Prosper.

"Is it true? Is he going home?" Matt asked Prosper.

"It's true. He told me yesterday."

"Are you sure you are not going to get axed?" Giorgio asked. "They do it that way sometimes, you know—call you back and then give you the boot."

"Well, I guess I will find out. I don't have much choice really."

"*Bastardi*, *bastardi*!" Giorgio shouted in Italian.

"I'll still come back and visit," Richard said.

"You better, man!" Matt said.

"I will send you a postcard."

"Postcards are gay," Matt said.

"I know, Matt," Richard said. "That is why you like them."

They all laughed, besides Matt whose brain was working to come up with a good comeback. He just needed some time.

"OK," Matt said to the table, "let's go inside and get really pissed tonight."

"One for all, and all for one," Giorgio said.

The band started playing the Rolling Stones's "Jumping Jack Flash," and the party was on. Jonas, the bar owner, came over and asked Richard if it was true that he was leaving tomorrow. Richard told Jonas that it was true and that tonight was his last night, for now at least. Jonas's reply was that they had to get really pissed.

That night would go down in Richard's memory as one of the best nights ever, not that he remembered all that took place, but it was all worth it. It was very early on Saturday morning when the Three Musketeers stumbled out of Midnight Oil. Prosper had left just after midnight; he had a life. The drunk trio looked at the Fullerton Hotel and the Maybank Tower to get their bearings. They walked along the deserted street, the five-hundred-meter walk taking them an hour.

At one point they had to restrain Giorgio, who wanted to jump in the river singing some Italian pop song that was a tribute to the ocean. When they finally arrived at the taxi stand on Circular Road, they could barely stand. A taxi arrived, and Richard embraced his friends and said good-bye. When the taxi drove off, he saw Giorgio running toward the river again, shouting "swimming, swimming, swimming is good" and Matt wrestled him down halfway to the river. Richard closed his eyes and fell asleep in the taxi. These are my friends, he thought. Yes, my friends.

An older Singaporean man saw the two drunk ang mohs wrestling on the pavement. One of them seemed like he wanted to take a bath in the river, and the old man shook his head in disbelief and spoke out loud, "Only ang mohs." The old man sat down next to the river on an old empty bench. He opened his little metal lunch box and took out his breakfast. He looked around at all the high rise buildings around him. Some seemed to reach into the sky, he thought. When he was a boy he used to come swimming and fishing here at this exact point. All his boyhood friends were long gone, so were most of the buildings that he had played in as a boy. He touched the old wooden bench he was sitting on with his old hand, and caressed the wooden surface, the wooden surface he knew so well—the bench had been there when he was a boy and would probably be there when he was gone. And there he sat watching time pass before his old eyes. He watched the two ang mohs finally stop wrestling and retreat into the shadows. "Now that is a sight that also has stood the test of time" he said to himself; then he drank his kopi, and ate his kaya toast.

CHAPTER 13

Saturday, 12 January
Somewhere in the Jungle, Borneo

The old man lit the wooden pipe. He had just finished the meeting with the elders. "So now you know what to do with him?" he said as he exhaled the sweet white smoke.

"Yes, I understand," another man replied. "Have I ever failed you?" He continued, "We will use the hunting potion. A small dose works with people too."

The old man nodded his head in agreement. "When you have him, take the normal way. He must not see!"

"I understand. Not to worry. Relax. We will do it as we usually do."

The sound of chants outside the simple hut were getting louder, signaling that it was time to eat.

"I see a storm coming—a dangerous storm, a man-made storm. They will throw everything at us. We must be ready, or we all fall. All of this will fall down. We must get to him first, before they do," the old man said as he extinguished his pipe.

His companion said nothing. He knew that the old one always spoke in riddles; it kept his people alert.

The old man picked up his old Motorola mobile phone and dialed a number. Far away on a small fishing boat, another old man picked up his mobile phone and listened to the command: "Keep an eye on him. Use whatever resources you need!"

The old man on the fishing boat confirmed the instruction received with a short reply. "It will be done." Then he got undressed, put on his swimming googles, strapped a backpack on his back containing his gear, and put on the simple traditional *Sirat* loin cloth that served as his swimsuit. He waited for the darkness to fall, then he dove into the ocean and started swimming toward the Singapore shore line.

CHAPTER 14

Saturday, 12 January
Singapore

Richard spent his last day in Singapore getting his bags ready and relaxing. He made some more phone calls to friends and family. He went down to MacRitchie Reservoir for a run. MacRitchie Reservoir was the large water reservoir situated at the middle of Singapore Island. The artificial lake-like water reservoir was surrounded by lush jungle forest. The area was a reprieve from the busy streets of Singapore. Here one heard no traffic, only the sounds of the water and the animals in the jungle. There were several walking and running trails encircling the reservoir, even a golf course. It was like stepping into the jungle and back in time. He took the twelve-kilometer run around the reservoir, through the humid jungle forest. On the way, he met a group of Italian men who ran counterclockwise, and they greeted him, "*Buongiorno.*" Richard laughed out loud. You have to love the Italians, weather in Rome, Naples, Timbuktu, New York, or the jungle; in traffic as in life, they found their own way of arriving at the destination. He passed an old Singaporean man who looked to be in his eighties, bravely jogging in the hot temperatures. What a man, Richard thought. Hope I am like that when I get old, he mused. He passed two Indian Singaporean women in their jogging-adjusted traditional saris and bright-pink jogging shoes, a perfect example of tradition meeting the modern world. At one time he was passed by three pretty, Singaporean, twentysomething girls in their brightest and tightest jogging attire, all with the mandatory iPod on the arm. They ran twice as fast as Richard, and in a moment they were past him and gone. After his run Richard had a drink and rested at the snack bar at the reservoir's entrance. He would miss MacRitchie Reservoir that was for sure.

He closed the door of the black-and-white bungalow that had been his home for the past five years. He handed the keys to the agent responsible for the house. He said good-bye to Youssef, the gardener, and shook his hand. Youssef told him, "For what you have done for me, I will be eternally grateful, Richard. Go now with Godspeed; we will meet again, sooner rather than later, God willing. It is written." Richard got into the taxi that was waiting for him on the road outside and left.

He boarded the giant A380 plane, flight SQ348, and got a window seat. He flew business class. The young, beautiful air stewardess greeted him and showed him to his seat. She addressed Richard by his name, one of the bonuses when flying business class on Singapore Airlines. Richard was always impressed with this extra attention to detail. The stewardesses had a list where they could see all the names of the passengers in business class, and they used that list very well. The giant plane lifted off into the night, only this time it was different; this was good-bye in its most pure and crystal way. The phrase "no regrets" seemed empty now—his mind was all but clear, and regrets, well, he had a few. He looked down and saw the city lights of Singapore disappear below him. The city had been his home for the last five years. As the lights disappeared below him, night was all around. The lights went on in the cabin, and the dinner service started.

Richard had gone back and forth to Zurich countless times over the years. He usually flew back once a month to visit clients and the head office. He had developed a special procedure over the years for the twelve-hour flight: drinks, dinner, music, movie, drinks, sleep, breakfast, music. Going to the toilet was a bit difficult to work into the schedule, so it was left as a joker in the program. Richard also enjoyed flying business class on Singapore Airlines because he did not have to worry about the potential guy from hell sitting next to him, as he would in economy class.

The beautiful stewardess removed his dinner and asked him if he wanted more wine. "Top up your wine for you, Mr. Lardelli?" Top up was one of those brilliant expressions of English that had been adopted into everyday use in Singapore. Top up your petrol, top up your wine, top up your cash card, top up your bank account, top up your plate. Richards's all-time favorite was the sign he had seen in a restaurant in Singapore, next to the coffee machine: "Thank you for topping yourself OFF." He sat back, sipped his wine, and put on his headphones. He thought of Louise and missed her. After listening to some music, he switched to the movie menu on the interactive handset—the movie classics menu—and selected his all-time favorite, *Lawrence of Arabia*. He watched the movie, and his mind traveled far away into the land of Arabia and the desert. After the movie, the stewardess helped him fold out his seat into the horizontal bed, and he fell asleep straightaway.

He woke up as breakfast was being served. They were flying somewhere above Asia Minor. The captain told the passengers that they would be landing in Zurich in about two hours, ahead of schedule, at 7:15 a.m. local time. He declined the offer of breakfast, instead choosing to lie on the reclining seat bed and look up at the cabin ceiling. In a few more hours he would be home, but home to what and who was he now? Was he an accomplice to a cover up? Was his silence a proof of his support for the alleged criminal activities of the Strydsteen family? The price was obviously his silence, but it went against all he believed and against his conscience. What Maximillian was trying to sweep under the rug was not right—something drastic had to be done.

He sat up and felt something hard on the bed below him. He reached down and found that it was little Mary's special rock; it must have fallen out of his pocket. He had no recollection of putting the rock in his pocket, though; he was convinced he had placed it in his suitcase. He looked at the rock in his palm and closed his hand around it. The little rock felt warm, and it fit perfectly in his hand. At this moment Richard realized that the universe was telling him something, that finding this rock in this very instance was no coincidence. It was time to wake up and act; otherwise, he would miss it all. He made up his mind in that moment that he was going to set things right and he was not going to miss it all.

He asked the stewardess for some paper and an envelope. He started writing and completed the short note in five minutes. He sealed the envelope and put it in his pocket. He was not going to miss it all.

Mr. Ueli Schweizer, immigration officer at the Zurich Airport, had just finished his morning coffee in his office. He had just finished reading the *Blick Zeitung*, a daily Swiss tabloid. It was time to go to his morning shift at the passport control and immigration counter. He always liked the busy morning shift when all the overnight intercontinental flights came in. He took his newspaper and put it into his jacket pocket. He straightened out his large moustache, the one that was in eternal fashion among countless Swiss German men in uniform, and made his way toward passport control. One of the first passengers he checked was a forty-something Swiss man, well-dressed and quite handsome, Ueli thought. He looked at the passport and scanned it. Then he spoke to Richard in Swiss German.

"*Guete morge, Herr Lardelli. Von woher kommen sie?*" ("Good morning, Mr. Lardelli. From where are you coming?")

"Good morning, from Singapore," Richard always spoke English to the Immigration officers.

"*Ach so, sind sie hier im geschäft oder ferie?*" ("Are you here in business or vacation?")

"Both."

"*Das isch aber rechts so.*" ("Sounds good.")

"Yes."

Richard took his check-in bag from the trolley belt, and two minutes later he was outside the customs area walking through the lines of awaiting families, mothers, fathers, girlfriends, boyfriends, husbands, and wives. There was no one waiting for him—yet another sign from the universe, he thought. He headed straight to the nearest kiosk where he bought some stamps, and then he walked over to a mailbox, where he mailed the letter he had written on the plane.

He then went upstairs to the departure floor. He sat down on one of the benches and took out his laptop and went on the web. He went to the Singapore Airlines site and booked himself a ticket back to Singapore that same morning, flight SQ347, leaving at 11:30 a.m. Before going through the security check, he stopped at a jewelry store and bought a gift for Louise. It was expensive, but it felt so right.

Ueli Schweizer, the Zurich Airport immigration officer, had just finished his break. He was on his way to his late-morning shift. He adjusted his moustache and sat down in one of the passport control booths; this time he was checking departing passengers. Ueli was not surprised to see Richard again. He had seen it all, really, in his thirty years at the airport—millions of passengers, countless fake passports, the myriads of fashion choices. Besides, he had been informed by phone just a minute earlier that Richard was coming back. Ueli stroked his moustache. Thank God my moustache is always in fashion. My only constant and loyal companion through all these years on the job, he thought to himself.

He looked at Richard on the other side of the glass window and addressed him in English this time.

"Already back?"

"Yes."

"Did you forget something?"

"Yes, my life."

"I see. Are you sure there is nothing else you have forgotten here as well?"

“No, I have and understand everything now” Richard replied and smiled.

“That pleases me. Sounds good.”

As soon as Richard walked away toward the planes, Ueli picked up his old Motorola 1991 mobile phone and dialed the number. “He is going back. He is on his way now, Singapore flight SQ347.” The voice at the other end acknowledged the message with a short and blunt “Good. It was written then.”

Ueli wondered what Mr. Lardelli had done. It had been a while since he had spoken to the old wise one. Whatever it was, he knew that the man boarding the plane would soon be in for one hell of a ride. One thing was for sure: it was never boring working for the old wise one.

Richard later boarded the plane and flew into the gray, rainy, Zurich sky. He was on his way to his new life.

Far away in a distant land and time zone, the candlelight in the tower glowed—a new candle, a new light, a signal to be seen near and far. The beacon had been lit, the first of three.

CHAPTER 15

Monday, 14 January
Singapore

Maximillian von Horstenbrik sat in his office and looked out the window. Below him he could see the Singapore River and the city. He had the corner office, so the view was spectacular from the twentieth floor.

He was pleased with himself. His plan had worked out according to his expectations. In the space of a few days he had most likely guaranteed himself a few more years as the head of Rossi & von Horstenbrik Cie Bank in Singapore. It was necessary, the word was out that some of the senior board members in Zurich felt that Maximillian had outlived his purpose in Singapore, and should retire. He had successfully removed that self-righteous Richard, installed his nephew Yann in his place, and removed the imminent threat of being discovered. If this did not work, well, he had a plan B, and plan C in store as well. On top of this he had met a new girlfriend over the weekend.

It had been a cunning plan, but not without risk. Yann, his nephew, had come to his office two weeks ago with a long, white face, literally shitting bricks. He had received the first money transfer on the Strydsteen account—the account Maximillian had given Yann, the one Maximillian had himself opened a few years ago. When Yann had received the funds on the account, he had been forced to do some research on the file, as most of the client information was missing. He had gone to the Internet and found all the articles about the client's father, Alain Strydsteen, the pending court case in Paris, and of course, some information on Bernard Strydsteen. Yann had never dared to question Maximillian; he was, after all, his uncle and his protector. Yann would not question him now, either; it was too uncomfortable an experience, and a von Horstenbrik does not question another von Horstenbrik. He had explained that he had called Bernie to ask about the funds that had been received in the account and the funds origin, and Bernard had said that it was his father's money, and that he was only keeping the funds for his father until the court case was finished, just to be safe. This was, of course, always a big worry to banks when such activities were discovered. The account holder was depositing someone else's funds in his account and pretending like they were his. In Bernard's case, his father was also a person under investigation for, among many charges, money laundering. Bernard was, however, honest about it and declared the origin of funds as his father's. He was not committing any crime as such; parents often send money to their children for all sorts of reasons. The worry for Yann was that Bernard declared that he was keeping the funds for his father in his account. Yann was not sure if Bernard was either stupid or smart. In any case, the activity in the account was a concern and worry. Yann had told Bernard not to receive any more funds until further notice, and Bernard had not taken this communication lightly and promptly hung up the phone on Yann. Then Yann got scared and had come see to Maximillian. Yann always came to him when he had a problem. He was "Uncle Maximillian" when faced with problems, and when there was no problem he was just "Mr. von Horstenbrik."

Upon receiving the news from Yann, there was no way he, Maximillian, could intervene. Of course neither Alain Strydsteen, nor his son, were going to take any phone calls from the head of a bank in Singapore inquiring about funds transfers from Alain into the account, especially not Alain Strydsteen who was currently being investigated for, among other charges, money laundering, human trafficking, and the financing of illegal rain forest depletion and lumbering. Maximillian did not care about the alleged criminal activities of Alain or his son, Maximillian reasoned in numbers – if it was up to him, they could ship the whole population of Africa into the Amazon rain forest, and let them cut down the trees, it meant nothing to him. His social standing and where he was in life at this moment—meant everything, and he would do anything to protect that.

What Maximillian feared was going to happen had happened, and it was going to get worse. It had all started a few weeks ago and had culminated with that one phone call from Alain Strydsteen that he had received last week, when he had been advised that the "red wine was on its way." Even though Alain Strydsteen had advised him of the transfers, he had hoped that Alain would not actually send the ten cases of "red wine." But Alain had gone through with the money transfer just as he had said.

First, $500,000 had arrived, and then $10 million had been credited to the account. Maximillian had told Yann to accept the first funds transfer to the account, the second transfer, Maximilian had approved himself; there was no other way, he reasoned. The stakes were too high. He just had to accept the incoming funds, and the funds kept on coming. Alain could not be crossed. Why had they been so stupid and transferred funds now? Maximillian thought to himself. Why had the imbecilic son not just said his father was sending him money as a gift? It would have been a much more simple solution. The son was obviously stupid and arrogant, spoon-fed and spoiled, Maximillian thought. Now they had a potential hot potato in their hands that he, Maximillian, had to solve.

Of course the fact that Richard had discovered that Maximillian had been noted as one of the directors of the Curaçao company that was sending the funds did not improve the whole situation. How the hell did Richard have access to the Curaçao company registry? Maximillian had no idea that it was public. This was something he had missed, and it was a potential disaster. The compliance department, who would of course block the account—it was inevitable after Richard's e-mail—had no knowledge of this fact. Richard had not mentioned it in the e-mail. Luckily, Maximillian had time to erase his tracks. Hell, the compliance boys would probably launch a suspicious funds transfer activity review into the account, and eventually they could even inform the local financial authorities. Maximillian was not worried about this as much as his own name appearing in the investigation. If the bank reported the case to the local financial authorities and regulators they acted exactly by the book, and it was always better to release information voluntarily regarding suspicious activities than to have the authorities ask you. This was true in all financial centers around the world. Rossi & von Horstenbrik would be seen as complying and acting correctly by reporting a suspicious activity.

Maximillian would have to find a solution, and fast, if it came out that Yann was the responsible banker when the funds came in. It would surely guarantee that Yann would not stay for long in the offices of Rossi & von Horstenbrik; he would be called home to Zurich, as far away from Singapore as possible. Yann was Maximillian's ticket to a few more years in Singapore. With Yann responsible for the Tiger Lady and the Lawrence account, Maximillian would need to remain in Singapore to supervise Yann and his work. Yann was family; he would keep quiet and be loyal. If Maximillian could get someone else to handle the troubled account of young Strydsteen, someone who could take the fall should things go wrong, it would be so much easier—yes, Richard could be the scapegoat, he devised.

Richard had, for such a long time, been a thorn in his side. Richard had gained the respect and trust of Lawrence and the Tiger Lady, and they had both explicitly asked for their accounts to be handled by Richard upon his arrival in the Singapore office. Maximillian had never understood this; neither of the clients had ever even met Richard when he arrived in Singapore. Maximillian did not speculate any further into the reason why the old, eccentric Lawrence and the stingy Tiger Lady were interested in Richard; they were just two crazy old dragons.

Richard had, over the years, also gained the respect of local fellow employees, and this Maximillian detested. No, this time the old fox was going to outsmart the young fox. Yes, he would pin the potential debacle on Richard before the storm hit. Maximillian needed to act quickly if he was to have any chance of achieving his goals, and he had. Maximillian was quite pleased with himself. He had called the head of the bank in Zurich, who was also a von Horstenbrik family member. Maximillian had heard that the head of the Asian private client group was not happy with his job in Zurich, so Maximillian had convinced him to tender his resignation immediately, or face unspecified consequences, and the Zurich banker had promptly resigned. Maximillian had the perfect replacement candidate who was also available on short notice. The head of the bank in Zurich also had a niece who desperately wanted to work for a year or two in the bank in Singapore—a perfect scenario for all—you give some, you take some. Maximillian would ask Richard to take over the troubled account and to offer "help" to Yann and the bank. Richard could not say no; he was too loyal to do that. Maximillian would also send Yann away just so he would be at a safe distance the moment Richard took over the account. Richard would take over the account and find the uncomfortable facts about the background of the client just in time for the second transfer of funds to come in. When this happened, Richard would be the responsible banker of the relationship and take the heat and the fall. At this point, Maximillian would offer Richard a way out, transferring him back to Zurich and a good position there in the head office. Richard had been in Singapore for five years, so it was even almost credible and logical. When the real storm hit, if it did, Richard would be long gone and back in the head office, far away from any local investigation.

It was a brilliant plan, Maximillian had thought; he would guarantee himself a few more years in Singapore, he would get rid of

Richard, and he would make the bank look good to the authorities if things went that far. The bank would, after all, be seen as having acted in an exemplary way by bringing the suspected case to the attention of the authorities. The only snag to the whole plan was that Richard had not acted the way he was expected to. On the contrary, Richard had put the whole plan into jeopardy. Maximillian had not expected that Richard would play Sherlock Holmes and discover his involvement with the setup of the Curaçao company that had sent the funds. Another worry, of course, was the fact that Richard had sent the e-mail to the bank's compliance department as well, where he recommended the closing of the account along with the presentation of some of his findings.

After the first meeting with Richard, Maximillian had immediately had his contact in Curaçao amend the corporate documents of the Curaçao company, so that the registrar now showed no sign of Maximillian von Horstenbrik as director. Maximillian had helped set up the company and account for Alain Strydsteen at the Gibraltar Bank. Maximillian had also agreed to act as a company director, at Alain's insistence. In hindsight, it had been foolish, but Maximillian had never imagined in his wildest dreams that Alain was going to use the account to send funds to Rossi & von Horstenbrik Cie Bank in Singapore, and besides, he had had no choice; Alain had dirt on him. Alain was obviously in a lot of trouble and desperate to get his money as far away from Europe and the ongoing French police investigation as soon as possible. Maximillian again thought how stupid he had been to befriend Alain Strydsteen all those years ago, but now it was too late.

Another worrying factor was that Massimo Rossi, Maximillian's deputy, had yesterday taken an abrupt leave of absence and seemed to be unreachable. Maximillian had, of course, called the Tiger Lady and Lawrence to communicate Richard's departure; this was before he had communicated the news to Richard himself. Lawrence and the Tiger Lady did not seem surprised at the news, though, but who could have told them? The only possible culprit was Massimo Rossi; he was the only other person in Singapore who had known. Maximillian decided he would have to keep a close watch on dear Massimo and even eventually come up with a plan to have him transferred back to Zurich as well. The whole plan was far from perfect, but it was the best he could do, Maximillian thought. He had survived far worse over the years, and Lady Luck had always been on his side. He just had to ride the storm out, the way he always did. Should it all go wrong, well, then there were many people in the bank involved now, and it's always better if there are many hands caught in the cookie jar.

CHAPTER 16

Monday, 14 January.
Singapore

Richard caught a taxi and left Changi Airport behind him, destination downtown. His new life had started. He had sent his resignation letter to the bank in Zurich on his short pit stop there. The bank would probably receive the letter, mailed in Zurich, today or the day after. He would be contractually bound to work for the bank for another three months, as this was his official notice period. However, he knew that he would be put on gardening leave immediately. Gardening leave was the term used for the practice of letting a departing employee go, effective immediately and with full compensation. It was standard in the financial industry among traders and private bankers or other key employees who had extensive client-serving roles or access to sensitive bank information. There was no interest for the bank to have the resigning employee sit around in the bank for the remaining period of his or her notice period; the risk was too large that the time would be used to try to move clients or access sensitive information—information that the departing employee might bring to his or her new employer. It was considered better, and safer, to let the employee go immediately with full pay. During the remaining notice period, the employee was usually not allowed to take up other employment. It was called gardening leave, because one could supposedly work in the garden during the leave and that was about it.

Richard knew he would get the call any day now from the bank's human resources department in Zurich. They would confirm the receipt of the resignation letter, and he would be placed on gardening leave with immediate effect. There was no way that they would oblige him to report to work for the remaining time of his notice period. They might ask him who his new employer was, if any, but this was of no concern for Richard because he had none.

He had decided to take a break from working as a banker—he was fed up and wanted no part of the whole thing anymore. Also, something in his mind had changed since his near-death experience off the coast of Singapore. Life is precious, no matter how bad things are or what misfortunes have happened. He was going to set things right. He held no grudge against his former employer, the bank. The bank had been good to him, and he had been happy there. It was just time for a change. Also he wanted no part in the dirt that Maximillian was trying to wipe under the rug. He could not support the alleged activities of the Strydsteen family, it went against his conscience. He knew however, that his voice meant little, and speaking out can sometimes be dangerous. So what could he do and how could he make a difference? To be a whistleblower and for one moment of glory spend the rest of your life on the run? Too keep quiet? Was there another way? Now his future was wide open, and he had left his comfort zone and opened the door that led into the unknown—and yes, a voice inside him told him that in the end justice would be served. He opened up his mobile phone and saw that he had several missed calls from both Lawrence and the Tiger Lady.

He got out of the taxi at Novena Velocity Shopping Center, in the residential district of Novena in downtown Singapore. After picking up a new mobile phone and a quick lunch at one of the Japanese restaurants on the second floor of the shopping mall, he caught another taxi. He called Prosper and told him he was back in

Singapore, and that he needed a place to stay for the night. Prosper was surprised that he was back so soon. Richard told him that he had resigned and was now a free agent, so to speak. Prosper invited him to come over to his place that same evening for dinner so they could talk some more.

Richard got out of the taxi at one of his regular drinking places in Little India. The bar was on the small, busy street called Dunlop Street. He greeted the bartender. Jim, an English bloke who had worked there for years.

"Wow! Fancy seeing you here so early. Bad day in the office?" Jim saluted him cheeringly.

"No just in need of a drink and couch for a few hours. Just back from some traveling, mate," Richard replied, tired.

"No problem. Pint of ale for you as usual?" Jim asked.

"Yes, sure, sounds great," Richard replied.

Twenty minutes later he was sleeping on the couch in the corner of the small bar.

At 7:00 p.m. he arrived at Prosper's flat with his suitcase and the duty-free bottle of whiskey he had purchased at the airport for Prosper. They ate a quiet dinner on the balcony, as Prosper's wife and children had already taken their dinner earlier.

"So you really did it? You left the bank?" Prosper asked him.

"Yes, it felt right," Richard replied.

"Wow! This is like a movie, man. You are insane!" Prosper countered.

"Hey, you only live once, man," Richard replied, laughing.

"What are you going to do now, just be a bum?" Prosper asked, smiling.

"Yes, why not? A gardening bum," Richard replied.

CHAPTER 17

Tuesday, 15 January
Singapore

Richard awoke late the next day. He had slept on the couch in Prosper's living room. He had not even heard when everybody had left the apartment in the morning. It was 10:00 a.m. now and high time for some breakfast and coffee.

After a light breakfast, Richard called one of his friends from Midnight Oil, Georgie "the Elvis" Fernandes. Georgie was a regular down at the bar. He was a thirty-something guy from the Philippines. Georgie was quite a character, to say the least. Georgie was known in the bar as Georgie "the Elvis", and this was the name he went by. Georgie had come to Singapore many years ago as a musician in a rock band from Manila, Philippines. His band was one of those many bands from the Philippines that made a living in Singapore playing at all the live music bars and venues. They played cover songs and had made a decent living for a while when they had first come to Singapore, several years ago. The singer in the band, Joy, had been Georgie's girlfriend, and she was from Manila as well. She soon left Georgie for a Singaporean man, who was also a music producer, a very convenient combination as she was now a recording artist in her own right. Georgie "the Elvis" and the Singaporean music producer were now a distant memory of Miss Joy; they had both been dumped along the way. The band in which Georgie "the Elvis" was the drummer had stuck together and still did some gigs now and then, but those gigs occurred rarely; however, at Midnight Oil he was a star in his own right. Georgie was not Elvis Presley, and he would never be the man himself, but he sure made one hell of a go at it. He was living his dream, so who in their right mind had the right to judge him? Many people never realize their dreams because they feel that their dreams are impossible to realize, and they let fear rule them. Luckily, there are people who follow their dreams, step out of their comfort zone, and step up to the task, people like Georgie "the Elvis."

Georgie Fernandes was a man of many talents, and he needed a job to be able to support himself and stay in Singapore. Over the years, he had worked as a bartender, producer, cook, teacher, real estate agent, tour guide, and private detective. Georgie "the Elvis" was a multitalented man and always held down several jobs at one time. He was called Elvis because his greatest hero and source of inspiration in life was Elvis Presley. He dressed like Elvis, talked like Elvis, sang like Elvis, and well, yes, he drank like Elvis too. Georgie was happiest when he stood at the bar counter of Midnight Oil with a beer in one hand, wearing his one-piece white Elvis bodysuit, his hair fixed like Elvis's, and if there was a Elvis song playing it was even better. He was even happier when he was on the stage doing his Elvis show; he lived and breathed Elvis. For all his eccentric traits and behavior, Georgie had a heart of gold and would do anything to help out a friend. Richard had helped Georgie out once several years ago when he was broke. Georgie had foolishly taken a loan from a loan shark; he was broke, unemployed, and his then-girlfriend Joy had just left him. He could not come up with the money, and the local loan shark had already started harassing him. The loan-shark's men had started threatening him and had sprayed the door to his apartment with red paint. The paint-the-door procedure was a common illegal modus operandi used by the loan sharks, a way to threaten, to make the person know that they could get to him. To let everybody else in the neighborhood know that here lived someone who did not repay his debt, and ultimately to inflict shame and loss of face. Richard had given Georgie the money to settle his debt. Georgie had repaid Richard in the following months; however, he had remained grateful for the help and had assured Richard, "I owe you big time." Yes, Georgie "the Elvis" was the man to call today.

Georgie had at one time worked as an English teacher in one of the private language schools down by Orchard Road at the heart of the Singapore shopping district, teaching English to foreigners. This had been one of his many jobs held in his multipurpose career. Georgie had developed what he called the "Elvis method" of teaching. Georgie was not going to teach the Queen's English, he was going to teach the King's English, the King's English being, of course, Elvis the King himself. The Elvis method consisted of playing Elvis Presley songs on a CD player all throughout the class period. The method was highly popular with the students but less so with the principal and management of the school. Georgie's career as a teacher was short-lived, and he was forced to move on eventually. It was during this brief teaching career, however, that Georgie had laid the foundations to his real estate career. Many of the students were in need of short-term accommodation during their stay in Singapore, the cheaper the better. Georgie had seen his opportunity and provided a service, helping the students and booking them into simple, cheap rental accommodations all over Singapore. The rooms were often small single rooms in houses or apartments, with cheap short-term leases. Georgie had once told Richard, "If you need a place to stay that's cheap and a little under the radar, I am your man." Now Richard needed a place to stay far away from the usual expat areas and the financial district—under the radar.

They agreed to meet up later that day in Little India by the exit of the Buffalo Road, Little India MRT Underground Station. Georgie had told him he had something suitable there for SGD$800—a single room with a shower and air conditioning, and yes, it was under the radar. Richard took the room.

During the afternoon, the bank called from Zurich, confirmed the receipt of Richard's resignation letter, and told him, as he had expected, that he would not be required to report for work anymore. He wanted to call Louise, but decided to wait; he first wanted to move in and get settled in his new place. Then he could plan a surprise for her at her uncle's food stall. He needed some time to organize the surprise first. The gift he had bought in Zurich for Louise needed to be presented in the right moment, and he had to be sure that she felt the same way.

Chapter 18

Wednesday, 16 January
Little India, Singapore

Richard moved into his new place the next day. The old house was situated on a small, quiet road adjacent to a large road that ran parallel to the more or less well-defined border to the Little India district; some called the border the curry line. The curry line was where the sweet smells of curry and jasmine filled your nostrils, eliminating all other smells of modern cities, and where the Little India district began.

The house was an old three-story independent house, or "landed property" as they were sometimes called. It had been built sometime before the Second World War. From the outside it looked rundown, but it had that quaint feel to it, the way a home should feel. The old concrete house was surrounded by a two-meter-high wall that encircled the property. There was a large garden with several palm trees and lush bushes that hid the house from street view. The house was one of three independent houses that stood in a row next to each other. The rest of the quiet street was composed of various small, traditional, low-rise Singaporean shop houses. The garden and plot that belonged to the house were so large one could build a small condominium on it. Just the land of the house was worth a fortune in today's real estate market. So sad, Richard thought, that in modern Singapore so often many of these old houses, all with history of their own, were being torn down and replaced by modern condominiums and apartment blocks. These lovely old houses, where generations had lived and grown up, were disappearing one by one. Often a whole large house was occupied by some older persons who owned the house and refused to move, but why would they? It was their home. So often as soon as the last occupier died, the heirs would move in and quickly sell the house and land, and before you knew it, there was another modern condominium in its place. One could not blame the children and heirs really; the profits from selling the land could be huge. Richard had had one of these old houses on his street where he used to live in the Katong area. That house had been occupied by an elderly Chinese Singaporean man who used to spend all his time in his lovely little garden. The only time he had visitors was when his children and relatives came to visit once a year for the Chinese New Year celebrations. During these few days of festivities, the man would erect a party tent in his garden for all the family and relatives who paid a visit, as was tradition during Chinese New Year. The garden would be decorated with the traditional Chinese red paper lanterns that glowed in the dark; it was a beautiful and heartwarming sight. One day Richard had seen an ambulance parked outside the old man's house and later found out that the man had passed away. Two months later the demolition trucks arrived, and the old house was no more. After another two months, the foundation for a small condominium had already been completed. Just like in any other metropolis in the world, land was scarce. Times changed and people's needs changed with it, and you cannot obstruct change—or can you?

The house Richard was to live in was composed of three floors with a common kitchen on the second floor and a common bathroom and shower on each floor. It was a traditional Singaporean property with the stairway in the middle of the house. The wooden stairway spoke each time he stepped on one of the steps, each step a different word in the wood language. Each floor had five individual rooms—in total there were fifteen individual rooms in the house and one small apartment on the top floor where the owner, Madame Tsui lived.

The house had been in Madame Tsui's family since its construction in 1933. Her husband had passed away ten years ago, and their children had all started their own families and now lived elsewhere. Upon the death of her husband, her children had tried to convince her to sell the house and cash in. But the old woman had refused; she had lived there her whole life and was not going to move now. Besides, none of the children had offered to take her in to live with them, as was often the tradition. Left with no income and a large house, she had started to rent out the individual rooms, mostly to young professionals working in the city center. The rent was inexpensive, and the house was centrally located as well. The rooms were in high demand, and none of them were left unoccupied for long.

The madame had a strict process for accepting new occupants to live in her house. Each new occupant had to go through a short interview with the madame herself and one of her nieces. She might have been old and frail, but there was never any doubt who was the commander-in-chief of the house. The interview took place in the common kitchen on the second floor of the house. After a cup of tea and some questions, the madame would speak her verdict, and the applicant was either notified yes or no, and that was it.

Richard had passed the test with flying colors—at least that was what he thought. It was difficult to know what Madame Tsui thought; she hardly spoke any English at all. Her niece translated from Mandarin Chinese into English. After the interview, the madame had spoken the magic word, yes, and Richard was accepted into the order of Madame Tsui's castle. The niece told Richard that he was the first ang moh that had lived in the house. After this translation, the old woman had looked at Richard and said, "You me first ang moh lah." What a charming character she was, the old madame. Richard replied, "Thank you." What else could he say? The madame had then laughed and spoken in the Chinese dialect to her daughter, who translated to Richard, "My mother thinks you are very quiet." Richard had no time to reply before the old woman laughed and looked again at Richard. "You me first ang moh, the quiet ang moh lah." She spoke in broken English. Great, she did speak some English after all, Richard confirmed. This was surely the beginning to a very fruitful and communicative relationship.

Richard had moved in straightaway that same day after his interview. The room was simple and clean—wooden floor and white walls, a double bed, a desk, closet, air conditioning, refrigerator, and TV. It was no larger than ten square meters. There was a large window with a glass door, and the door led to a small balcony facing the rear of the house. The room was on the second floor, adjacent to the kitchen. The guests kept the common space and their rooms clean in Madame Tsui s house; it was her house and her rules. These living conditions were light-years away from what Richard was used to; his room was about the size of the guest bathroom in the black-and-white bungalow he used to live in. He imagined telling his friends that he was living in a room the size of a bathroom; they would, of course, never believe him. Luckily, he had been able to cancel the shipment of his belongings back to Europe, and he was having them stored in a storage facility instead. All he had now in the room were his two suitcases, his laptop, and his mobile phones, along with a healthy dose of expectation. He spent the first night in his new home getting used to the sounds and ways of the house; the young couple upstairs were seemingly into nocturnal furniture moving. As the couple upstairs continued to move furniture, creating a new life and beginning, Richard went to sleep thinking of his future.

CHAPTER 19

Thursday, 17 January
Maximillian's Office, Singapore

Maximillian had heard of Richard's resignation from the human resources department in Zurich. This was not what he had expected, but he could live with it. In fact, maybe it was even better this way, he thought. His plan had worked out almost to perfection, until yesterday, when the shit had really hit the fan. Bernard Strydsteen, the twenty-eight-year-old student and client of Rossi & von Horstenbrik Cie Bank in Singapore had been nabbed in a routine border control inspection between Italy and France on the Côte d'Azur, on the French Riviera side of the border. He had been traveling from Italy in his red Ferrari sports car. Under the driver's seat the police had found an attaché suitcase with 200,000 euros in cash and some very interesting documents. The documents were especially interesting to the police after they found out that Bernard was the son of Mr. Alain Strydsteen, the famous French shipping magnate who was currently under investigation for human trafficking and money laundering. The documents included bank statements from three different banks in Zurich, Gibraltar, and Singapore, and the bank accounts were all in the name of the same Curaçao-registered company. Rossi & von Horstenbrik Cie Bank was one of the banks. The other documents were a complete set of corporate documents, including share certificates and articles of association of the company.

What a fantastic performance by Bernard, getting nabbed with all the eggs in one basket, Maximillian thought. Bernard was now being grilled by the police, who naturally, were very interested in all the documents, in addition to the 200,000 euros in cash—not a brilliant move either. The amount was well above the allowed limit for moving cash across the border of the European Union without declaring it. The police had, of course, been tipped off; they always were, and it did not take them long to realize who Bernard's father was and that he was currently involved in a court case involving money laundering and human trafficking. Maximillian was sure there was nothing random about stupid Bernard being stopped by the police. Why the hell did he have to take his Ferrari as well? He thought. "What an idiot!" Maximillian cursed out loud.

The newspapers had inevitably gotten ahold of the story; they always did. In the headlines one could read, "Rich Daddy's Boy Nabbed in Police Control," "Ferrari and Cash: The Lifestyle of Bernard Strydsteen," "Swiss Bank Account and Ferrari: Not Bad for a Student," and "Where Did He Get the Money?" The total value of money in the bank accounts with Rossi & von Horstenbrik Cie Bank was over $100 million. Bernard declared an income of $20,000 and bank accounts of $10,000 to the tax man in France, yes, Bernie had really outdone himself this time. The words in the headline that got the most attention were "Swiss Bank Account." Whenever the European press wrote about a famous person or not-so-famous person, if "Swiss Bank Account" was part of the headline, it was always news that sold. If it was not confirmed that the person had a Swiss bank account, the headline could always be changed from "Swiss Bank Account" to "Swiss Bank Account?" and sell just as many papers.

The discussions and negotiations between Switzerland and its neighbors regarding the Swiss banking secrecy had been going on for years. The Swiss maintained their banking secrecy, while their European neighbors wanted it dismantled. Year by year, the Swiss banking secrecy was being dismantled, piece by piece, client by client, secret by secret. Many neighboring countries felt that too many potentially undeclared fortunes of their citizens were being stashed away in Switzerland, far away from the tax man in these citizens' home countries. Switzerland was, of course, an independent country and not part of the European Union, and as such it had its own laws, the banking secrecy being one of them. Over the last years the Swiss had made several concessions and compromises with some of their European neighbors, and in particular with the United States. The treaties were constantly being renegotiated, and it was sometimes difficult to understand what the current status of the treaties was. One thing was clear: the European Union and the Americans, along with some Swiss political parties, were determined to eventually dismantle the Swiss banking secrecy; this was the end game. For whose profit and gain? Well, that was still to be decided; nothing is constant, not even history. Richard thought that the Swiss banking secrecy, seemed to be dying a slow death. All these changes had resulted in more and more Europeans who had money in Swiss bank accounts now starting to move their bank accounts in Switzerland to their home countries. Other account holders chose to move their funds to other financial centers that had yet to adopt international tax treaties and that operated under strict banking secrecy laws as well—countries that had yet to yield to international pressure. Europe was also coming out of the worst financial crisis since the Great Depression, and governments needed money: tax money. In the end, it's all about the money.

One of the banks mentioned in the newspaper articles was Rossi & von Horstenbrik Cie Bank. Bernard Strydsteen had accounts with the bank both in Zurich and Singapore. Of course the papers made no mention of the fact that Rossi & von Horstenbrik Cie Bank in Singapore had acted by the book and had promptly notified the respective financial authorities of the suspected activity in the accounts and that the cases were currently under investigation. The accounts had also been blocked and frozen in both jurisdictions, pending the investigation. The Rossi & von Horstenbrik communications officer in Zurich was surely getting a few phone calls these days. Singapore and Gibraltar had only been mentioned briefly in the articles; the amounts deposited in both places were too small, with the bulk of the funds deposited with Rossi & von Horstenbrik Cie Bank in Zurich. Bernard would now have to come up with some logical explanation why he had over $200 million stashed away in three different banks in undeclared bank accounts, and where the funds had come from. Some of the other involved banks had so far explained that they had not known that the father of young Bernard was under investigation for money laundering, a fact that the press and the financial regulators in Singapore, Switzerland, and Gibraltar were not impressed with. To know your customer was basic and fundamental in banking. The shit had really hit the fan, and it smelled.

Maximillian had anticipated some hiccups along the way, but not this. Richard was gone, and he knew of Maximillian's involvement with Alain Strydsteen and the debacle with the Curaçao company that had sent the funds. Luckily, Bernard had not had those corporate documents with him in the car. Had the regulators seen Maximillian's name on any documents? No. If so, the regulators and the police would have already knocked on Maximillian's own door by now. One thing was for sure: Richard knew too much, and his loyalty could no longer be guaranteed. He had left the bank, but he was out there somewhere. Would he leak and spill the beans to the press?

The only bright side to Maximillian's day was that his deputy CEO, Massimo Rossi, had agreed to return from his holiday early and had taken it upon himself to visit all the bank's key clients in this difficult time. He was now on his way to Borneo to see Lawrence, and after that, he would travel to Hong Kong to see the Tiger Lady.

CHAPTER 20

Friday, 18 January
Somewhere in the Jungle, Borneo

Thomas Holzstam sat next to his elderly father, Andreas Holzstam, alias Lawrence, by the campfire. It was nighttime, and the darkness of the jungle surrounded them. Besides the sounds of the river, it was quiet.

"Maximillian von Horstenbrik called again. He is sending Massimo Rossi to see us," Thomas told his father.

"Of course he is. He has no choice."

"He wants to brief us about the Strydsteen debacle. It's all over the newspapers in Switzerland. He wants to brief us about Richard's departure as well."

"Sure he does," Lawrence said.

"So it is all going as we planned."

"Yes, all like we planned. It was only a question of time before the young Bernard would get caught, was it not, my son?"

"Yes, our time, our making."

The old man played with a wooden stick in the flames of the campfire. He moved the stick in and out of the fire. He watched the stick catch fire, removed it, then threw it into the nearby river.

"Good. Now that the Strydsteen family is out of the way, we move on with step two of the plan," Lawrence explained.

"Do you want me to have Richard taken care of?"

"No, not yet. Have our people in Singapore watch him closely, though. They have already been informed what to do when the time comes. For now we let destiny play out its course."

"Do you think he will try to come here?" Thomas asked.

"Everything has its time and place, my son. We all have our paths in life. He just does not know his yet."

"But you do?"

The old wise one poured himself a glass of vintage single-malt whiskey. He did not answer his son. There was no need; he was the boss.

The old man was, in many senses, very much like his son, and in other ways they could not have been further apart. Physically, they were alike, like two pears. In character, they were oceans apart. Thomas was a monument to organization, his father, most likely mad. They had one common denominator, though: they both lived and cherished to be in control.

"You know that all roads in life must come to an end," Lawrence said. "The question is not how it ends. The question is what will you do when you come to the end of the road, if you have to choose between two evils, right or wrong, choice or no choice, what will you do then, and why, that is the question?"

CHAPTER 21

Saturday, 19 January
Little India, Singapore

Richard decided to go for a walk near to his house. He already knew Little India like the back of his hand, so there was not much to get to know really. Little India was this bastion of Indian and Tamil culture in Singapore, with all its shops, food, smells, and people. The district was more or less situated very centrally, in the middle of the Singapore city center. This district was predominately settled by people of Indian descent, Tamil to be exact. Singapore had several districts that were historically settled by a majority of one ethnic group. There was Chinatown, Kampong Glam (or the Arab Quarter as it was sometimes called), and there was Little India. Still today, Little India was a center for the Tamils and other people from the Indian subcontinent. Indians, and particularly Tamils, were one of the three major ethnic groups that composed modern-day Singapore. Tamil was also one of the four national languages, along with Chinese, Malay, and English. Singaporeans with Indian origins were the smallest major ethnic group of the Singaporean population today. In the Little India district, however, they were, as one could expect, a majority. Of course, all people of Indian origin, whether Singaporean of Indian descent or immigrants, did not live in Little India. However, it was a popular area to visit, especially on the weekends, as there were many shops selling produce and products of

Indian origin. The district was also home to many foreign workers who flocked there on the weekend.

Sunday was the busiest day in Little India, by far, a melting pot of sights, sounds, and people. There was no other place like it on Earth. It was like being in another country or another dimension, Richard thought. Thousands and thousands of people of Indian origin would descend upon Little India on their day off to meet their friends and family, to shop, to eat, to drink, to socialize, and to be seen. Many of these were the immigrant workers who worked all over Singapore and who had their day off on Sunday.

In Little India one could buy anything from used computers to Indian-made aftershave. Many of the small shops were also relatively inexpensive, at least compared to some of the major downtown shopping areas. Many of the guest workers did their shopping here on the weekend, not because they found the area quaint or nice, but purely out of economic necessity. If you can buy a pair of jeans and a T-shirt for under ten bucks, well, it speaks for itself, really.

For Richard, chaotic Little India was a reprieve from the other so well-organized streets of Singapore. Crowds of people walked up and down the narrow streets lined with shop houses, their movements almost like the waves on a river. Richard felt at home here, despite how weird it sounded that an ang moh would feel at home among the curry stalls and Bollywood DVD street vendors. The only explanation was, he thought, that he must have been Indian in a past life.

CHAPTER 22

Saturday, 19 January
Little India, Singapore

There were people of various origins and backgrounds living in the house with Richard. There were Singaporean, Indian, Chinese, Filipino, Malay, and Indonesian people, and of course him, a middle-aged, soon-to-be unemployed ang moh. Richard had wanted to live somewhere a bit under the radar and away from the usual expat residential areas of Singapore, and Madame Tsui's castle fit the bill perfectly.

He had no economic need to live under these relatively simple living conditions, but it fit his agenda for now. It was a new experience, and Richard would, during this time of living in Madame Tsui's castle, experience and see a new side of Singapore's people and culture and, not least of all, a new side to himself. It marked the start of probably the biggest adventure of his life. Stepping out of one's comfort zone is always a challenge. Within the past week, he had resigned from his well-paid job, escaped death, moved out of a house he had had all to himself, left his home country behind, and moved into a small room in an old house close to the Little India district of Singapore. So yes, he was well out of his comfort zone here, and it fit his agenda.

Richard's next-door neighbor in the house was a thirty-something, relatively attractive, Chinese girl. Her name was Lynn, and she was a secretary in some technology company. Lynn always wore short skirts and see-through tops. She had helped Richard with the washing machine on one his first days in the house. Lynn was nice and very friendly, and made no secret of her availability. The other rooms in the house were occupied by mainly singles and one-parent families with children. There was a young Malay couple who never seemed to leave their room; their TV was always on, and it was loud. This was the couple that lived above Richard, the couple he would hear every night. There was an Indian lady who cooked in her room, and when she did, all floors of the house were engulfed in the smell of curry and freshly baked bread. The niece of Madame Tsui had taken Richard on a tour of the house on his first day there. They had walked from floor to floor, and she had pointed to each individual door and said, "Number three, India," "Number five, Malaysia," and "Number eleven, Singaporean." So much for confidentiality, Richard thought, and wondered if she pointed to Richard's room and said, "Number ten, quiet ang moh," when she took other people on the house tour.

When you live in a landed property and share common areas and bathrooms, it's really quite a unique experience. No one dared to walk barefoot in the house. There were signs written on the walls by Madame Tsui that read "NO BAREFOOT." There was no please written on the sign; people got the message. The kitchen was also a common area, and whenever someone used it, it was up to the user to clean up after himself or herself. A cleaning lady would clean the common areas once a week, but her performance was really more of the cosmetic nature; she was not the most detailed cleaner. Yes, the madame ran the house almost in a military fashion, and she was the commander in charge. Everybody also had their own pots and pans for cooking, and they were neatly organized inside a large kitchen closet and marked with the owner's name and room number. Richard would eventually learn the importance of those name tags.

The small side street on which the house was situated was quiet and well kept. Most of the homeowners were Singaporeans of Chinese origin. All the houses had a fish pond in the garden, which was always close to the entrance gate, just like the Feng Shui teachings proscribed. Many of the houses also had the traditional Chinese lanterns at the gates. Some of the houses had their own security guard at the entrance, while others did not. Madame Tsui's castle had no security guard. Richard had a small balcony outside his second-floor room.

Prosper had been Richard's first new guest in the house. Prosper had expressed himself very diplomatically when he saw Richard's room. "It's very different," he said. After the house visit, they had both taken a walk down to Little India for some Tamil food. They had lunch in one of the many simple street restaurants that line the streets of Little India. They had both had a classic South Indian meal, served on the traditional banana leaf, and they both ate with their hands, as was tradition. The South Indian and Tamil cuisine was mostly vegetarian and quite spicy. The restaurant owner had eventually brought them some spoons; they were making too much of a mess and making a scene.

They talked about the latest gossip in the banking sector—who was leaving which bank and for how much, who had been fired, and who had gotten too drunk at the annual bank dinner. Prosper told Richard that several people had asked about him and where he was now. People had heard that he had resigned and gone back to Switzerland. Prosper told Richard that he had answered all questions with the standard, "I have no clue." Richard told him that he would like to lay low for a while, and the longer people had no clue where he was, the better.

"Well, you can't get much more under the radar than this, man," Prosper told him jokingly.

The only people who knew Richard was back in Singapore were Prosper, Matt, Giorgio, Jonas, Georgie "the Elvis," and Youssef the gardener. Richard was keen on keeping it that way as long as possible.

"What about that girl you used to talk about? What was her name? Wait, Louise, right?" Prosper asked.

"I have not called her yet. She has no clue that I'm here. I want to get organized first and then surprise her," Richard responded.

"OK, but really, what are you going to do now? Are you going to live in Little India for the rest of your life?"

"And if I did?" Richard responded.

"You got to get back in, man. Come back to the city. You are a banker, man. This is all nice and exotic, but it's not you," Prosper said.

"How do you know? Maybe this is me," Richard responded.

"OK, but Louise will want you to have a job, man," Prosper continued.

"I want to be my own boss now. I'm thinking of starting a company. It's as simple as that, you know," Richard responded.

"Just call her, man!" Prosper said, raising his voice.

When they had finished lunch and as they walked toward Prosper's car, Richard felt they were being observed. He turned around several times to look behind him, and he told Prosper about his suspicions. Prosper just looked at Richard and replied, "You paranoid Swiss freak. Now I know why Anna called you Enigma, you weird man. I don't understand you, man. You eat off banana leaves in Little India, share a house and toilet with a hundred people, and you think someone is following you."

He was probably right. Richard was different from most people. He surely had control issues and often thought he was being followed. Once, he had even thought about seeing a therapist to talk about these issues. Besides that, Anna was not the first girlfriend who had called him Enigma. There had been others.

CHAPTER 23

Saturday, 19 January
The Holzstam Estate, Santubong, Sarawak

Thomas Holzstam, son of Andreas Holzstam, watched the news on the TV. It was one of the European satellite channels. The news mentioned the Rossi & von Horstenbrik Cie Bank in Zurich. The shares of Rossi & von Horstenbrik had nose-dived during the last few days and had fallen by more than 30 percent. The bank in Zurich was surrounded by angry demonstrators. There were also rumors that the bank was having financial difficulties, and as a result, some clients had started taking their money out of the bank.

Thomas turned the TV off and sat down by his large wooden office desk. He took out a piece of paper and wrote down a message, then placed the paper in an envelope and sealed and stamped it with the red and blue dragon, the Holzstam family seal. He called the old English butler, Jones, into the room. "Take this message to Lawrence," he told the old butler. Jones took the envelope and left the room.

Jones walked up the old wooden staircase and arrived at the third floor of the large house. He opened the door that led to the winding staircase of the small tower, which shot up like a minaret on a mosque. He climbed the stairs and arrived at the small platform. He lit the single candle in the lantern on the table. He walked down the stairs and closed the door behind him. The signal had been given;

soon they would arrive. The small light tower had functioned as a means of communication for decades for the Holzstam family, and of course, it had been built by Lawrence. It was eccentric, but then again this house was the epicenter of eccentricity. Afterward, the old butler left the large house and walked over to one of the security guards at the main gate of the estate. He handed the envelope to the guard and said, "They will come soon."

One hour later two Iban tribesmen dressed merely in loin cloths and T-shirts, with spears in their hands, approached the guards at the gate. The older of the two tribesmen, his body covered in tattoos, took out a candle from his backpack and lit it, one candle only. The guard gave the tribesman the envelope; no words were spoken. With the envelope in hand, the tribesmen silently slid into the shadows of the jungle.

The Dayak and Iban tribes were part of Sarawak's many ethnicities. Sarawak was also populated by people of Chinese and Malay origins, among many other indigenous people. The Dayaks and Ibans were probably most famous in the West for their ancient custom of headhunting: the battle ritual, when in battle, the tribesmen would collect enemy heads as trophies.

CHAPTER 24

Sunday, 20 January
Little India, Singapore

After having a lovely afternoon pint of beer in a Bollywood theme Pub, Richard made his way back to the house. He stopped on the way in one of the small, family supply stores located in a small shop house on Buffalo Road. Inside the small shop, one could buy anything imaginable: rice, vegetables, bananas, eggplants, spices, curry, chickens, meat, beers, whiskey, toothpaste, condoms, underwear, saris, T-shirts, porcelain, aftershave (musk aftershave seemed to be popular in Little India), and even a tennis racket. The Tamil owner at the cash register had a moustache that looked like it was about to fly away by itself. When Richard paid for his items, he received a complimentary bag of onions—what a bargain. Richard thanked the man and complimented him by saying, "Nice moustache!"

It was like that in Little India when you shopped, especially in the small stores. You often received a little gift along with your purchase. This mostly happened in the stores that sold fresh food and produce. Many years ago Richard had bought a suitcase in one of the many shops that sold them in Little India. It had been just before Christmas that he had bought it. When he had opened the suitcase a few days later at home, he had found a small red ornament to hang on the Christmas tree for decoration. The cashier must have slipped it in when he hadn't been looking.

Back at the house, Richard cooked his pasta and tomato sauce on the gas stove. Several interested residents opened their doors in the hallway to see who was producing these new exotic scents from the kitchen. He sat down by the kitchen table and ate his first meal in his new home. He had used some cooking utensils that belonged to someone else, and afterward he cleaned them well and put them back in the same place from which he had taken them.

The next day when he awoke there was an envelope on the floor; someone had slid it in under his door. He opened the envelope and read the handwritten message, which said, "No use my kookking pot." The letter was signed with a single capital letter T, but who was T? T was obviously not in command of the best English grammar. He could not understand how someone had noticed; he had cleaned all the pots so well.

Later that morning as he was walking from the bathroom back to his room after his shower, dressed merely in boxers and slippers, there she was waiting for him in the kitchen. Madame Tsui blocked his way and raised her finger as she spoke, "No use my kookking pot!" He told the madame that he was sorry and that he did not know. She had replied with a brief "OK" and walked away. At least he was wearing slippers and he was not walking barefoot; that would surely have been a disaster. He retreated to his room and spent the rest of the morning there. Madame Tsui sat in the kitchen the whole morning eating smelly durian fruits, and he did not feel like encountering her again that day. In the afternoon, when the smell had evaporated and the madame had excused herself to the bathroom, he managed to slip out of the house.

Out of the house, he walked down to Serangoon Road, one of the main roads in the Little India district. He walked all the way down the heavily trafficked road until he arrived at his destination, the Mustafa Center. Mustafa Center was the large twenty-four-hour department store located in Little India, a multistory department store where they sold absolutely everything. Thousands of shoppers crowded the department store on a twenty-four-hour basis. Sometimes it got so crowded that the workers did not let people in as a safety regulation. Imagine that in the Western world—a department store being so busy it had to close its entrances. The main reason Richard liked the Mustafa Center was that one could shop there any time of day or night, and one could find almost anything there at relatively good prices. The saying was always that if you were looking for something and did not know where you could buy it, Mustafa Center was a good place to start.

On this particular day, it was busy as usual, and the aisles were jammed with shoppers. If one had to lose an overspending girlfriend or a stingy drinking pal, this was the place; one just had to slip into the relentless river of people passing by in the aisles and be carried away by the current.

After his shopping spree, Richard headed down to one of his many regular Little India drinking joints on Dunlop Street. He sat down in the beer garden and talked to some fellow thirsty ang mohs.

Chapter 25

Wednesday, 23 January
Maximillian's Office, Singapore

Maximillian was on the phone with one of his golf buddies, another Swiss banker, who insisted that he had seen Richard in town again.

"What do you mean you saw Richard? He is back in Switzerland," Maximillian responded to his friend in an irritated voice. "It's impossible," Maximillian responded again in an even more irritated voice.

Deep down inside he knew it was true. Richard had been seen in Little India. Maximillian himself never put his feet there; it was beneath him, he thought. His golf buddy had snapped a photo of Richard at the Pub in Little India, The picture had been taken three days ago. Two minutes later Maximillian's mobile signaled an incoming message. He opened the attached picture, and yes, sure enough, there he was—Richard drinking a beer in Little India.

Richard was back. What to do now? Maximillian had enough on his plate, and this was definitely not what he needed right now. Richard knew about Maximillian's involvement in the Curaçao company, and he was the last person Maximillian wanted around. No, Richard had to be taught a lesson. Reason had to be talked into him. First Maximillian had to find out why Richard had come back and what his intentions were. The only logical explanation he could find was that Richard was going to take him on and leak the news; he surely has a plan, Maximillian thought.

The best defense is a good offense, as the saying goes, and he was not going to sit around and wait for Richard's move. No, he must act now. Maximillian picked up his special mobile phone, the one with a cash card from a European country and the SIM card that could not be traced directly to his name.

"Hello, who is calling?" said a voice.

"Asian bird of prey calling," Maximillian replied.

"What color is the bird?" the voice asked.

"Green."

"Is your dog with you?"

"I have no dog," Maximillian replied.

"What can we do for you, my Asian bird of prey?"

"I have a little job for you. A little bird has escaped from the nest and needs to be found—well, maybe some heavier tools will be needed when he's found."

"I understand. Send me the details the usual way. I will contact you upon receipt."

"Price?" Maximillian asked.

From his personal laptop, Maximillian would later, per instructions, provide details to the man he had just talked to. He would leave a message on the home page of an anonymous web page on the Dark Net, or Deep Net as it was sometimes called. The Internet that is not accessible to the public—the one sometimes used to purchase and sell illegal products and services.

"Same as usual," the voice answered. "I am sure we can come to an agreement. It all really depends on how far your little bird has flown and how heavy the tools are that we need. "

Maximillian hung up the phone and turned it off. Several times before he had used this special service to solve problems on a global basis. It was usually nothing hardcore, just following people around, maybe talking a little reason into them, but, sometimes, more was required; these guys were very persuasive, and they were all professionals. This time he might ask them for some additional services that required a little more involvement and involved a certain degree of discretion, and above all their silence. The best part was that they operated all over the world; you called and they came. The person he had spoken to was just an agent, a middleman; it was always done this way.

CHAPTER 26

Thursday, 24 January
Little India, Singapore

Richard had, over the last few days, been busy and had spent most his time in one of the bars or at the gym. He had also found himself a new regular lunch restaurant in Little India. He had taken his lunch there now for three days in a row. The restaurant was a small family restaurant run by a family from Madras in Southern India. It was situated on a small, busy street full of other restaurants. The owner of the restaurant, Sunil, had noticed the new ang moh in the neighborhood, and when Richard entered for the fourth day in a row for lunch, Sunil showed him to his now regular table by the window, facing the street.

Sunil always placed the ang mohs at the window; this way other ang mohs would see one of their own kind, and the chance of them going into Sunil's place was improved. Ang mohs always ate with other ang mohs—at least Sunil banked on this. Sunil had decided not to be too friendly with the new regular customer—best not to scare him away—but he did not want this new source of revenue to move one door over to his archrival and competitor, Hassan, and his North Indian Muslim restaurant. Today, the ang moh ate his food on the banana leaf quietly, did not make a mess, and, Sunil noted, he liked his food rather spicy. Sunil looked outside and saw Hassan trying to convince some ang moh backpackers into coming into his restaurant, but they walked past Hassan and instead entered Sunil's restaurant. Fantastic! What a good day today was; his plan had worked. Ang mohs eat with other ang mohs, Sunil thought.

Arnold, Louise's uncle, was driving his small pickup van on the same small, busy, Little India street where Richard was having his lunch. Arnold passed the small Indian restaurant he had heard served excellent *roti prata*, the small Indian pancakes that he adored so much. He was on his way to pick up some chickens for his food stall at Bedok South. This was a new supplier, and it was only the second time he had ordered from this supplier; the first order had unfortunately been fried to pieces a week or so ago, due to a little beer glory in the booth. Only one chicken had made it through the beer bonanza feast, and that was the one Louise and her ex-ang moh boyfriend Richard had eaten. His regular supplier in China Town had suddenly jerked up the prices by one dollar per chicken; the supplier had modified the price due to inflation. Arnold had decided to take his business elsewhere and found this new supplier. The new supplier in Little India had offered one whole chicken for fifty cents below the old price he had enjoyed from the China Town supplier. Arnold was making now a dollar fifty Singaporean per chicken, a bargain he could not refuse. The chickens were also fatter than the ones from China Town. The Indians must feed them pancakes, he thought, and started whistling a happy, catchy tune.

Arnold looked over at the restaurant where he wanted to stop for pancakes as he drove by it. Speak of the devil, sitting in the restaurant by the window was that ang moh that Louise had been dating, Richard. What the hell was Richard doing in a restaurant in Little India? He was supposed to be back in Europe. Arnold decided to solve this mystery at once. He stopped the van and parked fifty meters farther down the road; he had to find out what this ang moh was up to. This ang moh had broken Louise's heart. He had left in a hurry and not stayed in touch—what a bastard. No, Arnold had one or two things to say to this arrogant ang moh. He hurried back to the restaurant but, unfortunately, Richard was nowhere in sight. He asked the owner who stood in the doorway, the one who smiled at him as he tried to shove a menu into his hand.

"Where is the foreigner in the window?" Arnold asked.

"He just left," Sunil replied.

Arnold inquired where he had gone, and Sunil proudly responded that the foreigner had just left. Then he added, in a proud voice, "Ang moh is a regular customer of mine. I think he lives around here. Comes here every day."

"This is not an everyday ang moh," Arnold said out loud and walked away.

Why was the man looking for him, who was this ang moh? Sunil thought.

Chapter 27

Friday, 25 January
The Apartment of Edwin, Bedok South, Singapore

Edwin had summoned his old friend and retired police officer, Arvin Singh, to his apartment for a meeting. Edwin had received the news of Richard's return to Singapore from his brother Arnold, and he was determined to find out what Richard was up to.

Since his departure, Louise had been depressed and out of character. Both Edwin and Arnold had tried to cheer her up and had advised her to move on with her life. The problem was that she seemed a completely different person now. The once joyful and sparkly Louise was just a shadow of her former self. Edwin had not seen his daughter like this for a long time. The last time was ten years ago when his wife, and Louise's mother, had passed away. Nothing seemed to cheer Louise up, and Edwin was determined to get to the bottom of this whole affair. Since nothing had seemed to work on Louise, he had decided that he had to approach the problem from another angle. Edwin suspected Richard had probably just lied to his daughter and had probably left her for some other woman, the way ang moh men usually did. He had surely made up the story of leaving Singapore just to get Louise out of his life. Louise was a proper girl, and Edwin was convinced that Richard might have left her because he did not get her into bed, or if he had, he was no longer interested in her afterward. Whatever Richard's motives were, Edwin would find out. If Richard was indeed seeing some other girl, Edwin could confront Louise with the facts, and she could move on with her life; she would get some closure.

Arvin Singh had been his friend since their time together in the police force. Arvin was a Sikh with Punjabi origins. After leaving the police force, Arvin had, for many years, run a small detective bureau together with his sons. The detective bureau had its offices not far away from Edwin's apartment in Bedok South. The firm was now run by Arvin's sons, but Arvin still had a hand in the management of the firm. Arvin was a very tall man, with wide shoulders, and he was sixty-five years old. He had a large gray moustache and white beard, and when he wore his black Sikh turban he did not go unnoticed. Edwin explained to Arvin the story and background of Louise's relationship with Richard and why he wanted Richard found and followed. Edwin explained his motives, briefed Arvin about Richard, and gave him details of Richard, including a photo. Edwin gave the address of the restaurant in Little India where Richard had last been seen. Arvin listened attentively and asked few questions. They agreed on a friendly rate for the job with a handshake; there was no need for contracts or mandates because they knew each other too well.

Before parting, Edwin joked with Arvin that he was the perfect man for the job: "With your height and your turban, you will blend in perfectly in Little India."

Arvin laughed and replied, "I have other disguises as well."

Edwin had countered, "Yes, but a turban is a turban, my friend, and you cannot take it off, can you?"

They both laughed at Edwin's joke and agreed that Arvin would report to Edwin as soon as he had some news.

As Arvin was leaving the apartment, he ran into Louise. She greeted her father and asked him what Arvin was doing there. Edwin looked at Louise and responded, "Oh, just taking care of some business."

CHAPTER 28

Saturday, 26 January
Singapore

Richard was having lunch with his friend Youssef in a food court. It was good to see Youssef again; he had been a faithful friend for many years. Richard had called Youssef some days ago to tell him that he was back in Singapore. Youssef had been Richard's gardener at his house in Katong for several years. Youssef was a thirty-two-year-old Singaporean of Malay origin, and he was a Muslim. Youssef told Richard that he had been fired by the new occupant of Richard's old house on the same day he moved into the house. The young banker named Mr. Yann von Horstenbrik had not been impressed with Youssef's CV and past. Richard said he was sorry to hear that, and that he would ask around if any of his friends needed a gardener. Youssef also told Richard that he had become a father again; his second son had been born a few days ago, and he had named the boy Mehmet Ali.

Youssef told Richard jokingly, "I wanted to name him Richard after you, but it's not a Muslim name, so it was sort of difficult to proceed, unless you convert and call yourself Mehmet Ali."

They both laughed.

"I'm honored, but think I will stick with Richard and my faith. We can still be friends, though," Richard replied, and they laughed together again.

Youssef was only joking, but Richard knew that he held Richard in high esteem, not only as a friend and ex-employer, but also for what he had done for Youssef.

Richard had met Youssef in a bar close to his house a year after his arrival in Singapore. Youssef had been unemployed and was looking for a job. He had a young wife and newborn baby to feed at home. The whole meeting with Youssef had been born out of coincidence, the way coincidence often dictates who we meet in life; sadly, most people do not recognize that everything happens for a reason.

Richard had been sitting alone one Sunday afternoon in a bar close to his home and reading a book when, out of nowhere, Youssef, dressed in white trousers, white shirt, and black tie, had sat down next to Richard by the bar counter. Youssef was dressed for a job interview, although Richard did not know this at the time. When Youssef was ordering his Tiger Beer, he turned to Richard, pointed to the book he was reading, and said, "*Seven Pillars of Wisdom* by T.E. Lawrence. Great book, great man!"

They had started talking about the book then; apparently, Youssef had read the book several times. They started talking about history and T.E. Lawrence, the man known as Lawrence of Arabia. Not only had Youssef read the book several times, the man was a walking history book of the life of Lawrence of Arabia. They talked for an hour or so about the book and Lawrence of Arabia. Youssef had spoken like a history professor, yet Richard realized that he was not; he was too young, and the tattoos on his neck seemed to indicate that he came from a whole different background. Finally, Richard asked him why he had read the book so many times. The book was good, but why read it so many times? After all, there were many other good books. Youssef's answer had been casual, blunt, and not the one that Richard had expected: "I read it in prison. Did some time in Changi prison for gang-related crimes. I'm clean now, for many years. Now, to answer your question. Well, there aren't that many books in Changi Prison, and an unknown benefactor just kept sending me the same book over and over, so there was not that much choice really."

Youssef then told Richard his story, and what a story it was. He had been part of a gang when he was twenty-three years old. He had been young and stupid and had thought that it was cool to be in a gang, but it had been a mistake. He was arrested and charged with causing hurt to a member of a rival gang. He had also later been charged with possession of some illegal items. Youssef told Richard that the items had not been his; they had been given to him in a bag by the woman who lived next door to him. The woman, bruised and scared, had one day knocked on his door, and asked him to get rid of the bag. Youssef had not had the heart to say no to her, so he had given in, especially because some of the contents in the bag could be used to hurt her. Her husband had a history and reputation of having a heavy hand, a hand often used on her.

Youssef had perhaps committed the classic sin: he had done wrong for all the right reasons. Youssef had tried to get rid of the bag and its content, but the content was later found and traced back to him. This along with the other pending charges had guaranteed him an extended vacation in Changi Prison. In the end it did not matter Youssef told Richard, he was guilty as charged. He passed his years in prison reading and promising himself that when he came out he would be a new man, a better and reformed man. It was in prison he had first come into contact with the man that had changed his life. Youssef had not wanted to elaborate on the identity of the man. "Did you meet god?" Richard had asked. Youssef had looked at Richard and smiled, "god is always with me my friend – no this man is smaller than god but he sure is larger than life, come to think of it, for some he is probably god"

That day in the bar Youssef told Richard that he had left his criminal past behind and was now currently looking for a job as a gardener, which was his profession. Youssef could have been a scholar; he spoke about history with a passion that was contagious, but with his past that would sadly never happen. Youssef went on and told Richard that he had just been laid off from a job in a gardening nursery store. Someone had stolen some cash from a cash register in the store. There had been no security camera to catch the thief, but it was quite clear that it was one of the employees. The ensuing police investigation did not have much to go on, and there was no evidence, so the owner of the store had blamed the weakest link, Youssef, because, after all, he had a past. It did not matter that Youssef had had no access to the cash register and that he was a gardener working outside the store. The owner had to make an example—he could not lose face—and someone had to pay the price, and Youssef was the man. He had been let go with the explanation that he was no longer needed; no other reason was given. The owner had also already told several employees that it was Youssef who had stolen the cash. None of the other employees said anything, however; they did not want to lose face or lose their jobs as well.

Richard felt for the man. Youssef struck him as honest and sincere. He had no reason to tell Richard of his past, yet he had, Richard knew how to appreciate this. Sometimes in life we find a person to tell our past to without reservation. This can happen after years or a lifetime of trust and friendship, or it can happen on the spot with a complete stranger. When you are on the receiving end, and the person seems to be telling the truth, you will know; you will feel it in your bones, and you will feel that this is happening for a reason. Youssef stood for what he had done. Was he proud of it? No, but he had told his version of the events, he had done the time and paid the price. Finding a job when you have a history of doing time is surely not easy, Richard thought. Richard was also impressed by the bluntness with which Youssef spoke about his past. Youssef had left his CV and contacts for references with Richard that day.

Richard believed him and decided on the spot to give the man a chance, it felt right. After having checked out the references, a few days later he had communicated his decision to Youssef. Everybody deserves a second chance, he thought, and Richard needed a gardener for the large garden at his home—everything happens for a reason. The man had made a mistake, done the time, and would pay for it all his life, and Richard sympathized with him. Richard also knew where he was coming from, when he spoke about losing face, and the *Kiasu* mentality that existed in Singapore and Asia. To lose face is never good, but in some Asian cultures it was really exaggerated, Richard thought. People made mistakes; it's part of being human. A mistake means just that, however—an unintended action or intended action that leads to an undesired outcome, Richard believed. Unfortunately, in Youssef's case, he had committed a crime.

So Richard had decided to give Youssef a chance. After all, he was a man who stood for what he was, a man out of the ordinary. *Kiasu* literally means "to lose esteem or face, to stand out from the crowd, to be different from your peers." The concept of Kiasu is deeply rooted in many cultures in Asia, particularly in the Chinese and Japanese cultures. It had different names in different cultures, but its concept was the same. Of course the concept of Kiasu had several positive aspects to it as well. It is good to win and get ahead in life; to loose is never good, or is it? To do the wrong thing is never good, but sometimes we make mistakes, and what do we do then? In the end, it all depends on what we do, and if we can live with our mistakes, at least this was Richard's opinion.

It was Youssef who had introduced Richard to the bar, Midnight Oil. Richard had many times visited the simple home of Youssef and his lovely young wife and son. He had met many of Youssef's friends, and almost all of them were ex-offenders. They all lived honest lives now, as they had picked up the pieces of their lives and started anew. They were like a fraternity; their pasts bound them together, but they also stuck beside one another because their original families and friends had turned their backs on them after they had gone to prison. Youssef's fraternity of friends and their families were so tightly knit that any newfound friends were looked upon with suspicion, experience had taught them so, and Richard was no exception. Youssef's friends had accepted Richard, however, because he was someone who had given Youssef a chance and believed in him, and that was something that did not happen often to one of them. The proof of acceptance had come in the form of an invitation. Richard had been invited by Youssef and his family to their simple but homey one-room apartment, along with some of Youssef's friends, all ex-offenders, to break bread at the end of Ramadan. There were people from all walks of life and from all sorts of professional backgrounds—manufacturing, business, transportation, gardening, finance, construction, etc. They all had one thing in common: they had all done time. It's really true that if you don't have a family or your family turns its back on you, then you find your own family, Richard thought. It was at this event that Youssef had told him, "If you ever need help with anything, Richard, you let me know, OK?" Richard had thanked Youssef, but Youssef had sensed Richard's hesitation and said, "Anything, Richard. We are the Kiasu brothers. We are not worried about losing face. We lost ours a long time ago."

Most Singaporeans, Richard knew, and he knew people from many walks of life, were extremely proud of their country and achievements, and no country or system was perfect. However, some of these people felt that Singapore was in the process of losing its identity in the fast economic development that was taking place in their country. Some felt that the foundations, heritage and values they held as precious was losing its appeal to the new generation—Youssef was one these people.

Youssef was always the first in his building block to display Singapore's national flag from his balcony in the month leading up to National Day; he was fiercely nationalistic, and his humble beginnings and personal history had no impact on his conviction. "My children might not be proud of me when they grow up, but they can be proud of their country and of themselves. This I can teach them—God willing." Youssef used to say.

Youssef should have gone into politics; he spoke his mind with no restraint and answered only to his own conscience. Youssef had been at the bottom of life and come back. No, Youssef had been below the bottom and looked up—an experience only those who have been there recognize. One thing was for sure: Richard would have voted for him in any country, for any political party; the man stood for his actions and lived by his word. In the end, it's all about people, not left or right, up or down, or rich or poor; it's about what someone believes, and about what that person does with those beliefs, Richard thought.

When they had finished their lunch at the Little India restaurant, Richard noticed an elder Sikh man sitting at the table next to theirs. The man had been reading a newspaper the whole time, and when Richard looked at him the man looked the other way. Richard got the distinct feeling that the man had been watching them the whole time.

Richard leaned over the table and said to Youssef, "That Sikh man behind you, I think he is watching us."

Youssef responded causally, "That, my dear friend, is a man from my past. He was a prison guard at Changi Prison."

Youssef's bluntness was his trademark, and Richard knew that he was not joking, his school of life had taught him so. His words left no room open for interpretation, what he said he meant.

"Are you not going to say hello to him?" Richard asked.

Youssef responded again quickly and bluntly, "What happens in prison stays in prison, but I can tell you that he is an honorable man and a good man."

The elder Sikh man stood up, paid for his soft drink, and grabbed his newspaper. Youssef turned around toward the man just then, and the man looked at Youssef and nodded his head in recognition. Youssef answered the gesture with a similar nod of the head, and then the man walked off. It was really true—what happened in prison stayed in prison. A few seconds later, Youssef nodded his head to Richard and said, "He is a good man."

Richard and Youssef said good-bye after their lunch, and they agreed to stay in touch. Youssef wanted to introduce Richard to a nice girl—a girl from his past who wanted to meet Richard. "She is only in town for a while. She is from Borneo. Her name is Suva, and she is lovely," Youssef told Richard.

"Thank you, but really there is this girl that I really like now, and frankly, I think she might be the one. You know, just have some things to take care of first before—well, you know how it is," Richard said.

"No, Richard, I have no clue what it's like out there. I have a family, remember?"

CHAPTER 29

A Day like All Others in January
Marseille, France

Mustafa al Taqwa and Joseph Salwa had now spent over six months in the French immigration center in Marseille. They had spoken to the police, immigration officers, doctors, and countless officials. The day they had stepped on the SS *Botaki Star* freighter and had been herded into a shipping container in the small port in the Congo now seemed like a lifetime ago. Now they were stuck in a makeshift barrack together with another fifty or so men, waiting for the immigration police to decide what to do with them. They were sure they would eventually be shipped back to Africa, and back to the misery and the lives they had wanted to escape; only upon return, their lives would be even worse. They had spent all their money to make the journey, and many were in debt back home as well. If they had a life upon return in Africa, that life expectancy had now surely been cut in half. The famine, the desperation, the pressure to support their families, and finally the greed of the debt collectors would end their miserable existence on this earth.

Mustafa al Taqwa positioned a simple prayer carpet on the floor; it was time. He faced the direction of Mecca and completed his prayers. Joseph Salwa touched the small brass cross on his necklace, raised it to his lips, kissed it, and in silence he whispered, "God help us. Show us the way."

The next day two police officers entered the barrack accompanied by a white man. The white man wore a suit and tie, and spoke to the crowd of desperate men in English with a distinct German accent. The words that came out of his mouth were the words of salvation and hope. The man had kind blue eyes, Joseph Salwa noted.

CHAPTER 30

Saturday, 26 January
Rossi & von Horstenbrik Cie Bank, Zurich, Switzerland

At the head office of Rossi & von Horstenbrik Cie Bank in Zurich, the storm had hit in full force. The large, old, stone villa, which had been the bank's head office and epicenter since the bank's founding in 1888, was under siege by journalists. The old house was surrounded by a large garden and stone walls that separated the journalists from it. The bank was in crisis mode. The news of the past days had put the public eye on the bank. It was not just the news of the unfortunate young man with a Ferrari, son of a suspected money launderer and human trafficker, who maintained accounts at the bank. There was also news of the rapid fall of the bank's shares on the Zurich Stock Exchange, and that the bank had recently announced several plans to cut their number of employees in Switzerland. Finally, some key corporate and private clients had spoken publicly and said that they would stop doing business with the bank as a protest against the possibility that the bank was sheltering and aiding suspected human traffickers. The bank was also in meetings with the labor unions and financial regulators, and things were not going well. All these factors had led to the inevitable speculations of whether the bank was solvent or not. Would clients withdraw their funds? Would Rossi & von Horstenbrik Cie Bank survive?

Massimo Rossi, deputy CEO from Singapore, had flown into Zurich that morning straight from Singapore. Massimo had been on the road for a week, visiting Singapore, France, Hong Kong, Borneo, and Australia. Massimo had just finished a meeting with an important private organization of the bank: the Rossi & von Horstenbrik employee shareholder organization called the R & H Shareholders Club. The shareholder organization had been organized by the bank's employees who held shares in the bank. It was not an official entity of the bank and had no legal obligations to the bank. They met regularly, and over the years the club had grown. Many of the bank's Swiss employees were members. The members of the shareholders Club were all shareholders of the bank's common shares quoted on the Zurich Stock Exchange, in fact, they held the vast majority of the publicly traded common shares. The members were largely staff; in fact, no one with the title of director or above was allowed to participate in the organization. This was considered an important aspect of the club and one of the cornerstone ideas of the founding members; the organization wanted to have no responsibility or obligation to the bank. If directors or other employees with managerial positions were allowed to participate, the risk was too large that these persons would exercise undue pressure on the other members, or they might want to implement the bank's own views and ideas. Under such conditions, the existing members might be afraid to speak their minds and present their ideas, as they would be afraid of reprisals that would affect their employment at the bank. The bank had no official shareholder saving scheme like many of the larger banks had. Rossi & von Horstenbrik was considered too small an organization by the bank's management to institute such a vehicle. Also, the management of the bank had no interest in these matters. The Rossi & von Horstenbrik families had been the controlling shareholders since the founding of the bank, and they held the private, preferred shares, the ones that controlled the voting rights. These preferred shares commanded five voting rights to each ordinary share, which commanded only one voting right. The ordinary shares that were floated and publicly traded on the Zurich Stock Exchange represented 49 percent of the share capital; the rest was held by the Rossi and von Horstenbrik families in private shares.

The R & H Shareholders Club was not merely interested in investments; the organization had, over the years, taken a keen interest in making a name for themselves in the Zurich area as organizers of fund-raising activities for worthy causes. They regularly organized parties and events to raise funds for famine relief, medical research, and environmental issues. They were particularly interested in donating funds to organizations such as Greenpeace and other environmental groups. Environmental issues were important to many of the club's members. The organization's activities were not condoned by the bank, but over the years the management of the bank had realized that the activities of the R & H Shareholders Club reflected positively on the bank. It was always good to have the bank's name in the news in connection with organizations that practiced philanthropic activities. The philanthropic activities and fund-raising had, in fact, become the main activity of the organization.

Members of the club were not happy about the latest performance of the bank's shares, nor were they happy about reading about the bank in the news. The alleged involvement of one of the bank's clients in human trafficking was not something that went along with the ideas and morals of most members in the club. They were also losing money, and they did not like it. Nor did they want to be part of an operation that was described in the papers as "aiding and facilitating" such activities.

When Massimo Rossi finished the meeting with the representatives of the shareholders club, he was happy. The representatives had listened to and liked what they heard from Massimo Rossi. When Massimo left the conference room on the second floor, he had a large smile on his face. He then walked to the large room that had once been a ballroom and reception room for gatherings of the bank's wealthy clients. The room was still furnished with wooden furniture from the 1800s and large crystal chandeliers that hung from the ceiling. Massimo crossed the large wooden dance floor toward the balconies at the front of the villa. He looked outside and saw all the reporters and demonstrators that were literally camping outside the bank's garden premises. Massimo smiled. Today was a good day.

Outside the gates of Rossi & von Horstenbrik Cie Bank in Zurich, Fritz Zimmerman looked around at the crowd. Fritz was a reporter from one of the local newspapers, and he was a happy man today. Today he had enough news material to fill several pages of the small newspaper he worked for. For the readers of the local newspapers, the financial future and condition of Rossi & von Horstenbrik meant little; the future of the employees and the safety of clients' funds were also not priorities. The news was, of course, the large number of demonstrators of various backgrounds that had gathered around the bank. Just like any public event, various people and groups would descend on these events with their own political agendas; with the bank in the public eye, it was a good place to be seen and to create buzz around another political or nonpolitical cause. There were groups demonstrating for all sorts of topics and causes, and most had little to do with Rossi & von Horstenbrik Cie Bank. The banners and signs of the people demonstrating read, "Down with the World Banking Mafia," "We Want Change Now," "Wake Up and Join Us, Bankers of the World," "Workers against Human Trafficking," "Free Tibet," "Free the Congo," "United Africans against Imperialism," and "Where's Our Money?" Fritz's all-time favorite was the banner held by a group of old hippies standing on an old green Volkswagen bus with psychedelic peace signs and stars painted on it. The bus had Swiss license plates from the canton of Bern. The sign read "Free the Alps," and under the freshly painted banner text one could still read the old text: "Free Mandela."

Fritz snapped several pictures with his giant paparazzi zoom lens. As he concentrated his attention toward the Rossi & von Horstenbrik villa, he noticed someone standing in the window by the large balcony on the second floor. He raised his camera and zoomed in and saw Massimo Rossi. He was well dressed, surely in some very expensive, custom-made suit that would cost at least a month's salary for some normal Swiss factory worker. Mr. Rossi was smiling at the crowd, and Fritz took several pictures of him. Fritz smiled to himself. *This* was the scoop. He could already see the headlines in tomorrow's newspapers: "Rossi & von Horstenbrik Bank Deputy CEO Singapore Smiles at Demonstrators and Their Demands" or "Rich Director Frowns upon Demands of the People." He could even see the picture in one of the leftist newspapers that had a particularly clever editor. The caption published with the picture might read something like "Rich Man, Poor Man."

Fritz was excited. He would surely be able to sell the picture to many news agencies around the world. Maybe he would even get an offer to join one of the big newspapers now. Yes, maybe he could soon leave the little local newspaper, and its idealistic views, and join a real paper that reported on the lives of the rich and famous. It was so true, Fritz thought. We all have our own agendas for being here today. He looked again at the old hippies standing on top of the bus, shouting even louder now; they had also seen the well-dressed banker behind the window on the second floor. One of the hippies shouted, "Look, he is smiling at us. The bank boss is smiling at us." And one of the other hippies remarked, "Maybe he wants to join us?" It took only a few seconds for the group of people standing on the old Volkswagen bus to change their slogan. They started shouting in unison, "Don't be afraid, banker! Join us!"

Fritz took his camera and walked toward his car. He was done. On the way he stumbled upon a reporter from a well renowned American cable news TV network and crew who was lost. "Excuse me," the excited American reporter asked Fritz. "Can you show me the way to Rossi & von Horstenbrik Cie Bank, please?"

"Sure, no problem. I help you. Welcome to Zurich!" Fritz replied in his Swiss German accent and sent them on their way. Business was business, and this was his day; no one could take that away from him.

Fritz got into his car and honked the horn several times at the excited American cable network crew. Out of pure pleasure and happiness, the grateful camera crew saluted him with a unified thumbs up. He drove away, pleased with himself. He had a deadline to meet.

Much later that day, the American cable news reporter was not having such a great day. The reporter had reported live for five minutes in front of the majestic building that housed the renowned Swiss private bank in Zurich. This was going to be the young reporter's big international breakthrough on live intercontinental TV. It was exclusive all right; there had been no other TV crews there. The only problem was that the building he had positioned himself in front of was not the Rossi & von Horstenbrik Cie Bank in Zurich; it was the Zurich Opera House. The young reporter forever damned and cursed himself for listening to the man with the large camera zoom lens who had given him the directions and address. Never trust another reporter—it was so true.

CHAPTER 31

Sunday, 27 January
Changi Airport, Singapore

The two men took their luggage from the baggage claim and proceeded out through the customs checkpoint. The two large Caucasian men commanded respect in the eyes of the awaiting crowd outside. They looked like two gangsters out of a James Bond movie. They were dressed in black from head to toe, both with shaved heads and both very tall. Their muscles looked like they could pop out of their clothes at any instant. They both had an identical tattoo on their right forearm, a skull with the inscription S. They looked to be in their late thirties, maybe early forties. Their faces looked like they had been carved out of stone, and they had large scarred hands that looked like instruments in their own right. As they walked into the crowd, there was no need for them to say "Excuse me "or "Sorry." The people simply moved away, and a path was naturally formed in front of them. They walked toward the taxi stand and got into an awaiting taxi.

They told the taxi driver the name of the hotel in China Town where they desired to be driven. The taxi driver, a Singaporean of Indian descent named Birendra, took one look at the passengers and decided he would be quiet today. Birendra was usually a very talkative and chatty fellow, but one look at these two and he knew it was better to be quiet and concentrate on his driving. Birendra even decided to skip the normal practice of asking the customer which way they preferred to travel, by ECP or PIE Highway. Birendra just drove.

The two men checked into the hotel in China Town thirty minutes later. Upon checking in, they were given an envelope that had been left for them by delivery that same morning. One of the hotel staff wanted to help the two men with their luggage, but changed his mind when he took a closer look at them. Once they had checked into their two separate rooms, they both went to sleep and slept for the next twelve hours. It was always better to get enough sleep before the mission started.

CHAPTER 32

Monday, 28 January
Rossi & von Horstenbrik Cie Bank, Singapore

For the past few days the TV had been on constantly in Maximillian's office. Rossi & von Horstenbrik was in crisis mode. They had daily video-linked conferences with all of the bank's branches and their management all over the world: Zurich, Geneva, Lugano, London, Paris, Monte Carlo, Singapore, Hong Kong, Montevideo, and Nassau. The news of the bank had faded out a little in the Swiss media over the past few days, thanks to the fact that a famous Swiss female actor had been caught on camera involved in a very hot and passionate nocturnal meeting in a car parked in a Geneva parking garage. Her partner had been a well-known and beloved news anchor on Swiss TV; he was, of course, married and also happened to be a member of a church group that was famous for its antiabortion stand.

However, this quick breathing room from the media would not last. The fact was that in the past week no stone of the bank's history and current management had been left unturned. Everything was under the scrutiny of the media: the bank's directors, the Rossi and von Horstenbrik families, the potential involvement of the bank with the court case in Paris against the Strydsteen family, the financial condition of the bank, and of course, the dramatic drop of Rossi & von Horstenbrik shares on the Zurich Stock Exchange. It had also been speculated that the goods seized on the SS *Botaki Star* freighter in Marseille had been financed by funds deposited at Rossi & von Horstenbrik.

Young Bernard Strydsteen and his Ferrari did not escape the media's attention either. In fact, the young man's life since birth had been mapped out and hung out for the media to see and report on. The press had interviewed several of Bernard's friends and ex-girlfriends, and the result of that research was a tale of a lavish lifestyle with fast women and easy money; the press were having a field day with young Bernard.

As long as the media concentrated its attention on other issues than the bank, it was good news for Rossi & von Horstenbrik Cie Bank. The various Rossi & von Horstenbrik branches around the world had their hands full with concentrating on calming their customers—reassuring them that Rossi & von Horstenbrik would survive and that, yes, the clients' money was safe.

In Singapore the effect of the news had been minimal. The bank was a Singapore-registered entity and not a direct branch of Rossi & von Horstenbrik Cie Bank in Zurich. The bank in Singapore ran its own balance sheet separate from Zurich's. The assets of the bank in Singapore belonged to the Singapore legal entity, and the clients' deposits were booked and held under the name of the Singapore legal entity, Rossi & von Horstenbrik Cie Bank (Singapore) Ltd. This reassured the clients of the bank in Singapore, and the news in Zurich was deemed less important for them. Rossi & von Horstenbrik Cie Bank in Singapore was having no financial difficulties and its balance sheet and reserves were in order, as per local regulations. Maximillian cared little for the other branches. He was convinced that this storm would pass, and soon they would be back to business as usual. He knew from history that people have such short memories when it comes to finance and money.

During these past few days when Maximillian had been holding the fort in the Singapore office, his deputy Massimo Rossi had been busy elsewhere. Massimo had seemingly been able to reassure key clients Lawrence and the Tiger Lady enough that they had pledged to remain loyal and would not consider moving any of their funds elsewhere. Massimo had also apparently been able to calm the bank's employee shareholders club down in Zurich—surely not an easy task. Maximillian wondered what Massimo had told them; he would have to reevaluate his relationship with Massimo Rossi. Massimo was surely wining important allies at home in Zurich, and allies at home were always good. Maybe Maximillian would invite Massimo and his family to his house on Bali. The bungalow Maximillian owned in Seminyak was mostly empty and not used. Massimo and his young trophy wife would appreciate this gesture. Rosella was Italian, young and sexy, and although Maximillian usually preferred Asian girls, Rosella was a woman worthy of his seed. Forbidden fruit always tastes the best, Maximillian thought. A von Horstenbrik seed in the Rossi sphere of influence—now *that* was food for thought. The thought aroused him. To plant one of your own in the camp of the enemy—old Machiavelli could not have said or planned it better, Maximillian thought. Rosella and Massimo had been having some problems lately, and Maximillian had heard that Massimo had blocked her credit cards. It was understandable; she was a shopaholic. Maybe Rosella would be in need of some attention from someone else? Maximillian knew her kind so well, the young trophy wife who needed more than just love and safety; she needed to feel desired and in control. To cut off her credit card was not the way to go. It would only be a question of time before she would venture out to seek someone new, someone who paid, who could supply her with a new credit card. It was worth a try, Maximillian thought. He felt more aroused as he thought of what he would and could do to her, all the mental snapshots he could collect; it was risky, but he loved a gamble. He knew himself so well—sex was not the primary source of his arousal; it was the game instead, and it meant everything. He was five hundred-plus Max; he was irresistible.

He scrolled through the names on his mobile phone, and he found Rosella written in red capital letters. In his contacts list, all the female names were color-coded: blue for Done and red for To Do. Red and blue were his colors, his motto, his motivation, his destiny.

He dialed Rosella, and she answered straightaway.

"*Pronto*."

"*Ciao*, Rosella. It's Maximillian."

"Hello. What a surprise. Is anything wrong?"

"No, everything is fine. Sorry to disturb you, but I need your help."

"If there is something I can do, just tell me," Rosella said.

"I know Massimo's birthday is coming up soon. He has been working very hard, as you know, and well, I would like to arrange a little something for his birthday."

"*che bello!*"

"It will be a surprise; he must not know."

"I can keep a secret, Maximillian, come rain or shine as they say."

"I'm counting on it! Do you think we can meet one of these days to discuss how to organize it and who to invite?"

"Sure, let me know where and when you want to meet."

"I think it would be best during the day, when he is busy in the office, don't you think?"

"Yes, of course. Tell me where and when."

"How about my place, Friday, lunchtime. Shall we say noon?"

"Your place?"

"Yes, I want to show you the gift I have prepared…It's kind of big."

"OK. See you then. *Ciao*."

Maximillian hung up the phone. He smiled at the large mirror that was mounted on his office wall, and the mirror smiled back. The game was on.

CHAPTER 33

Monday, 28 January
Singapore

Youssef and Richard stood outside one of the coffee shops on Upper East Coast Road by the Siglap Center shopping complex. They had stopped for a smoke after the coffee. Richard noted that Youssef's secret friend from Changi Prison, the tall, distinguished Sikh gentleman, had also conveniently found his way to the Siglap Center. The man sat on a bench outside the McDonald's restaurant across the road from them. The tall Sikh pretended to be reading a newspaper, but Richard had no doubt that the man was following them.

"Hey, there's your Sikh friend again." Richard said.

"Yeah, you are right. He is wearing a new turban today—have not seen that one before. Let's wave to him, shall we?"

"I'm serious. The man is following us."

"Are you serious?" Youssef said. "You are paranoid, man."

"OK, what are the odds that you see the same person twice in two different places in a city of five million plus, all in the lapse of a few days, Einstein?"

"Oh, I don't know, Richard, but if I see the same person more than twice I think its destiny, God's will, as we say. Besides, it's only Mr. Singh, and he's a good man, Richard. Remember that."

"OK. Maybe you are right," Richard said.

"Loosen up, man. Live a little and stop worrying. Listen, when can I set you up with my cousin Suva? She is young and pretty and wants to meet you."

"I told you before, I have a girlfriend."

"OK, well, at least think about it. Anyway, you will meet her soon. It is written, my friend; it is meant to be. She is really beautiful."

"Nothing is written."

"If you say so, but, well, let's see if it's written."

They said their good-byes, and Youssef jumped on a bus. Richard got into a taxi, and as the taxi pulled away, he looked back and saw that Mr. Singh was getting on the back of a motorcycle that had stopped to pick him up. How convenient for Mr. Singh, he thought. How convenient indeed.

CHAPTER 34

Tuesday, 29 January
Somewhere in the Jungle, Borneo

The Malaysian workers and immigrant Indonesian loggers were busy with their old gasoline-operated automatic chainsaws. The two-hundred-year-old tree was dead now, lying on the ground. It had nurtured and given life for so many years. So far they had cut down twenty large trees today. The old ones were the most troublesome to force to the ground; just like humans, they had a history and deep roots, and did not fall easily. Where the large trees once stood a small opening in the dense jungle had formed a perimeter the size of a football pitch. The logging was done. The second stage was the clearing, then much later the foreigners would come with their money and their genetically modified seeds and crops. The multinational corporation in question had no research facilities or laboratories of their own, so they used the rainforest. They had been experimenting and testing the genetically modified seeds and crops for years, always far away from their home, always far away from the public eye, always far away from the rule of law. The new genetically modified insect- and disease-resistant crops, along with the chemically engineered fertilizer from their own biotech laboratory—the fertilizer that only worked as fertilizer for the genetically modified crops, and killed other similar non-genetically modified crops—needed to be tested, and the jungle was prime testing ground. The rain forest, the source of life, which perhaps held the cure for many diseases, a complex ecosystem that perhaps held the key to the future of mankind, was being used as the testing ground for these new biotech products. But why? Because there was profit in it; there was money to be made.

When the old wise one had first heard of these experiments, he had exploded in anger. The wise one rarely got angry or demonstrated any feelings, but he had said, "No one in his right mind ever tried to rewrite the Bible or other holy scriptures. He dares not! Yet some men today have no problem with rewriting the genetic codes of plants, animals, and people, destroying the rain forest in the process, altering life as it was created. Does the description of the Garden of Eden in the Bible not sound a lot like the rainforest? They dare not touch the Bible, but have no problem playing God in my backyard. This will not do!"

The group of loggers sat on one of the large tree trunks they had just cut down. They needed a break, and it was extremely hot and humid in the jungle on this day. From his vantage point high up in a tree, the old man raised his hand and signaled the girls to move forward. Out of the jungle they came: five young, beautiful, topless girls, each carrying a case of beer. The leader of this group of naked beauties walked in front of the other four girls, her long black hair covering her pear-shaped breasts, which moved up and down under her hair as she walked. The workers thought they were in a dream; they were speechless. What was this magic of the jungle—demons? The young, beautiful girl stopped in front of the group, put down the case of beer on the ground next to her, and grabbed a bottle of beer and opened it. She then handed it to one of the silent workers. "Beer, beer for a real man. You work so hard, you so strong, you so good!"

The other girls followed suit, and soon all the workers had beers in their hands. The workers were still speechless, but slowly, one by one, they drank, one beer after another. The girl with the long black hair, the leader of the group of jungle beauties, then started dancing, the way men like, and the other girls followed suit; she had trained them well. Like the mythological sirens in Homer's *Odyssey*, the women lured the men in. The men started talking and shouting, the arousal and testosterone levels in the little jungle opening were nearing explosive levels. The young girl and her girlfriends kept dancing, keeping the men at a distance, teasing them and urging them to drink more and more. She knew what she was doing; she knew the ritual so well: first the dance, then the talk, then what comes after. She knew how to keep the men on the hook of anticipation for as long as possible. That was the most profitable stage, and also the least dangerous. She had learned this the hard way, and had left that life behind a long time ago. But if she could help the old wise one, she would gladly go all the way with these pitiful, simple loggers.

During those years in the darkness of her past, she had told herself that offering herself to men like this was not a sin. If she did not take pleasure in what she was doing, then it wasn't a sin, she had told herself. It had worked for a while, until she realized that it was not just the house where she had practiced the oldest profession in the world that was constantly dark. Soon the faces of the countless men who bought her turned dark as well. In the beginning, she had remembered their faces, but after a while their faces had become blank, dark spots of nothing and nobody—bodies without faces, bodies without souls. Finally, the darkness had entered her heart as well, and there was no light to be seen. It was the wise old one who had rescued her, who had taken her away, who had given her a new family and a new life, who had given her hope—she owed him everything. Yet he had never asked for anything in return; that was the way he was, the wise old one. She had volunteered for the mission today, however; it was the least she could do. As the girls continued to dance, one by one the men fell to the ground, lifeless in a trance. The secret potion in the beer had worked.

Three days later, the group of men awoke in another part of the jungle, where they were all tied to a giant old tree trunk that lay on the ground, much like the ones they had cut down on that day when the beautiful jungle demons had possessed them and made them drink. Their bodies were smeared with sweet wild honey, and the ants were already at work. They were given an ultimatum: go back to their homes and never cut down a tree without permission from the wise old one, or remain tied to the tree and let the jungle animals do the rest. All but two had gone home and sworn never to cut down a tree again. The remaining two had no homes or families to go back to, and they stayed and joined the old wise one. The followers of the old wise one were increasing in numbers day by day, getting stronger and stronger.

Chapter 35

Saturday, 2 February
Madame Tsui's House, Little India, Singapore

Richards's friends Giorgio and Matt arrived by taxi at Madame Tsui's house, Richard's new home, and Richard greeted them at the gate.

"Wow, you have a whole house to yourself again," Giorgio said excitedly to Richard as he stepped out of the taxi.

Richard explained that it was not so. He was only renting a little room in the large house. Richard took his guests up to the second floor of the house and showed them his new home. His guests were silent. Giorgio seemed to be in shock. Giorgio sat down on Richard's bed while Matt took a seat on the chair by the desk.

Matt opened his mouth first. "It's a bit different from your old house. At least you have a fridge. Any beer in there?" Richard opened the fridge, took out three bottles of cold Tiger Beer, and handed one to each of his friends. Giorgio was wearing his best nonworking casual attire: cream chino pants, custom-made button-down shirt, and red socks with leather loafers. Matt wore a T-shirt with the Oxford University insignia, shorts, and flip-flop slippers.

Giorgio was way outside his comfort zone and in a part of Singapore he had rarely ever visited. In fact, Giorgio symbolized the epitome of some Caucasian expats in Singapore, maybe the epitome of ang moh-ness. Giorgio rarely went anywhere on the small island nation that was outside of his daily routine. Giorgio's vision of

Singapore comprised the premises of his condominium in Newton, the financial district of Raffles Place where he worked, the shopping area around Orchard Road, the entertainment hubs of Clarke Quay and Club Street, and finally Changi Airport. Giorgio had only once stepped out of his comfort zone. Once he had taken a girl to the Singapore zoo and night safari, but only because the girl had told him that she liked animals. Giorgio went anywhere if it got him to his desired final destination: in bed with a pretty girl. Giorgio was well into deep water here in Little India, and there was no girl in sight; in fact, he had only seen Indian men driving through Little India on the way here.

Giorgio pulled out some paper wrapping from the plastic bag he had brought with him and handed it to Richard. "Here. This is for you. Thought you might need these here, for the new environment."

Richard carefully undid the wrapping. He felt that there was something soft inside, and the paper wrapping had the emblem of Giorgio's tailor written on it. Matt quickly remarked that it was from both of them, although Giorgio had chosen the design and colors. Richard pulled out the three custom-made shirts, short-sleeved, button-down shirts. One shirt was red with yellow stripes, the second shirt was black with a blue circle pattern, and the third was green with black stripes. Giorgio proudly pronounced to Richard in his Italian accent, "Never been to Little India, but we thought these might help you blend in over here. Hear they like colors over here. *Bello, no?*"

Richard laughed and thanked his friends. Only Giorgio could come up with such an idea. All the shirts had his initials, RL (Richard Lardelli), inscribed in fine thread on the cuffs and collars.

Giorgio continued speaking. "Just because you move to Little India does not mean you cannot be stylish, my friend. The initials... Well, we cannot throw the whole social hierarchy out the window, can we now?"

Richard took Giorgio and Matt for a small tour of Little India. Matt knew the area well; he had gone drinking with Richard there many times over the years. When all bars closed downtown, Little India was always a safe bet to find alternate drinking venues. Poor Giorgio was really a fish out of water and walked a few steps behind Matt and Richard as they walked down Buffalo Road toward Serangoon Road and the heart of Little India. At a certain moment Giorgio told Matt and Richard, "*Mama mia*! This place is full of HPP!" HPP was Giorgio's politically correct term for dark-skinned people, and it stood for "highly pigmented person." Giorgio was surely very arrogant, but one could not accuse him of being unobservant; they were, after all, surrounded by Indians. Richard took them to Sunil's restaurant, and they sat down at the window seat that was by now Richard's regular seat. They watched the endless traffic and crowds of people passing by on the street outside. Richard ordered three South Indian meals composed of curry, rice, and vegetables, all served on the traditional banana leaf, and they ate with their hands. Even Giorgio seemed to adapt well to using his hands as utensils. Matt even jokingly asked Giorgio if he was sure that his background was that of a Roman noble and not Indian, but Giorgio was not amused by the comment.

The Tamil waiter came over after they had finished their meal and asked if they wanted to order more food. Giorgio wanted a coffee, so he said to the waiter, "One espresso, please."

The waiter looked at him questioningly and replied, "Sorry?"

Giorgio repeated, "One espresso," in a louder voice, but the waiter shook his head; he obviously did not understand.

Giorgio did not give up, however. He continued. "*Kaffe.* Brown water. After-food drink?" Richard and Matt looked at each other—yes, Giorgio surely had noble beginnings after all. Matt explained to Giorgio that the word for coffee was *kopi* in local jargon. Giorgio did not hesitate for a moment after learning this interesting new word, and he stood up and shouted out in a loud voice, "Three ang moh kopis, please."

The waiter understood and retreated toward the kitchen. Sunil, the owner, smiled and thought to himself that this ang moh definitely had interesting friends. Maybe he was indeed famous, maybe a movie star.

After lunch the three friends had worked up a thirst; the curry had been particularly spicy. They decided to go for a drink in one of the bars on Dunlop Street. They sat down at a table on the pavement and ordered three beers. Matt started the conversation and asked Richard what he was going to do now. Richard replied that he was going to take some holiday and chill out for a while. Giorgio told him that he had to get a job soon or people would start talking. Richard told them that eventually he would be back in Raffles Place but maybe doing something different, he said. He had some things to take care of first.

At one time during the conversation, Giorgio interrupted Richard and Matt abruptly. "Why do all Indian men in the Little India district have moustaches?" This was typical Giorgio. He was always studying the physical appearances of people wherever he went—so Italian.

Matt responded and told Giorgio, "They all have moustaches here in Little India because the temperature is always a few degrees hotter here than in the rest of Singapore. It's due to the general lack of air-conditioned premises in the area."

Giorgio listened attentively as Matt continued his explanation and told Giorgio, "Facial hair, especially moustaches, makes your face feel cooler. The hair attracts the humidity in the air, and the result—well, it's simple—your face feels dry and cool!"

Richard studied Giorgio. Surely he was not going to fall for this one, surely even Giorgio was not that gullible. Matt and Richard both looked at Giorgio and awaited his reply, but he looked perplexed. Giorgio's reply was swift and serious. "It is actually much hotter here than downtown. Makes sense. Maybe I'll get a moustache too. Always wanted to have a moustache!"

The friends finished off the evening in another pub on Dunlop Street, where they drank some more and watched a live band perform. Giorgio eventually excused himself and left. It had been a good day, Richard thought; a day spent with good friends, good food, good drinks, and good music. His life had changed dramatically in the past weeks, but when he had his friends around him he felt safe—yes, friends were good to have.

At the corner of the bar, in the shadows, stood a tall, elderly Indian man—a Sikh with a turban. He watched Richard and his friend carefully at a distance.

CHAPTER 36

Sunday, 3 February, Late Afternoon
Midnight Oil Bar, Boat Quay, Singapore

Jonas, the bar owner, was working the day shift by himself behind the bar. Sunday was a quiet day on Boat Quay, as most people were out and about and the financial district was empty on the weekend. There were only a few customers sitting outside in the bar beer garden by the river. Jonas was standing behind the bar, washing some glasses and talking to the only customer at the bar counter, Georgie "the Elvis" Fernandes. Georgie was wearing his standard Sunday attire: white bell-bottom trousers, a red long-sleeve shirt with two large neck collars that looked like airplane wings, and a thick gold necklace. His hair was perfectly permed like the King himself, and he wore the obligatory round seventies-style tinted sunglasses.

Two bald, very muscular men dressed in black sat down in the beer garden outside, and Jonas left the bar to take their orders. Georgie "the Elvis" saw that Jonas conversed with the two strangers for a minute or two. Jonas then returned from outside and started filling up two pints of lager along with two shots of vodka. Georgie picked up his conversation with Jonas again.

"Shit. Those guys look like Rambo."

"Yeah, for real. Heard them speaking some weird Eastern European language between themselves."

"They are so bald, man. Maybe they are porno actors," Georgie said.

"Georgie, you spend too much time on the Internet. Too much triple-X surfing. Too many boobs and bald heads, but they could be porno Rambos, maybe."

"Yeah, Porno Rambo One and Porno Rambo Two." Georgie replied.

"Yeah…PR-One and PR-Two," Jonas said.

Jonas and Georgie laughed.

Then Jonas took the two pints of beer and vodka shots out to PR-One and PR-Two. One of the bald men asked Jonas if he knew Richard Lardelli, and if he knew whether Richard was going to show up today at the bar. Jonas told them that he had no clue and that, as far as he knew, Richard had returned to Europe recently. When Jonas returned to the bar, he told Elvis that they were looking for Richard.

Elvis thought to himself, what had Richard gotten himself into now? Porno movies?

"Hey, maybe Richard is in the porno business too?"

Jonas laughed and looked at Georgie and replied, "Yeah, maybe he is a PR too…Porno Richard."

Jonas and Georgie burst out in laughter. They both looked at the men outside.

"Maybe PR-One and PR-Two are waiting for Richard…PR-Three…Porno Richard," Jonas said.

Later, as the two men outside were preparing to pay and leave after finishing their beers and shots, Georgie picked up his mobile phone and called Richard.

"Hi, Richard. It's Elvis."

"*Ciao*, Elvis."

"I'm down by Midnight Oil. Hey, there are two strange, bald, white guys looking for you here, man."

"Oh? Who are they?"

"I don't know, but they look scary, man. A bit like porno actors... Have you been a naughty boy and started in the porno business, man? I didn't know you were like that."

"Don't be daft, man. I have no clue who they are, Elvis."

"OK. Elvis will find out who they are."

"What are you going to do? Follow them?" Richard asked.

"I was a private detective once too, remember?"

"Yeah, and how well did that go?"

"Don't worry, man. Trust the Elvis."

And with that Elvis hung up the phone and returned to the bar counter.

The two bald muscle packages stood up and left the beer garden. They walked down the narrow walkway on Boat Quay toward Clarke Quay. Georgie followed at a safe distance behind them. Suddenly the men were gone, but where had they gone? At the same moment Georgie felt a hand grab him by the neck from behind. The grip around his neck felt like an iron fist. There was nobody in front of him; the street was completely deserted. He heard a voice speak to him, and the grip around his neck tightened. The voice said, "Don't move and be quiet." At that moment Georgie knew that his mission was over, and it had lasted only 150 meters.

He was led into a small opening in between two shop houses; the small space was no wider than half a meter. He was shoved forward along the walls, until they arrived at the opening at the back of the houses. Georgie was pushed into the small service road that lay behind the riverfront shop houses. This was where all the garbage cans, air-conditioning units, and bottle containers were situated. It was also where all kitchens and bars had their deliveries made. At night there would always be some activity on the small, quiet service road: some cook throwing out kitchen waste, some bartender smoking a cigarette while on a break, or some beer delivery men stocking up the bar supply. But today the street was empty, and no one was around at all. Georgie was shoved into the small street. One of the bald monsters then punched him in the face. They pinned him up with his back against a wall. One of the bald giants punched him again in the stomach. Georgie felt all the air go out of his body, and he could not breathe. PR-One and PR-Two surely knew what they were doing, Georgie thought, as PR-One slapped him in the face again. Then they spoke.

"Where is Richard?" PR-One asked.

"What Richard? I don't know any Richard, man. Who is he?"

"It's better if you tell us where he is, Mr. Elvis," PR-Two said. "You see, we know who you are and who your friends are. In fact, we know a lot about you. We are professionals and do this for a living."

"I'm serious. I don't know who Richard Lardelli is."

He realized it the moment he had said it. Shit. He had slipped up and not thought before speaking, just like usual.

"Good. Now we are getting somewhere, Mr. Elvis. Where is he?"

Georgie decided in that moment that he was not going to betray his friend; he was not going to say anything to these two Transylvanian thugs.

"You look like shit in that Elvis attire. Really laughable!" PR-Two said.

At that moment something snapped in Georgie's mind. Shit. He was not going to let these two Transylvanian Neanderthals insult Elvis, the King himself. You insult the King, you insult Georgie Fernandes.

"You can do whatever you want to me, but I will not tell you anything, man. The buck stops here, man...This will not stand."

PR-One and PR-Two looked at each other. After exchanging a few sentences among themselves in a strange language, PR-One looked at Georgie, then got only a few centimeters away from Georgie's face. Georgie could smell garlic and alcohol on PR-One's breath. PR-One one smiled at Georgie, and then he spoke.

"We are not going to hit you or hurt you, Mr. Elvis."

Georgie felt relief inside himself. His bluff had worked. What a performance by Georgie "the Elvis"; he was the man today. Georgie's rush of confidence lasted for about ten seconds, until PR-One spoke again.

"Like I said, we're not going to hit you or take your money... We're just going to *do you*."

"Do me? What do you mean...eh...by do me?"

PR-One and PR-Two looked at each other and smiled.

"You know...do you...doggy style...put the bread in the oven... widen your southern horizons."

Georgie realized in horror what was going to happen. He started shaking at the thought of the proposed treatment by these two giant Elvis-hating bald monsters. Georgie was not particularly homophobic, he had several friends that were homosexual, but this was beyond keeping an open mind—no, getting done by two giant, *botak* (*botak* was Malay slang for bald), Transylvanian, porno men, was in Georgie's world not on the map. Georgie would never be able to look himself in the mirror again, nor walk like a man, and worst of all he would surely never be able to listen to the King again in his life. This was too much for Georgie, so he told PR-One and PR-Two everything.

After he had told them all he knew, PR-One took Georgie's mobile phone. They told Georgie, "If you ever tell anybody about this, we will find you and finish the job we never completed." They left Georgie there by himself, sitting down next to the wall.

As they rounded the corner, PR-One gave PR-Two a thumbs-up. PR-Two smiled back at him and said, "It always works on macho guys with egos and no money," and they both laughed.

"Yeah, it's incredible. Tell them you will kill them, beat them up, torture them—nothing, but you tell them that you are going to *do* them, and they all sing like birds," PR-One answered with a satisfied grin on his face.

Georgie came to his senses after a few minutes. He felt better now. He had escaped the proposed special treatment by PR-One and PR-Two. He had betrayed his friend, but Georgie was still a man—yes, he was still a man—a man who had lived to fight another day. Georgie was going to make it all up to Richard. He was going to find his friend and warn him. This was the least he could do now. Nobody messes with Georgie "the Elvis," and this would not stand.

CHAPTER 37

Sunday, 3 February, Evening
Madame Tsui's House, Little India, Singapore

Richard had just come home from the pub on Dunlop Street in Little India. Richard poured himself a cup of tea; he was not alone in the house's common kitchen. Madame Tsui was sitting by the kitchen table reading the newspaper; she was up late. Richard heard a noise from downstairs; it was the thick entrance door that opened and closed. He heard some voices that he did not recognize, but he did hear them mention a name that he recognized: Maximillian. He went to the top of the staircase and took a peek. He saw two giant, bald, Caucasian men speaking to each other in low voices; they seemed to be speaking in some Slavic language. Richard immediately realized that Georgie the Elvis's detective mission could not have been that successful; they had found him. It had only been a few hours since Georgie had called him, telling him about two scary-looking botak men looking for him. Richard had not paid too much attention to Georgie's call, figuring that Georgie was probably drunk. Now Richard realized that Georgie had been speaking the truth after all. One look at these two characters and Richard realized that they were no friends of his; they looked like hired killers. Elvis had been right when he said that they were scary.

Richard quickly made his way back into the kitchen again. He looked at Madame Tsui and tried to think quickly. He could not go to his room or run, so where could he hide? Madame Tsui looked at him with that firm look of hers, the one a mother gives when her child has done something wrong. Richard could now hear the two men walking up the stairs. Madame Tsui looked at the stairs, and then she looked at Richard. Two seconds later Madame Tsui turned around and opened the door of the large kitchen cabinet that was behind her, and she told Richard, "Quiet ang moh problem have. Get in lah."

Richard wasted no time and quickly climbed into the large cabinet, and Madame Tsui closed the door behind him. There was barely enough space for him inside; he stood like in an *S* shape in the small compartment. He was surrounded by large, fifty-kilogram bags of rice and cases of bottled water. Luckily, there were no shelves, as they had all been removed to make room for the rice bags on the cabinet floor. He was surrounded by rice in a tight, hot, small place. Madame Tsui had obviously understood that he was in trouble. Richard could hear the men enter the kitchen then, and he could tell from the footsteps that they walked straight to his room. He could hear them calling his name while knocking on the door. He then heard Madame Tsui raise her voice and yell out, "Richard no here now lah."

He then heard the footsteps move toward the kitchen again, away from his doorway. One of the two men spoke. "Where is Richard?"

Madame Tsui wasted no time telling them who was in command here. "Get out of my house. I call police lah."

Richard heard one of the two men respond. "Madame, please, we mean no harm. We only look for Richard. He is our friend."

"Friend no allowed. Richard pay single-room only. Please leave house now lah!" the madame responded angrily.

Richard heard the two men leave the kitchen and walk down the stairs. The heat in the kitchen cabinet was building up, and the small, confined space started to lack air. Richard started feeling dizzy. It seemed like an eternity before Madame Tsui opened the cabinet door. Richard stumbled out, and in doing so he stumbled on one of the large bags of rice. The rice bag broke, and rice slowly started pouring out of the cabinet's wooden floor onto the kitchen floor. Madame Tsui raised her hands to her face. "Oh no, my rice!" she said.

Richard immediately apologized for the broken bag, not twice, but three times. Madame Tsui was screaming at him in Chinese, and she was not happy. Richard gathered from the first barrage of the Chinese verbal assault that the madame did not seem to be upset about the two men, but rather the broken rice bag. The old woman had maybe saved his life, and all he wanted to do was thank her and, yes, even take her in his arms and give her a good hug. Richard again and again repeated, "Sorry, sorry," "Thank you for the help with the two botak ang mohs. Thank you for saving me," he said. He then asked and pleaded with the madame, "How can I repay you? I'm so grateful."

The word, repay, seemed to have a magical impact on the madame, and she became quiet. After gaining her breath she told Richard, "You pay for rice, OK?"

Richard took out his wallet. He could see the madame's eyes widen as she saw the wallet. As Richard opened his wallet and asked the madame how much, the old woman's hand struck like a snake, and before Richard knew it, she had grabbed a Singaporean ten-dollar bill. She looked at Richard and said, "Ten dollar OK lah."

Before Richard had a moment to reply, the madame struck again and grabbed another ten-dollar bill out of his open wallet. "Twenty dollars better lah." The madame again eyed the open wallet in Richard's hand; he had one fifty-dollar note left in his wallet. The madame struck again, and the fifty-dollar note made its way into her hands. "Twenty dollar OK lah. Fifty dollar much more better lah."

What a delightful madame she was. Richard was happy that she did not accept credit cards as well. Richard again thanked her, and she responded with a witty comeback. "You have expensive friends lah." How could he respond to that? Seventy dollars was a small price to pay for someone saving him from two very scary-looking thugs. Richard was convinced that his two pursuers would not give up that easily, however. And who the hell were they?

Richard went upstairs, all the way to the top floor of the house. He opened the door that led to the roof terrace. He stepped out on the roof terrace and crawled toward the front of the house. He peaked over the ledge down to the street in front of the house, and, as he had expected, he saw one of his pursuers. The man was leaning against a light pole on the street below, smoking a cigarette and talking on the phone. One look at this character and Richard knew that this was not a very pleasant man. His first instinct had been right. The bald man was dressed all in black: black jeans, black T-shirt, and black sneakers. Richard could also see the large tattoos on the man's arms—no, this was no friend of his.

Richard returned to his room. It was time to pack his emergency bag. He had to get out of here and find a new place to stay, at least for a while, until he could find out what the hell he had gotten himself into. A voice in the back of his mind told him that Maximillian von Horstenbrik had something to do with this. The two guys had, after all, mentioned the name Maximillian. Richard's instincts told him he was in danger and that the police were not the answer now, but maybe later. Now he needed to get out of here, and his primal instinct of flight was too strong. He stuffed some trousers, T-shirts, underwear, his toothbrush, and his passport into the little sports backpack he had. He had to leave as soon as possible. The two men would surely come back during the night, and this time he would not have Madame Tsui to save him—and he sure as hell did not have any more cash.

Suddenly he heard a noise from his balcony. Someone was climbing up the ladder that was mounted on the wall next to the balcony. He heard the heavy breaths and the cranky noises from the old rusty metal ladder. Richard grabbed the old sun chair on the balcony and awaited his uninvited guest. He dared not look over the balcony and see who it was—no, he was going to hit the intruder in the face with the old sun chair upon his arrival. He saw one hand grab the balcony railing, and then another one. Richard was ready to strike. He was not going to wait for the intruder to reveal himself, and he struck with full force against the hands that were holding onto the balcony. A quick, painful scream was followed by, "Shit, man. It's me, Elvis."

Luckily, Georgie had a high threshold for pain; he had held onto the balcony and not fallen. Richard quickly helped Georgie up and onto the balcony.

"Shit, man. Why you hit me? That's really bad, man."

Richard asked Georgie "the Elvis" if he was hurt. "Of course I am hurt, man. Came here to help you, my friend, and you hit me. What kind of reception is that?" Elvis sat down on the other balcony sun chair and gathered his breath. "Hey, I'm so sorry," he said. "I had to tell them where you live. They forced me to tell," Georgie told Richard quickly, still catching his breath. "I had no choice, man. They were going to do bad things to me. Came here to warn you, man."

Richard told Georgie that they had already found him, and he told him about his recent narrow escape and how one of the men was waiting outside the house.

"I know, man. Why the hell do you think I came this way? To throw you a birthday surprise?" Georgie snapped at Richard in an irritated voice. "Look, you have to leave now. We have to get the hell out of here…I have a plan."

Great. Georgie had a plan. That's brilliant, Richard thought—not. Georgie explained his plan that they were going to escape over the garden wall at the back of the house. It was not that bad of a plan, actually. Georgie had obviously come that way, so he knew the way. Richard grabbed his backpack, looked over his room, and came back to the balcony. They then climbed down the rusty old metal ladder mounted on the wall until they touched the garden grass. Georgie told Richard to be quiet. "One of the porno Rambos is standing in front of the house. He could hear us."

"Did you just say porno Rambos?" Richard asked Georgie.

"It's a long story, man," Georgie replied, again in a pissed-off voice.

"I am not sure I want to hear that story, Georgie," Richard responded.

To climb over the two-meter-high wall topped with barbed wire they had to climb up onto one of the palm trees that stood adjacent to the wall. Before starting the climb, Richard touched the trunk of the palm tree eight times with his hand, just for good luck. Richard reached the branch that hung over the wall first, and he balanced his way out on the branch; it was like walking on a rope. When he passed over the wall, he jumped down onto the grass lawn on the other side. Georgie was next. He first pulled the Irish stunt—he first threw his wallet over the wall, so now he was totally committed to complete what he had started. Halfway through Georgie's balancing act it happened: the branch broke, and Georgie was left hanging in the barbed wire alongside the wall, luckily on the outside. His clothes were stuck in the barbed wire. Luckily, he was not hurt, but he was stuck.

"Are you OK, Elvis?" Richard whispered to him.

"Yes, I'm OK. This was not part of my plan, man."

Richard tried to release Georgie from the barbed wire, but it was impossible. Georgie was stuck.

"You have to leave, man. I will be OK. Leave!" Georgie whispered to Richard. "I will release myself!" Georgie then asked Richard for his mobile phone, and Richard gave it to him. Georgie's arms were free, so he dialed a number.

"Abdul, its Georgie. Need help, man. Can you bring a metal saw?" Georgie gave the address and directions to where he was and hung up the phone. Richard was not even going to ask who he had spoken to. "Get the hell out of here. I'll be OK," Georgie whispered to Richard, trying to reassure him. "You have my e-mail, man. Let me know when you are safe," Georgie told him. They said good-bye, and Richard left Georgie, who was waiting for "metal saw Abdul".

Richard was not going to leave Georgie to the fate of being found by the two thugs—no, he was going to do something for Georgie. He had to lure the two Balkan or Transylvanian Dracula warriors, or whatever nationality they were, away from the house. He had to get their attention and lead them away from the house to give Abdul enough time to arrive. Richard walked along the wall until he came to the end by the street in front of the house. He saw the bald man still leaning against the light post, still smoking, the other man was sitting on the pavement close by. It was now or never, he thought. He might as well go for it.

CHAPTER 38

Sunday, 3 February, 11:00 p.m.
Singapore

Richard ran into the street and called out to the two botak Neanderthals by the light post, "Hello there!" Then he sprinted down the road toward Farrer Lane. His two uninvited guests were soon in hot pursuit behind him. Richard sprinted across the large grass field, the one that was sometimes used as a multipurpose field. He looked behind him and saw that his two followers were gaining on him; they looked to be about fifty to seventy-five meters behind him, and they were closing in on him quickly. Richard arrived at the crossing of Race Course Road and Buffalo Road. As he ran across the busy Race Course Road, he almost got hit by an oncoming car.

On the large grass opening, opposite the Buffalo Road MRT station, a crowd had gathered to watch the chase. Hundreds of immigrant workers, who usually spent part of their Sundays sitting down on this peaceful open grass plot, had parked their behinds here today. Here they ate their food, drank their beers, and socialized with their friends on their Sunday day off. One of the workers saw Richard run across the road and almost get hit by a car. Then he saw the two gangster-looking fellows following in hot pursuit. It took only a few seconds, and then the whole pitch of people were on their feet and shouting, "Go! Go! Faster!" cheering Richard and his followers on. Many of the workers pulled out their mobile phones and started filming the chase that was playing out in front of them. A few seconds later the rumor spread among the workers that this was surely a movie shoot that was taking place in front of their very eyes. Some were convinced that this was probably an action flick, maybe even some Bollywood movie. "It's a movie, it's a movie," some started yelling. At least ten of the people on the pitch were standing up and cheering, "Look at us, look at us! Hello! Hello!" One of the workers said to his friend, "Where is the film team? I see no cameras," and his friend replied, "You can't see them because they are professionals; they blend in with the surroundings. They do it that way sometimes—makes it more realistic." The friend nodded his head in agreement. "Makes sense," he said. "That's why there is no retake." His friend agreed. "Yes, they are really professionals."

Richard ran into Buffalo Road, and in the process he almost knocked over some vegetable stands at the busy corner shop. The road ahead of him was jam-packed with late night Sunday shoppers. Richard switched his course from the pavement to the road, as there were too many people on the pavement. He sprinted down the one-way road, while oncoming traffic signaled and honked their horns at him. He looked behind and, surely as he expected, the two giant men were still behind him. As Richard and his pursuers were running on the road, the surrounding shoppers were not immune to what was playing out in front of their eyes. Many took out their mobiles and started filming. This was exciting—first the white man, followed by two large bald white men dressed in black, followed by a motorcycle driven by a large Indian Sikh with a red turban. This was better than the movies.

Arvin Singh, the private detective, had tailed Richard home after his pub visit that same evening; in fact, he and his helpers had kept an eye on Richard for several days. Now Arvin was in hot pursuit; it was quite obvious he was not the only person who was interested in Richard.

Richard had, by this time, reached the end of Buffalo Road and had arrived at the busy intersection. He took a left and continued running down Serangoon Road, practically running in the middle of it. A taxi pulled up alongside Richard as he was running and asked, "Taxi for you, sir?" and Richard nodded in agreement. "I meet you at taxi stand three hundred meter, OK lah? No pick up passenger on road. Cannot lah. Taxi stand, OK lah?" the taxi driver said. The taxi driver's sales pitch left Richard unimpressed, so he continued running. He looked behind him, and saw that his followers were still in pursuit. Richard started feeling tired. His legs were starting to ache, and he was losing his breath. The two bald giants who followed him were obviously in better shape because they were closing in on him fast.

Suddenly a motorcycle pulled up alongside Richard, and a tall Sikh man in a red turban was driving. The Sikh called out to Richard, "Hello, Hello." Richard was in no mood to buy a suit or entertain this traveling salesman, or whoever he was, so he kept running and tried to pick up speed. The red-turbaned Sikh did not give up, and he continued to drive alongside Richard. "Hello. My name is Arvin Singh. I think you are in dire need of some assistance, sir. Richard, let me help you, please," the motorcycle riding Sikh called out to Richard. Richard looked at him. The man seemed relentless, and he was clearly not going to give up. Richard was sure he had seen this Sikh somewhere before, but he could not place him. The man reminded him of the ex-prison guard he had seen in the bar, the one who Youssef knew, the one he thought had been following him and Youssef. Richards mind was in flight mode, and he could not think and reason properly, and even though the man knew Richard's name, Richard kept on running.

When Richard finally arrived at one of the traffic lights, the lights turned red, and his newly found friend in a turban was forced to stop. Richard continued and tried to pick up his running pace. His followers were still on his tail, even closer than before. He had only a few hundred meters left until he would reach his destination. It was hot outside even though it was well past midnight, and the heat in the air was unbearable. Richard's clothes were soaked in sweat, and he felt his trousers were glued to his legs, making his legs feel even heavier. The two bald followers were now only a short distance behind him, and he could hear them speaking and shouting to each other in some Slavic language. Moments later he saw an old Malaysian man, his face painted red and blue in what looked like some tribal ritual war paint. The old man was running parallel to Richard on the busy adjacent sidewalk. He wore tribal feathers in his hair, and wore only a loin cloth. The man was old but ran like his life depended on it. How many people were being chased on this road tonight? Richard thought. The old half naked man soon disappeared in the crowd—just like a ghost. There was something in the way the old man carried himself. Richard had seen this man before, he was sure of it. Richard finally arrived at the crossing of Serangoon Road and Syed Alwi Road, and he took a right and sprinted straight into the narrow Syed Alwi Road. His followers were caught on the other side of the road and were not able to cross because the traffic was too heavy.

Richard had arrived at his destination: the Mustafa Center department store. He looked back and saw his two pursuers still waiting to cross the road. Richard left his bag with the security guards at the counter by one of the entrances. Shoppers were not allowed to bring plastic bags into the shopping center; upon exit of the shopping center one could retrieve a deposited item or bag again. The way things looked now, Richard doubted he would see his backpack again. He entered the Mustafa Center and stepped into the chaos of the twenty-four-hour shopping experience.

The two hit men arrived at the entrance of the shopping center shortly after Richard. When Richard was taking his first step on the stairs that led to the basement level, he saw the men entering the door, and they saw him. Richard hurried down the stairs and almost knocked down a group of women in their black robes. He was lucky he did not knock them down and cause a commotion.

The basement was packed with shoppers, as always. He walked into the textile section, located next to the stairs. This was the section where all the Indian textiles, clothes, saris, etc., were sold. Richard hid behind one of the shelves that displayed Indian saris. He saw his followers come down the stairs, and they split up and started systematically searching between the aisles closest to the stairs. Bollocks, Richard thought. His plan was not going as well as he had thought. He had placed his bets on the fact that he would have lost the men on the small, crowded streets of Little India. It had not worked, and when he realized he would not lose them, he had set off in direction of the Mustafa Center. Surely here he would be able to lose them, he thought. It did not look good for him; they were professionals, and this was surely not their first chase. He saw that the two men had earpieces in their ears, and they were communicating with each other via radio. Who were these guys? KGB, CIA, MI5, underworld hit men? Richard had no idea, but they were good at what they were doing, that was for sure. One thing was for sure, he was sure that Maximilian von Horstenbrik had something to do with the whole thing. They were getting closer to his hiding place. It was only a question of time before they would find him now. They were only two aisles away from him, less than five meters away. As their systematic combing down of the aisles continued, Richard had to come up with some brilliant idea now if he was going to save the day.

Suddenly a small Indian-looking man approached him from behind and tapped Richard on his shoulder. The small man whispered to him, "Wear this and follow me." The man wrapped a large black linen sheet around him. Richard was speechless. Who was this unexpected benefactor? The man wrapped a small black scarf around his head that covered Richard's hair and mouth, then he placed a pair of dark sunglasses on Richard's face as well. While this efficient little man did his job, Richard asked the man, "Who are you?"

The man replied, "Shut up and do as you are told. If you want to get out of here without your two friends, be quiet!"

When the strange couple walked up the stairs to the ground level again, several people turned their heads as they saw a short Indian-looking man leading a much taller veiled character dressed in traditional attire, with face covered and sunglasses. Even the sales clerks at the watch counter took notice, and they had seen a lot of odd people. The odd couple continued toward the exit and walked out the door. Richard's savior kept a tight grip on Richard's arm. As they stepped out of the door, Richard remembered his backpack.

"I have to get my bag," he told his newfound friend.

"You got to be joking," the man snapped at Richard.

The odd couple stood in line at the security counter to retrieve Richard's bag. After receiving his bag from one of the security guards, Richard was led toward the street by his benefactor, the man still gripping tightly to Richard's arm. Richard noticed that the man was wearing an earpiece as well, so which search party did this guy belong to, he wondered. Obviously he was not with the two Balkan warriors. Maybe he was a friend of the Sikh on the motorcycle? In any case, all these guys seemed to be highly organized, and they were all after Richard, but why? The moment Richard thought about making a run for it, the man's grip on his arm tightened even more.

"Oh, forgot to tell you. I am a *Gurkha*. Served with the British Forces for over twenty years," the man said to Richard in a low voice.

Great, Richard thought. A Gurkha. That was all that was missing from the equation now. Richard decided it was best to do as the man said and come along; after all, he had saved him from his pursuers, but who the hell was he and who did he work for? The Gurkha raised his hand and seemed to be speaking to his wristwatch. "Package with me. Do you see me?"

An instant later a large black Range Rover with tinted windows approached on the road. It stopped alongside Richard and the Gurkha. The back door opened, and a large blond giant of a man, who sat in the back, called out to them, "Richard, it's time to go for a little trip."

Richard replied in a nervous voice, "Who are you guys?"

The man in the back seat responded in what sounded like a German accent. "We are friends of Lawrence, and he is waiting to see you. Get in now!"

Before Richard could answer he was pushed into the back seat, the door closed behind him, and the Range Rover pulled away from the curb. The giant blond with a crew cut spoke. "Richard, you have your passport?"

Richard answered, "Yes." He was then told to sit back, remove the black clothing the Gurkha had wrapped him in, and be quiet.

The Range Rover arrived at Seletar Airport less than a half an hour later. Seletar Airport was the old international airport that was still in use today, mostly used for smaller aircraft and private jets.

Within thirty minutes Richard was seated in a private jet next to the giant German blond man, who he had gathered from the conversation with the Gurkha was named Thorsten. The plane took off and flew into the night sky, flying in a southeastern direction. Richard again attempted to ask the man named Thorsten where they were going, but there was no reply from the German.

It did not matter. Richard knew where they were going. The only comment from the German during the two-hour flight to Richard was, "You are very lucky that you have Lawrence."

Chapter 39

Sunday, 3 February, Midnight
East Coast Park, Singapore

Louise walked along the foot and bicycle path that ran parallel to the beach and ocean. It was late Sunday night, and the park was almost empty at this late hour. There were only some late-night runners still out on the path. By the beach the fishermen and hobby anglers had arrived and taken their positions for night fishing, their fishing rods standing firmly in the sand with their lines out at sea. She walked down to the beach and sat down. She was alone.

Louise often came here alone at night when she needed to think. Her thoughts often traveled to Richard. Where had he gone? She had tried to contact him several times on his mobile, and via e-mail as well, without any success. She had even called the bank in Zurich, only to find out that he was no longer working there. She had, of course, read about the bank in the news; it was inevitable. She wondered if he was involved in any of the events mentioned in the news. She had finally been able to get in touch with one of Richard's friends, Prosper. He had told her that Richard had resigned from the bank and was now travelling. He said he had no idea where Richard was, but Louise suspected that he was not telling her the whole story. Louise was convinced that Richard had not done anything wrong, yet her intuition told her that he was in some sort of trouble. She was sure that he was out there somewhere, wanting to reach out to her, but for some reason he was unable to do so. She knew that Richard had feelings for her. She was sure of that. Had Richard gotten cold feet and left his feelings for her behind? Maybe he wanted a younger girlfriend at his side, one with less baggage. She had a three-year-old daughter and a marriage behind her—was this the reason? She knew they would meet again, but when and how? Why does love so often strike when the winds of change are blowing? When love strikes, so many emotions, conditions, and changes occur in one's surroundings. Is it the changes in one's surroundings and habits that let love strike, or is it love that sets the changes in motion? It was a mystery, she thought. Why was it that one always seemed to meet that "one person" when either oneself or the other person was leaving or moving on to something else?

She missed him. She looked out on the ocean and started crying. She saw the last planes approach Changi Airport. Was Richard on one of those planes? Would she ever be on one of those flights, going to see him in his home country? Could she ever leave Singapore and her home and get on a plane with her daughter to go somewhere far away and start a new life with him? She looked to her right at the skyscrapers of Marina Bay and the financial district. The skyline seemed so peaceful at night when the city was asleep. This was her home, and had been so for all her life. Would she be able to feel at home somewhere else? What is home, really, she asked herself. Is it where we feel safe and where our family and friends are? Is it where our history is? Can home also be a place we have not yet been to? Could it be so easy that home is merely where you decide it is in one given time? Maybe it is not even decided by you. The universe decides for you where you will be and with whom. Maybe it was much easier than that, she thought. Home is where your story begins. The question was which story, though. She missed him.

CHAPTER 40

Monday, 4 February
Sarawak

Richard and the small private jet touched down on one of the landing strips at Kuching International Airport. The flight had taken less than two hours. It was 3:00 a.m. and morning would come soon. Kuching was the state capital of Sarawak. Sarawak was one of the Malaysian states that was a part of Malaysia. The northern part of the large island of Borneo was made up of the Malay states of Sarawak, Sabah, and the independent sultanate of Brunei. The rest of Borneo was a part of Indonesia. The portion of Malaysia that lay on Borneo was sometimes referred to as East Malaysia.

The state of Sarawak had been formed in 1841 by the Englishman James Brooke. Brooke was an adventurer, explorer, and businessman, and he had helped the sultan of Brunei to combat pirates. As a reward, he acquired land that eventually become the state of Sarawak. He had proclaimed the state an independent monarchy and proclaimed himself as ruler, with the title of rajah of Sarawak. Sarawak became a British protectorate in 1888. The Brooke dynasty ruled Sarawak from 1841 until 1946, it's rule interrupted only during the years of the Japanese occupation during World War II. Sarawak was the only monarchy in Asia ruled by white monarchs. The White Rajahs, as they were known, were determined to protect the indigenous people of Sarawak from colonial exploitation. The White Rajahs united the many tribes and peoples of various backgrounds under one flag and nation. Although the White Rajahs ruled the country like a monarchy, their rule was appreciated by many of its citizens. Sure, there were many who opposed the rule of the White Rajahs, but there were also many who remained loyal to the rajahs even after their departure after World War II. The White Rajahs built hospitals, combated piracy, upheld the law, and in general tried to improve the living standards of the people of Sarawak. Profit was surely one of the main motivations behind the rajah dynasty, but still today, the rule of the White Rajahs is looked upon favorably by many people of modern Sarawak. Others claim that the White Rajahs ruled the country like their personal family property, and that they were cruel. History is like everything else in life; its interpretation depends on whom you ask. After the Japanese occupation and the end of World War II, the last rajah of Sarawak, his highness Charles Vyner Brooke, ceded the territory to the British in 1946. A portion of the Sarawak population did not favor living under British rule, some even supported the return of the White Rajahs, and the heir to the throne, Anthony Brooke. Upon Malay independence from the British, Sarawak eventually became a part of Malaysia in 1963. The fact that Sarawak became a part of Malaysia and did not gain its total and permanent independence, is still widely discussed by many. Some people in Sarawak even supported the return of the White Rajahs, and an independent Sarawak, even when Sarawak became a part of Malaysia, years after the Rajahs departure.

Sarawak was the home of the Dayak and Iban tribes, deep jungles and rain forests, long houses and rivers, beautiful coastlines, beaches, and a unique ecosystem of plants and wildlife. It was a land of mystery and beauty. It was the home of the feared head-hunters, a practice now outlawed, yet still surfacing in sporadic incidents now and then. Richard had been to Sarawak many times. He was fascinated by its people, its history, and its culture. He had traveled up the river into the rain forests and jungle. He had once spent time with an Iban family in their long house; in fact, he had lived with them for a week.

Now, after arriving at the airport and clearing customs and immigration, Richard's journey continued in another black Range Rover. They drove through Kuching, the state capital, and continued on the smaller roads toward their destination.

After about a one-hour drive, they arrived at the small, sleepy, seaside town of Santubong. Santubong meant "spirit in the boat" in the Iban language. Santubong were the canoes that had been used by the Iban to transport the dead on their last journey. The Holzstam Estate, also known as the Lawrence House, lay by the beach, its front facing the ocean and it's back facing the Santubong Mountain. They drove through the small village, with its traditional Malay wooden houses on each side. They arrived at the small private road that led to the beach and the Holzstam Estate. The large iron gates opened, and a security guard closed the gates behind them as they drove the last meters toward the large estate.

The large black-and-white wooden colonial-style house stood right on the end of the tree line, where the trees end and the beach begins. The house was a colossal construction, three floors high, and had several annexes and smaller separate bungalows in its immediate vicinity. It really was a majestic house, and its location made it even more spectacular. Richard looked up at the roof of the large house. He looked at the strange round tower that shot up from the roof like a minaret. This was the tower that was used to communicate with Lawrence, wherever he was, somewhere out there in the jungle. On top of the tower, even though it was still dark, he could see the Holzstam family flag with the red and blue dragon. The door opened in the same moment they stepped onto the doorstep.

Jones, the old English butler, appeared in the doorway. "Mr. Richard, good to see you. Won't you come in?"

Richard stepped into the large hallway, and he was immediately led into the large study and library that was used as a reception room. He was told by Jones to have a seat. The master of the house would be with him shortly. It was like a scene out of *Downton Abbey*. The room was decorated like a nineteenth-century English mansion with wooden brown armchairs and tables, and crystal chandeliers hanging from the ceiling. The large room was rectangular in shape and had to be more than 200 square meters in size. Three of the walls were covered by old wooden bookshelves, and the shelves were filled with books from floor to ceiling. There must have been more than ten thousand books in this large private library. Standing in the middle of the room, looking at all the books, Richard felt like he could almost hear all the voices from the millions of characters who lived in the books, all with different stories and different destinies. In the middle of the room stood a large wooden desk with three large cardboard boxes. Richard knew what the boxes contained; it was the registry of all the books. The thousands of titles were all neatly and alphabetically organized on small paper cards, and the book registry cards were the heart of the Lawrence Library. Lawrence's son Thomas had once told Richard that it had taken Lawrence several years to complete this card registry. It had all been done manually, and the cards were all handwritten. No computers were allowed in the Lawrence House; it was the way old Lawrence had wanted it, and that was the way it had remained. Richard looked at the only wall in the room without bookcases. He walked over to the wall and looked at the three giant portraits that hung there. The first portrait on the left was a portrait of Otto Holzstam, the founder of the Holzstam dynasty. The second portrait pictured Andreas Holzstam, or Lawrence, as he was known. Lawrence wore a white Arabic Bedouin outfit, with white linens wrapped around him just like Lawrence of Arabia had done, and he looked like a sheik with the white Bedouin head-cloth. Andreas's eyes were light blue, and Richard got a spooky feeling that they were looking down on him, staring at him, judging him. The third portrait was of Thomas Holzstam, the current master of the house, son of Andreas, and the official head of the current

Holzstam business empire. Otto had started the business and laid the foundations, and Andreas had made the business expand into a multinational conglomerate of various business interests. Thomas, the now official head of the business, ruled a powerful business empire, yet his role was only symbolic—old Andreas still pulled the strings from his domain deep in the jungle. The family company that Thomas had taken over in 1995 was composed of holdings in shipping, mining, manufacturing, minerals, and oil. It was one of the most powerful companies in Southeast Asia, and the Holzstams were one of the wealthiest families in the region. The Holzstam name was a name that had earned respect in the region, a name and family one did not cross.

Andreas, alias Lawrence, had ruled the business empire with an iron fist and had controlled the company's every move and expansion with his ever-watchful eye. A longtime bachelor, Lawrence had finally met the love of his life at forty years of age. She was Olga, a Russian girl twenty years younger than him. Olga's ancestors came from an old shipping family out of Vladivostok, Siberia. The young Olga had hit Andreas like a whirlwind, causing the precise, detail-oriented Andreas to lose his bearings. He had fallen for her like a rock. But the fairy-tale love story had lasted only two years. Andreas's beloved Olga was killed in a tragic airplane accident. Foul play was suspected but never proven. After this incident, Andreas rarely flew. Thomas was only an infant at the time of her death. Andreas was heartbroken and in despair. Richard had heard from many people that old Andreas had never recovered from this loss. It was said that this tragic loss was the beginning of the end of Andreas and the birth of the character that he would become, Lawrence.

Andreas's descent into eccentricity had been gradual and strange. The first signs had started soon after the death of Olga. Bit by bit he started to separate himself from his family and friends, to the point that he isolated himself and spoke rarely. He continued to rule the business empire and controlled it with ever-increasing precision.

The business grew, and so did the profits; however, the ever-increasing moods of Andreas made him an impossible person to have to deal with. He slowly isolated himself in the family estate at Santubong, Borneo. By this time the Holzstams were so wealthy they could buy a small country if they wanted; however, all Andreas wanted was to stay in the large house.

It was during these first years of self-proclaimed isolation and depression that Andreas had developed symptoms of obsessive-compulsive disorder, or OCD, and general anxiety disorder. It had started as it often does, with opening and closing doors repetitively, touching doorknobs and windows repetitively, and counting and avoiding steps on the stairs. Every action he took had a special procedure, and it always had to be repeated in the same manner. Like many sufferers of OCD, he believed, or rather his subconscious told him, that if he did not repeat certain procedures for certain everyday tasks, something terrible would happen. Every thought led to a specified action or procedure. It started with small, innocent procedures of everyday tasks, but had eventually become such an obsession that he could no longer live like a normal person. Andreas had to control everything and everybody around him, and the obsession of repeating certain everyday tasks in a certain manner no longer just applied to himself; it applied to everybody around him as well, and it became unbearable.

Then the anxiety started, the fear of everyone and everything, and the sleeplessness, a mind constantly running at high speed in fight-or-flight mode, with the inevitable thoughts on cause and effect. The ever-present questions: "If he did this, what could happen? What are all the possible outcomes? Was he still in control?" He constantly feared being in imminent danger and battled with endless moral thoughts of what was right and wrong—if one would have done that differently, what would or could have happened? It was at this time and in the vortex of his distorted mind that Andreas had decided to isolate himself completely from his family and the rest of the world, and he moved to the third floor of the large house in Santubong. Isolation was, of course, another symptom of his OCD and anxiety disorder—the need to place himself in safety from any possible threats or actions he might undertake voluntarily or involuntarily. The fear of hurting someone or losing face became too much for him, and there was only one way to deal with these thoughts and feelings: isolation. Only his son Thomas and the butler Jones were allowed on the third floor. It was during these years in exile on the third floor that Andreas had come to identify with T.E. Lawrence, or Lawrence of Arabia, as he was also known.

Lawrence of Arabia was a British intelligence officer who had been one of the leaders of the Arab revolt against the Ottoman Turks during World War I in what was then Arabia. The young officer had captured the attention of the world during those World War I years of 1916–1918. Lawrence of Arabia led the Arabic Bedouin tribes in the deserts of Arabia, dressed like an Arabic sheik, spoke their language, slept in tents, rode camels, and blew up the Ottoman Turks' railway system far behind enemy lines. His feats and heroic conquests were publicized in the press as the feats of an almost mythological character or god. He had captured the imagination of the whole world. In the eyes of the Western world, he had been some sort of cross between Robin Hood and Billy the Kid; he was good and bad at the same time, a person who was many persons, many characters, and who lived many lives all at the same time.

Andreas had been fascinated by the character of Lawrence of Arabia. He had read all the books there were to read about the man. He had seen the epic 1962 film *Lawrence of Arabia* starring Peter O'Toole uncountable times. He had even memorized most of the dialogue of the movie itself. Thomas Holzstam, Andreas's son, had explained once to Richard that his father became Lawrence to escape from himself. Thomas had explained that it was his eccentric father's theory that if one lived the life of someone else, a person who has already lived, there are no more unknowns; the path is already written and can be followed. If his father was no longer Andreas, he had no need to control every single action or task he undertook. If he was no longer Andreas, nothing bad could happen to him because he was now Lawrence. Thomas had gone on and explained that his father had chosen Lawrence of Arabia because he symbolized all that Andreas had ever wanted to be: a man who had lived his life on his own terms. A man who had stepped out of his comfort zone and had ridden out into the desert and the unknown to meet his destiny. Andreas had never had any choice in life. From the moment he was born, he had been destined and groomed to take over the family business and to make it even more profitable and powerful. He was raised to rule like a king, to be ruthless when needed, to be compassionate when it was profitable, and to put the interests of the company before himself and his family. The pressures and expectations had been immense on the young Andreas, and all these pressures had finally taken their toll on him, causing him to step into the eccentric world of living the life of another person, his alter ego and safe zone.

The third floor of the large house had gradually been converted into some sort of version of the fable *A Thousand and One Night* and the film *Lawrence of Arabia*. In fact, the whole third floor looked like a set from the film; the furniture, porcelain, carpets, textiles—everything was inspired by the film. To symbolize the desert, the living room had even been covered in sand, which only Thomas and the butler Jones had been allowed to carry up in sandbags to the third floor. Andreas had also built a small toy railway, and its tracks covered the floor of the third floor and went from room to room. Once Andreas had even tried to blow up the railway with firecrackers, all to reenact the railway raiding scenes from the movie *Lawrence of Arabia*. The man had been beyond all logic and far away from reality. No phones, TVs, or computers were allowed on the third floor; in fact, nothing that had been invented after 1916 was allowed. When he occasionally had to travel away from his sanctuary it was always by boat. During these years, all communications to the outside world were handwritten notes that Andreas left to Thomas and Jones the butler. The communications were often only quotes from the movie itself. Over time Thomas and Jones learned how to decode the meaning of the cryptic messages; they used to call it Lawrence code. The code was thereafter adopted by Thomas to communicate with many others in the Holzstam business empire.

To have a father who thinks he is Lawrence of Arabia living on the third floor of the house in complete isolation, to have a father who had chosen this life—what psychological scars this must have left on Thomas. But Richard did not even want to think about that.

One day in 1995, fifteen years after Andreas's self-proclaimed isolation on the third floor of the Holzstam Estate, and on the sixtieth anniversary of the death of Lawrence of Arabia, Andreas came out of isolation. He came down the stairs, officially handed over command of the Holzstam business empire to his son Thomas, walked out the door, and stepped into the jungle. The last words that he spoke were to his son Thomas. Thomas had pleaded and begged for him to remain in the safety of the house, to get treatment, to get help, but it had all been futile. Finally, Thomas surrendered and realized that his efforts of convincing his father were useless. He had asked his father why the jungle, and the old man had replied, "That's where it all started. That's where the future lies." Now Andreas was out there somewhere in the jungle, in the heart of darkness. Although his son Thomas was officially in command of the business empire, the old man still pulled the strings and ran the whole show from somewhere out there in the jungle—a global business empire commanded by an eccentric through smoke signals, handwritten notes, and couriers.

Thomas Holzstam entered the room and shook Richard's hand with an iron handshake. Thomas was almost an identical copy of his father. This is what Andreas must have looked like when he was young, Richard thought. Thomas was tall, with blond hair, blue eyes, and broad shoulders. Thomas was forty-two years old, but he looked much younger. He had recently become a father for the first time, his baby son had been born only a few months ago. Thomas was married to a Russian girl who originated from a Russian shipping family, just like his mother had.

"Richard, good to see you," Thomas greeted him.

"Good to see you again, Thomas. Thank you again for probably saving my life," Richard said.

"Oh, you're welcome. We thought you were a little bit out of your element and needed a helping hand. I'm sure you are wondering why you are here," Thomas said.

Thomas was old school northern German, he got straight to the point with no verbal distortions. When the Holzstams said something, they meant it. When the Holzstams did a deal, the handshake meant everything. Paper and signatures meant little; a man's word was everything.

"Yes. At this point, yes, very keen actually."

Well, you will have to wait a little bit longer, I am afraid. Now it's time for you to get some rest. It's been a long day, and it's best to rest now."

"I see. But can't you even tell me a little bit?"

"It's really not up to me to decide. You know who calls the shots here, Richard. The man has a plan for you, and in time it will all be revealed to you. You are not a prisoner. You are a guest, Richard. You are free to leave whenever you want, but if you leave now you will never know why you are here. What do you want to do?"

"I want to stay, Thomas."

"Excellent. Then I will see you tomorrow."

The old butler, Jones, entered the room to tell Richard that one of the guest bungalows had been prepared for him. He was accompanied by Jones and a security guard to the bungalow by the beach. After Jones and the security guard had left, Richard more or less collapsed on the bed, and he was asleep within one minute.

CHAPTER 41

Monday, 4 February
Santubong, Sarawak

Richard woke up to the sounds of the ocean and wind; it was Monday. He looked at his wristwatch; it was past 11:00 a.m. He decided to go for a swim. He threw himself in the warm, salty water and swam straight out toward the nearby reef. After passing the beach break, he arrived at the reef. The water was shallow here, and he could see the ocean bed below him, maybe five meters deep at the most. He started treading water and looked toward the beach. It was still early, and there were no people around. He saw a large ocean turtle swim past him, heading out toward the open ocean. The turtle had probably spent the night at the beach laying eggs. Turtles often used the beach at the Holzstam Estate; as it was a private beach there were rarely any people around. As he treaded water, he started thinking of the past day's events and what it all meant. He thought about the Holzstam family—what was their interest in him? Who were the bald thugs who had followed him? What did they want? Obviously, nothing good. Who was the Indian man in a Sikh turban who had attempted to stop him and help him? Was the Sikh man the same man that he thought had been following him and Youssef earlier, the ex-prison guard that Youssef knew? Why this sudden interest in Richard? After a few moments of reflection, he started swimming back toward the beach again.

When he came back to his bungalow, Richard took his breakfast on the small porch outside. The breakfast was served by two young Malay girls who giggled and smiled at Richard while they were serving him his breakfast. After breakfast, he decided to go for a walk and think some more. He thought of Lawrence—why had the old man saved him? What was his game? Why was the old eccentric interested in him? What did Richard have that Lawrence was interested in? Richard thought about the motives for Lawrence's departure into the jungle. What had caused him to leave the safety of his home and step out into the jungle? Most people would spend their retirement relaxing and watching their grandchildren grow up, but not Lawrence. He had gone all the way and chosen the unknown and the jungle, but why? The old man still ran the whole business empire from his self-proclaimed Lawrenceland, far away from modern civilization. Richard had once heard from Massimo Rossi that Lawrence was the new white rajah. Massimo had told him this when he had drunk a little too much at a cocktail party in Singapore, and the next day, he had told Richard that it was just a made-up story. Richard never thought more of it at the time. But now—the return of the white rajah. Was it possible?

Richard could understand the fascination of Lawrence of Arabia. Richard had himself been fascinated by the story and life of Lawrence of Arabia. During his years in university in Milan, he had once written a research paper about Lawrence of Arabia. His professor had asked for permission to send the paper to one of the large Italian newspapers. Richard's paper had been published. The twenty-page research paper had been split up into three parts and published in the weekly Sunday Culture section of the paper for three consecutive Sundays. This had been Richard's first experience with publishing. He had later also written a research paper about the global destruction of the rain forest, in particular about the Amazon and Borneo Rain Forests. This later research paper had also been published by several European newspapers. Yes, Richard had made something of name for himself and had over the years been approached by several newspapers to write about various topics, most concentrating on the environment.

Richard's interest in Lawrence of Arabia had at first been purely academic. However, the more he read about the man and legend, the more his fascination for the complex character of T.E. Lawrence developed. Richard had, like Andreas Holzstam, been fascinated by the young officer who had left his comfort zone, faced his fears, stepped out into the desert, and had, against all odds, been successful. Richard had also seen the epic movie *Lawrence of Arabia* countless times and read all the books; however, his interests had stopped there. Andreas, on the other hand, had become Lawrence himself. He had not only been fascinated by the legend, but also had gone all the way and lived it.

Richard walked back along the beach to his bungalow. He looked at his watch and realized that several hours had passed. He had been so deep in thought that he had not realized how much time had gone by. It was now afternoon, and the sun was at its zenith above him. His arms and legs were sunburned, and he felt a headache coming on. He decided to walk back to the bungalow for a nap. He was not supposed to meet Thomas until after 5:00 p.m. He lay down on the comfortable double bed in his bungalow and fell asleep.

Later Richard was awoken abruptly by someone tapping his shoulder. He had slept heavily and felt dazed and confused. When he opened his eyes, he saw two Iban tribesmen dressed in traditional wear: red *Sirat* loin cloths and feather head garments. The two men also had spears in their hands. Great, Richard thought. This was all that was missing—to be woken up by Iban tribesmen. Richard did not have time to sit up or speak, because someone grabbed his shoulders from behind and held him down.

"Don't make a move, and be quiet. The less you resist, the easier it will be for you." The voice came from behind and had a distinct British accent. "We are not here to hurt you, only to guide you on your way, on your path," the voice continued.

Richard was terrified, but he dared not speak. His body started to shiver and shake from the fear. Before he could even try to say something, the same person who had spoken to him placed a black textile hood over his head. It all went dark for Richard, and he could only hear his own breathing. They grabbed his feet by the ankles and his shoulders from behind, carried him out of the bungalow, and placed him on the ground. He could see nothing; it was all black in front of his eyes. He heard footsteps approach, and then the footsteps stopped. It was quiet and the only sound Richard could hear was the sound of the palm trees rustling in the wind.

So this was it. This was how it would end, Richard thought. He thought he would see his life flash before him, images of his life and pictures of the people he loved. Is that not what's supposed to happen when you are about to die? But he saw no pictures. All he heard was the sound of the ocean and the wind. So it was all fake—when you go, you just go—no images of your life flash before you. There's no drum roll or gun salute; you just go, and that's it.

Finally he heard a voice he recognized. "Richard, sorry, but it has to be this way." The voice belonged to Thomas. "It's for your own protection," he continued.

"Thomas, is that you?" Richard finally managed to break his silence.

"Yes, it's me, Richard. Don't be afraid. It's all good," Thomas continued in a low, reassuring voice close behind him.

"I don't want to die, Thomas!" Richard yelled out.

There was silence, and again, only the sounds of the wind and the ocean surrounded him.

"This is for your own protection. You are going to meet Lawrence. You are going on the path that leads you to the truth, and it is written."

These were the last words Richard heard and could comprehend. A moment later he felt a prickle in his left arm, probably a needle of some sort, and then it all turned black. The three Iban tribesmen carried Richard's seemingly lifeless body toward the Range Rover parked nearby.

"Take him to the house by the two rivers!" Thomas told the leader of the tribesmen.

The old Iban man nodded and replied, "Yes, boss."

Chapter 42

Tuesday, 5 February, Early Morning
Maximillian's Apartment, Singapore

Maximillian's special mobile rang, and he picked it up and answered.

"We lost the bird at the Mustafa Center," the voice on the other end said.

"You lost the bird at Mustafa Center?" Maximillian replied. "Now what?"

"Yes."

"Where is the bird now?" Maximillian asked.

"We will come back to you when we have more information. Oh, by the way, we are not the only ones interested in this rare bird," the voice said.

"What do you mean?" Maximillian questioned.

"I mean, we are not the only ones interested in this bird."

"Look, you need to find the bird now. I will raise the premium."

"OK."

The conversation ended.

So they had found him at last. Maximillian was sure that they had probably found Richard at that pub down on Boat Quay, the one he had tipped them off about. Now they had lost him again. Richard had to be found *now*, Maximillian thought. If Richard spilled the beans and talked, he would endanger everything that was important for Maximillian.

"Soon, my dear Richard, you will be mine!" Maximillian said out loud as he lit a Cuban cigar.

CHAPTER 43

Tuesday, 5 February
Edwin's Apartment, Singapore

Edwin had heard from his friend, the private detective Arvin Singh that Richard had disappeared. Arvin had tracked him down in Little India a few days ago and had been able to locate where he lived. They had first spotted him in a restaurant, the one that Arnold had tipped them off about. They had followed him for a few days. They found nothing really extraordinary; over the past days Richard's activities had been rather boring, as Arvin had said. Richard had gone in and out of restaurants and shops in Little India, gotten a six-dollar haircut from a barber on Dunlop Street, gone to an ATM, and spent most of his time in a pub in Little India. He had always gone home early and alone in the evenings. One day he had spent with two friends, wandering around Little India, and another he had been seen with a man that Arvin knew, a man named Youssef, who was an ex-convict. Arvin had for many years worked as a prison guard and correctional officer at Changi Prison. When Edwin heard of the meeting with Youssef, he interrupted Arvin and asked him, "Who is he?"

Arvin responded calmly and told Edwin that he knew Youssef from the time he had been working as a prison guard. "The man did time for gang-related crimes in his youth, and he has been clean since release. We checked it out and found out that he was working as a gardener for Richard for several years—that probably explains their friendship.

"Interesting object you gave me to investigate, Edwin. Not really the everyday ang moh, is he? I mean, here is a wealthy private banker who hires an ex-convict and has lunch in a restaurant with him like the best of friends. Most people I know would keep their distance from anyone who has been to jail, let alone hire them. Don't you agree?"

Edwin nodded in agreement. "Yes, he is a bit of an enigma, our friend Richard!"

Arvin continued his recollection of events. It was on the fourth evening that they had spotted him running out of the landed house where he was renting a room, followed by two mean-looking, bald, Caucasian ang mohs; the two botak men looked like mercenaries—two dogs of war who seemed very keen on catching Richard. The chase had led all the way to the Mustafa Center, where both Arvin and the two dogs of war had lost Richard; he had disappeared. Arvin explained that he had even blown his cover, as he had realized that Richard was in some sort of trouble and probably in danger. But Richard had refused Arvin's offer of help and had turned his back on him.

Arvin also informed Edwin that most likely, the two bald ang mohs were not the only people interested in Richard. Arvin had taken note of a black Range Rover that had been observed at most places Richard had been to in the past days. The car seemed to be ever present on the streets of Little India, wherever Richard ventured. "I had the feeling myself that I was being watched, quite odd actually. Whoever they are —they are pros" Arvin told Edwin with a tone of resignation in his voice. Arvin also learned that Richard was no longer working for the bank. The person they had spoken to at the bank's human resource department had said, "We are not at liberty to discuss the terms of Richard Lardelli's departure." After losing Richard in the Mustafa Center, Arvin had ordered one of his aides at the scene to follow the two bald ang mohs instead. The aide had tracked them down at a small hotel in China Town. Arvin had also sent another one of his assistants to watch the house where Richard appeared to be staying. The aide had watched the house day and night, but there had been no sign of Richard so far.

After this whole report, Edwin gave instructions to Arvin to keep watching the house and to keep watching the two ang mohs in the hotel in China Town. They agreed to keep in touch and to speak as soon as there were any new developments.

Edwin tried to put some of the pieces of the puzzle together. Richard was in Singapore, not working, and he was being followed and chased by two angry ang mohs who look like contract killers. There existed the possibility that there were several entities interested in Richard and his whereabouts. Arvin had been a private investigator for many years, and if he felt that he was being observed—well quite frankly, he probably was.

Richard lived in a landed house in Little India where he was renting a room—not really a normal address for an ang moh banker like Richard. He was spending his days eating curry and getting drunk in bars in Little India, even getting six-dollar haircuts. He appeared to be friends with an ex-offender as well. All of this did not sound like the best match for his Louise- no this was bad news indeed.

Edwin had doubts, however. He had liked Richard from the beginning, and his first impressions were rarely wrong. To employ an ex-offender was, in Edwin's eyes, a service to society, but sadly his view was not shared by everyone. Edwin had been a police officer for enough years to know that many offenders went in and out of jail because they were labeled as outsiders and as bad by society. Life as an outsider and the difficulty in finding employment once they were out of jail regrettably caused many to break the law again. Edwin's gut feeling told him that Richard was in some sort of trouble—yes, something was not right. Why was he hiding out in Little India? The guy had enough money not to work another single day in his life.

There were too many question marks—question marks that Edwin was determined to find the answers to. And he always did. Louise walked into the apartment just then with her young daughter, Mary.

"Hi, Dad. Just ran into Arvin on the stairs. You guys still work together?"

"Yes. In fact, we are working on a little something. Indeed we are."

"Probably following some cheating spouse around, eh, Dad?"

"No, just some ang moh who seems to be in a little bit of trouble."

Little Mary interrupted the conversation. "Ang moh Richard, Mommy's special friend, in trouble?"

"Why do you say Richard, Mary? Why do you say that?" Louise asked.

"I don't know. It just came out that way, but maybe he is in trouble."

"Mommy's special friend is far away, and he is not coming back. OK?"

"Why? Everybody I like leave. Dad left. One day you will leave too, and I will be alone."

Edwin bowed down and held Little Mary tightly. He had tears in his eyes. "Mommy will never, ever leave you," he assured her. "We will always be here for you in one way or another. We are a family, and don't you ever forget that!"

Little Mary wiped a tear from Edwin's face. "Ang moh Richard will come back. I gave him a special rock," she said.

CHAPTER 44

Wednesday, 6 February
Somewhere in the Jungle, Borneo

Richard awoke out of his deep, dazed sleep. He felt tired and drugged. His head was heavy, and he had some problems breathing under the black hood, which was still in place. He sensed that he was lying down on some sort of stretcher and was being carried. He heard the sounds of the jungle around him. He felt like he had slept for days. The heat was unbearable, and he was sweating heavily. He heard several men speak in some tribal language; the voices were all around him. He counted the voices and guessed that his abductors were four men. He tried to speak, but his mouth did not seem to respond; he tried to move his feet, but his feet did not respond either. What had they given him? He tried to remember, but his brain did not seem to work at all. He felt tired, and then he fainted again.

When he awoke a second time, he was lying on a firm floor, and he could hear the sound of water and feel vibrations; he was on a boat. He realized that he had retrieved some senses in his body. He could now feel his feet as well as his hands, which were tied together and rested on his stomach. He was lying on his back, and the boat was rocking more heavily now, the vibrations from the hull growing stronger. He heard the outboard engine loudly behind him; they were going faster now. He did not smell any salt in the air, so he guessed they were on a river. He tried to raise his head, but he was too tired. He felt that he was slipping away again, and then it all turned black.

When he awoke the third time, he felt that he was being carried on the stretcher again. He could hear the sound of sand below and knew he was no longer on the boat. He suddenly detected the sounds of the jungle again and the smell of vegetation; the humidity in the air picked up again. He heard the sounds of many people in the distance, first far away, then closer and closer. A few moments later he heard the sound of children laughing, and then he felt small hands touching his body and little voices speaking some strange tribal language he had never heard before. The only word he could recognize from the children was "Lawrence, Lawrence." Richard started feeling dizzy again and fainted.

Richard awoke again and opened his eyes. He was staring up at a ceiling made up of palm trees and wood. Suddenly four little eyes appeared above him. Two little Iban boys were staring down at him, and they smiled. The two little boys soon disappeared and left Richard alone again. He continued staring up at the ceiling. He recognized the distinct long wood beams in the ceiling holding up the palm and grass that made up the roof, and he knew now where he was; he was in a long house.

The long houses were long, wooden, rectangular-shaped houses often built on wooden stilts or pillars that elevated them from the ground. Long houses were common in Asia from India to the Pacific Islands. The houses were often constructed by bamboo wood, this mainly thanks to the strength of the wood and its abundance. The houses were built on stilts elevated from the ground for various reasons: to keep livestock, to protect the houses from floods and water, to keep produce and other utensils, and to protect against predatory animals and other threats. The long houses were often the homes of many families, or even a whole tribe. The inside area was often separated by a long wall in the middle that ran from one short side of the house to the other short side. The wall separated the house into sections. On one side of the separating wall each family or occupant would live in their own separate living space or room, and on the other side the open corridor would be used as a communal space, an area used for everyday life, such as cooking, washing, eating, socializing, etc. Some long houses could be over fifty meters long and house over a hundred people. The occupants would usually make up a large extended family, and they would usually all come from the same tribe or family. The Ibans and Dayaks, two of the ethnic peoples of Sarawak, often lived in long houses still today. Even though the families and occupants lived in a rather loosely knit community within the long house, there would usually be a strict social hierarchy observed within the house. Every tribe and family had a head or chieftain, and the long house was no exception. The head of the tribe or family would, under normal circumstances, be the head of the long house.

Richard felt water on his face and sprinkles of water in his eyes, and he sat up and cleared his eyes. His arms and legs were no longer tied up. He was lying on a simple bamboo bed in a small room. He looked to his right toward the open doorway, where several small Iban children were standing and looking at him, most of them naked or wearing only loin cloths. They were smiling and giggling and making funny fart noises with their mouths. One of the little boys was wearing a baseball cap that read Tokyo Giants. Another little boy had a plastic water pistol that he was pointing toward Richard. He was obviously the guilty one; the little rascal had woken Richard up with his water pistol. Boys will be boys, even in the jungle, Richard thought.

The crowd of children suddenly scattered and disappeared, and in the doorway a man dressed in traditional Iban costume appeared. He looked to be in his fifties. His face looked old and weathered, but his muscular, naked torso and arms looked like those of a twenty year old. The man approached Richard and spoke: "Hello there, old chap. How do you feel?" He spoke in perfect Oxford English, which surprised Richard, to say the least. "You are still feeling the effects of the potion, Richard." The man smiled at Richard as he spoke.

"Potion?" Richard answered. He realized that he still felt dizzy.

"Not to worry. All-natural ingredients. No funny stuff in it," the man answered.

"Natural ingredients?" Richard questioned.

"Yes, all-natural ingredients. We sometimes use it to put our livestock to sleep," he answered Richard in his perfect Oxford English. "Look, the potion is still in your body. A few more hours and you will be back to normal again," the Oxford Iban replied.

The man introduced himself as Situ, son of Bitu. He went on to explain that Richard was in the long house of Bitu, his father—the long house by the two rivers in Lawrenceland. Richard felt the effects of the potion take hold of his body and mind again, and he started feeling dizzy and weak.

"Lawrenceland," he managed to reply with his last energy before he passed out again.

When Richard awoke the next time, it was all dark in the room, and the man who had introduced himself as Situ sat by him on a chair next to the bamboo bed. "Are you ready to meet the enemy, Richard? It's time."

Richard was led forward by Situ along the corridor toward the meeting with his enemy, as Situ had said. Even though Richard had no idea what lay ahead of him, he felt no fear. Something told him that he was not in enemy land at all; these people were too friendly to be enemies. A feeling of familiarity or déjà vu came over him. It was strange because he had never been here before, yet it felt like home.

As they walked down the corridor, many occupants of the long house joined the procession and followed behind. The walk through the corridor seemed to go on forever; the long house was at least fifty meters long, Richard surmised. Finally, they arrived at the end of the corridor and entered a large room. Richard guessed this was the chieftain's room. Richard was ordered to sit down on the floor facing the stage-like platform that was elevated above the ground. On top of the platform sat one old man, one man only, with one lit candle in front of him, one candle only. The old man faced Richard and said nothing; there was no expression on his face whatsoever. The old man was wearing a tribal head garment with red feathers and a red loin cloth, and that was all. The old man's body was covered with tattoos from his face to his feet. Richard looked at the wall behind the old man. On the wall there hung three large portraits, three old samurai swords, and, to Richard's horror, six or seven small human skulls. The skulls, some with hair still on them. The skulls seemed to be very old, and they had probably been smoked, Richard guessed. The smoking of skulls was a process Richard had read about several times. After heads had been taken, they would often be smoked as a sort of traditional ritual, but some argued that it was done mainly for conservation purposes. In any case, the smoking of heads had been an important feature among the headhunters for centuries. The heads were trophies, and although they were the heads of enemies, they were treated with respect. Richard counted the skulls that hung from the ceiling again and hoped his head was not going to be one of them.

"Welcome. I'm Bitu, and this is my house," the old man said as he introduced himself. He also spoke with an Oxford English accent, just like his son, Situ. Situ sat down next to Richard on the floor facing Bitu on the elevated platform. The old man looked like he was at least one hundred years old.

"Welcome to my house, Richard—the house by the two rivers," Bitu said again.

"Thank you, sir," Richard responded.

"I trust you had a good journey, and that you are feeling rested?"

"Yes. I'm happy to finally be here, sir."

"Good."

The old man's English was really exceptional; he spoke just like a university professor. Richard wondered how this was. It was not very likely that Oxford University ran an exchange program with the long house. The skulls suspended from the ceiling would not be the best publicity for possible exchange students back in England, or would they?

"I believe you probably have some questions, Richard, so go ahead," Bitu said.

When the old man had finished his sentence, he made a gesture to the people that sat behind Richard and Situ on the floor. Richard looked back and saw that the other occupants of the long house who had followed them into the room stood up and, one by one, left the room.

"So, go ahead, Richard. What are your questions?"

"Where am I? Are we still in Sarawak, or are we in Kalimantan, Indonesia?" Richard asked.

"We are still in Sarawak, yet fairly close to Indonesia. But for all practical purposes we are in Lawrenceland."

"Lawrenceland?" Richard asked.

"Yes, Lawrenceland."

"I do not understand."

"I need to start from the beginning," Bitu said. "I need to tell you how it all started."

The old man then stood up and lit a long wooden tobacco pipe. The smell of sweet tobacco soon filled the room.

"I was born in this long house in 1922. I have been the head of this house and family for many moons, just like my father was before me. You might wonder why I speak such good English. Well, it's all because I served in the armed forces of the White Rajah as a ranger. I also served with the British Forces for many years. I was a reconnaissance scout and served with a British military intelligence unit during the Japanese occupation of World War II. See those Samurai swords up there? See the skulls? They are the skulls of Japanese soldiers who came to our village uninvited. Three of them were officers, hence the swords. I also served with the British during the Malay Insurgency in the 1950s and 1960s on the Malay Peninsula.

"I see that you are looking at the three portraits on the wall. The first portrait on the left is his highness, Mr. Charles Vyner Brooke, the last rajah of Sarawak. He ceded his throne and Sarawak to the British in 1946. The portrait in the middle is that of Mr. Anthony Brooke, the heir to the throne, who only recently passed away. The last portrait is that of a man you already know, Richard. I am talking, of course, about Andreas Holzstam, the old wise one, or Lawrence as he is known here. When the British took control of Sarawak upon the departure of the last rajah, many of us still supported the rajah. I was one of them. My long house and several others in the area remained loyal to the rajah, as the rajahs had been good to us and our country. When we finally realized that the rajah was not coming back, we laid down our arms. However, in our hearts we still remained loyal to the White Rajah dynasty.

"When Sarawak became part of Malaysia, our hopes of the White Rajahs returning were finally shattered. On the map we are Malaysians, but in our hearts we are foremost people of Sarawak, and nothing can change this. The heir to the throne, Anthony Brooke, never regained the throne of Sarawak. We supported Anthony Brooke, and an independent Sarawak, but unfortunately, this never came to be.

"Many years ago, in 1995 to be exact, some of my hunters found a white man by the riverbed far away from here. The old man was in delirium and suffering from dehydration and malaria. My hunters brought him back to our long house. My people did not realize who the man was. However, I knew the moment I saw him that it was Andreas Holzstam. The Holzstams were known throughout Sarawak; they were one of the wealthiest families there were. I had heard the stories about the old eccentric and about his isolation in the house at Santubong. We took the old man in and cured him. It did not take long before the rumor had spread out near and far away that we were curing an old white man who had been found by the river. Rumors are a powerful thing, and after a while, we started receiving visits from other long houses. They had all come to pledge allegiance to the rajah—yes, they had heard that the rajah had returned to his people again.

"By this time, Andreas had recovered and was able to walk around and speak. Andreas Holzstam, with my help, tried to explain to the visitors that he was not the white rajah, that he was merely a simple man who had lost his way in the jungle. His explanations went on deaf ears, however, because no one believed him, and they thought he was merely humble and cunning. Andreas Holzstam explained to me that he had left his former life to find a new life in the jungle. He explained that he wanted to help us improve our lives, and in exchange, he wanted to stay with us. For me it was an easy decision; he could stay.

"You see, Richard, we are a poor and simple people, and with Andreas's help we could improve our lives and the lives of our children. Andreas soon sent for help from his house in Santubong. One day several boats came up the river all stocked with food and medicine. He built a small clinic and a movie house down by the river. Andreas soon started to dress himself in long, white, Arabic-looking linens, and he looked like Lawrence of Arabia. The sight of the old man dressed like that only helped to convince many people that he was indeed the rajah; although slightly eccentric in his ways, the rajah had returned. The months went by, and as time passed, Andreas, or Lawrence as he preferred to be called, continued to ship goods and materials up from the house at Santubong. Soon he had built a small school for the smallest children and another movie house as well, and this is how it started.

"Now almost two decades have passed, and he is still here. Lawrence has financed the education of many of our brightest and most promising students, and with his help, we now have people in business, education, engineering, and medicine, spread out all over the world. We have people in England, Switzerland, Germany, Singapore, and Hong Kong, among others. These young adults are our ambassadors and eyes to the world; they safeguard our interests and existence. It's a perfect fit, really; he wants to help us, and we are happy to receive his help. There are no words of gratitude that could express what he has done for my people.

"Now, Lawrence no longer stays with us. He is old now and lives in his own long house up the river. He still comes here every now and then by boat or canoe. Now what happens when Lawrence dies? This is the question we all ask us ourselves. Will all this good he has created just go away? Will someone new take over, and then what will happen? This is where you might come into the picture, Richard."

Richard sat on the floor. He was mesmerized by the fantastic and incredible tale he had just heard. It was too good to be true—what a man, what a story. He felt so small.

"So where do I come into the story? Can I help?" Richard asked.

"You sure can, Richard. But how? Well, only Lawrence can tell you this. He is waiting for you now."

Bitu gestured to Situ and Richard to stand up, and he told them that the meeting was over and that it was time to rest for the day. Richard was accompanied to his small room again and told to get some sleep. Tomorrow would be a long day—the day he would meet Lawrence.

CHAPTER 45

Thursday, 7 February
Deep in the Jungle of Borneo

Richard awoke early. It was still dark outside. The first rays of sunshine were starting to hit the long house roof, and he could feel the temperature rising. He looked out through the small makeshift window in the wall. Outside there was silence. Only a lonely Iban tribesman stood watch by the nearby river, where the morning mist lay like white smoke. He heard footsteps approaching in the corridor outside his room. A short Iban woman entered the room holding a plate in her hands. She approached Richard and said, "Good morning, sir," and put the plate on the small table next to his bed. The plate contained a small cup of coffee and freshly baked pancakes. Richard got up out of bed and started eating his breakfast; the coffee was very good. He was hungry. He realized that he had not eaten for—well, he did not know for how long. How long had the journey to the long house taken? He guessed several days, because he did notice that he had lost a few kilos. He ate the breakfast quickly and drank at least a liter of water with his pancakes.

After he had finished the breakfast, Situ appeared in the doorway. He had changed into Bermuda shorts and a T-shirt, abandoning the traditional loin cloth. "Good morning, Richard." He saluted Richard. "Ready for the last part of the journey?"

Richard replied that he was ready and anxious to start the journey as soon as possible. Situ handed him some clean clothes to wear: a white T-shirt, white shorts, and white sneakers. Great, like a lamb before the slaughter, Richard thought. He went outside and did his morning toilet in some bushes behind the house, washing his face by the river and brushing his teeth. He had been given a small disposable toothbrush and a small tube of toothpaste the night before. The toothbrush read "Malaysia truly Asia." He chose another trail back to the long house and told Situ that he was ready. Situ again placed the black hood on Richard's head. "Sorry, but it has to be this way, Richard," he whispered to him as the hood was slipped over his head.

Richard did not mind or attempt to resist; he was, by now, used to traveling with a hood. Situ led Richard toward the river and helped him get into the waiting canoe. The canoe pulled away from the riverbank, steering toward the middle. In the canoe with Richard were Situ and two other Iban men who were paddling. The canoe picked up speed and steered away from the long house by the two rivers, which soon disappeared out of sight behind the river's bend. Bitu, the old chieftain, stood on the shore and watched the canoe disappear around the bend. May God protect him, he thought.

All Richard could hear as the canoe traveled upstream was the sound of the paddles hitting the water and the sounds of the surrounding jungle. The heat was tremendous. The sun was up now, and he could feel its intense rays against the back of his head. Situ must have read Richard's mind then because a straw sun hat was placed on his head. "For the heat, old chap," Situ told Richard as he placed the hat on Richard's head.

The journey lasted what Richard guessed was several hours. Every now and then the hood was partially removed to let him drink water from a plastic PET bottle. Not much was said on the boat, besides Situ conversing with the two men paddling. Richard could hear the sounds of the jungle surrounding him, sometimes nearer and sometimes farther away. After what seemed an eternity, Richard heard the sounds of the jungle getting nearer; the sounds of insects, monkeys, and birds seemed very close to the canoe, and the heat and humidity were increasing. Suddenly the canoe stopped close to one of the sides of the river where the jungle was so thick, almost like an impregnable wall. Situ called out in some tribal language, and a voice answered. Suddenly a part of the jungle opened in front of the canoe, and a well-camouflaged door was pulled open. The door and gate were so well covered by lush twigs and leaves that it was impossible for the naked eye, even at a close distance, to know of its existence. The door swung inward into another narrow and shallow canal. Two Iban tribal men who operated the door saluted Situ as the canoe steered into the small canal inlet. The camouflaged secret door closed silently behind them as quickly as it had opened. The canoe and its occupants continued their journey on the small canal, deeper into the jungle, deeper into Lawrenceland.

Richard, who had no idea of the secret canal or where he was, started to feel uneasy. He sensed that they were now on a small waterway; the jungle was close as sounds of animals and insects were all around. He could feel insects and ants crawling down his back, and the intense heat and humidity almost caused him to faint. A few minutes later they encountered another canoe traveling in the opposite direction. The two canoes passed by each other with only a few centimeters between them. One of the passengers on the other canoe, another white man, pointed to the hooded Richard, and Situ answered him with a thumbs-up. The other white man reached out and tapped Richard on the shoulder lightly as his canoe passed.

"What?" Richard said as he felt the tap on his shoulder.

"Just checking to see that you're OK," Situ answered.

The other white man was a man Richard knew well, and his name was Massimo Rossi. Eventually the canoe Richard was travelling on, reached the end of the canal and another secret door. Another well-camouflaged doorway opened, and the canoe slipped through it. The canoe now entered a large lagoon of shallow water, almost the size of a small lake. The small body of open water was surrounded by thick rain forest, and some of the trees reached well above thirty meters in altitude. For someone who saw the sight for the first time, it truly looked like a Garden of Eden. This is what the world must have looked like when it all began.

Richard had spent most of his time during the journey reflecting on his life—the protected, comfortable life he had lived back in Europe and Singapore; it had all been so easy and safe. Sure, he had stepped out of his comfort zone many times—switched jobs, moved to other countries, switched friends, and switched girlfriends—but all of that was nothing compared to what he was experiencing now. He had lived a life always on the borderline—to be or not to be—always moving along with the flow of things, always adapting to new rules and conditions, always adapting to new people, groups, and places. He had always been an outsider. He had friends from all possible social and ethnic backgrounds, but he never identified himself as one of them. It was like he was constantly moving forward in life toward something unknown, following a river. Today, for the first time in his life, he felt at peace with himself; he was not afraid of what lay ahead of him. He was on this canoe for a reason, and he hoped that reason would help him understand who he was and where he was going. Then fear grabbed ahold of him again. What if he was asked for something he could not deliver on, agree with, or, heaven forbid, make up his mind about. One thing was for sure: this was the end of the river. Was it his last journey as well? He wondered. Then he felt calm again. There was nothing else he could do, he assured himself. He was at the end of the line, and if this was the end of the line, why did it feel like home?

The canoe steered toward a clearing in the jungle on one side of the small lagoon. A small wooden landing with several canoes tied to its sides shot out from the dense jungle. Several people waited on the landing. The canoe was tied to the landing, and Richard was helped to disembark, and his hood was removed from his head. The bright daylight hit his eyes, and he had to cover his eyes for a moment before he could open them again. The first thing he saw was Situ standing in front of him and smiling.

"Welcome to the end of the river, old chap. End station," Situ said.

Richard turned around and looked out on the small lagoon. Dense rain forest jungle surrounded the lagoon and all the canoes and small boats around the small landing. It reminded him of the MacRitchie Reservoir Park in Singapore, only here there was no comfort zone to retreat back to, no nearby taxi to take him home. Situ took Richard's arm and started leading him toward the jungle. At the end of the landing, he saw an opening in the dense forest, the beginning of a trail.

Then he saw him: Lawrence. He was standing in the middle of the trail. A tall elderly man wearing a white Arabic Bedouin linen, he looked like a sheik or a holy man. He had gray shoulder-length hair, distinct facial features, piercing blue eyes, and a large mouth. He looked just like the man in the portrait. Situ and Richard arrived at the beginning of the trail, standing right in front of Lawrence.

"Welcome, Richard. Welcome to the end of the river! I am so happy that you are finally here and that you have arrived safely," Lawrence said.

The old man spoke English with a distinct German accent. Richard was speechless. He had thought about what he would say when he finally met the man, but now he could not speak a word.

"Don't be shy, Richard. You are safe now. I don't bite, OK?" Lawrence said.

Richard finally managed to speak. "Good to meet you, sir. I have also been waiting for a long time for this moment, sir."

"Good. So the feeling is mutual. That is an excellent start, indeed. Now walk with me," Lawrence instructed him.

They walked up the trail that led into the jungle, Lawrence holding Richard's arm as they walked. Situ walked behind them. Ahead of them another Iban man led the group, carrying an old double-barrel shotgun in his hands. They walked in silence, and after a few hundred meters they reached an opening in the dense rain forest. In the middle of the opening stood another large long house. The house was twice the size of the long house by the two rivers, and it looked much newer and more majestic. On the roof of the house a flag blew in the wind, a flag with a red and blue dragon on it. This was the house of Lawrence, the house at the end of the river. Around the long house stood several small huts and houses. The long house stood on poles and was elevated roughly a meter or two from the ground. Next to the house Richard noted a large Bedouin-looking white tent—yes, this was definitely the home of Lawrence, Richard thought. Around the house several people were going about their daily chores of washing and preparing food on small fires. Several Iban children were kicking a football around, and some elders were sitting in a circle on the ground listening to an old radio.

"The men are in the forest today for the hunt. This is my home, Richard. Hope you like it."

"It's beautiful, sir. Never imagined it to be like this."

"Yes, this is home," Lawrence replied.

Next to the long house stood a large, modern, garden nursery glass house full of plants, with at least fifty large solar panels positioned on top of it.

"That's my greenhouse. Keep all my cherry blossom trees there. I have one tree for every day of the year brought out. The solar panels on the roof power the air conditioning to control the temperature inside. I have a Japanese gardener, Mr. Suzuki. He does his best to try to time the flowering to have at least one cherry tree blossom for each week. There are twenty separate temperature compartments inside the greenhouse to facilitate all the different flowering seasons and times. We try to keep at least one blossoming tree outside for everyone to see and enjoy," Lawrence explained.

Richard was accompanied to a room in the long house, and shown inside. "This will be your room, Richard, "Lawrence told him. The old man stood in the doorway as Richard sat down on one of the simple wooden chairs that stood next to a desk. "Please make yourself comfortable," the old man continued. "I have some chores to take care of and will be back tonight. Then we will talk about the future, Richard."

Richard nodded his head in agreement. "Sure. Sounds great, sir. Looking forward to it," he replied.

"Please feel free to wander around as you please, Richard. I highly recommend that you go for a refreshing swim down by the landing. The water is pristine, clear, and quite cool and refreshing. Just watch out for the sea monster, OK?" Lawrence laughed, turned around, and walked out of the room, leaving Richard alone.

Richard decided to take Lawrence's advice and go for a swim. It had been days since his last shower. He felt dirty and had noticed during the morning's boat ride that he smelled like sweat. He left the room and walked down the long corridor. When he passed an open door, he saw someone was in the room, someone who caught his attention, causing him to stop and stare. Inside the room he saw a young, beautiful girl, naked, washing her long black hair. The water droplets on her smooth brown back, along with her long black hair, awoke something in Richard. At that moment she turned toward the open doorway and smiled at Richard. She had a beautiful face, dark eyes, and large, pointed breasts. She kept smiling at Richard while she continued to wash her hair, and she made no effort to cover herself up. "Hello," she said. Richard quickly left the doorway and the young washing beauty behind. He felt ashamed of himself for peeking at a naked girl, like some old pervert. The young girl had not seemed to mind, though. She had not been ashamed of her nakedness and beauty at all. Maybe it was the way of the jungle, Richard thought happily, as he walked down the trail that led to the landing by the lagoon.

He arrived at the small landing by the water and sat down. He looked around and saw a few fishermen casting their nets into the water. The fishermen were sitting on wooden poles, which stood in the middle of the lagoon at least fifty meters from the shore. Some children were playing on the small sandy beach close to the jungle. Richard got undressed and slipped into the water naked and unnoticed, at least so he thought. He started swimming toward the middle of the lagoon; the cool water felt great. At one point he turned around and started treading water; he looked back on the landing and at the jungle behind. Then he saw her, the washing beauty from the long house. She was walking toward the landing, topless, her perfectly shaped, pointy breasts covered by her long hair. He had already seen them back in the room at the house, and his imagination started working; it's so true that sex is all in the mind. She wore only bikini bottoms, and her long black hair blew into her face as she stepped onto the landing. There was no need for imagination anymore; her body and her breasts were visible now in all their glory, and even better than the image in his memory. She started waving at Richard and making signs for him to come back toward the landing, and Richard started hastily swimming back toward the landing.

As he was swimming back, it happened. The sight of the twenty-something beauty, along with the primal simplicity of the jungle and its ways, had taken their effect on Richards's libido; it was unstoppable. He stopped about five meters from the landing and decided it was better to stay at a safe distance, to give it some time. The young beauty called out to him. "Hi, me Suva. How long you stay water?"

Richard replied that he would stay in the water for at least another twenty minutes. Suva did not seem amused by his answer. Richard had figured that twenty minutes would give him enough time to think of something to combat his libido reaction, like painting toy soldiers or building sand castles. Suva waited at the landing, then she called out to Richard again, "I wait for you back at house." Then she turned around and started walking away. To Richard's horror, he saw it too late; she was holding his shorts and T-shirt in her hand. He started calling to her. "Suva, wait!"

Suva turned around and replied, "I wash clothes for you. You get back later, OK? When you come, I come, OK?" And then she was gone. Her last cryptic comment did not diminish his libido reaction, and the more he thought, the stronger it got; sex *is* all in the mind. Ten minutes later he was back to normal size and swam back to the wooden landing, where he stayed in the water.

One of the young boys playing near the landing had seen the whole incident and started laughing. He disappeared into the jungle only to soon reappear again with something in his hand. He walked onto the landing and called out to Richard, "It's OK. Clothes for you." The boy handed him a set of shorts. Richard was barely able to squeeze into the boy-sized sport shorts, and it took a good two minutes for him to get into them.

He decided to get back to the long house as soon as possible. He walked up the trail toward the house, away from the water. The shorts were so tight that it hurt when he walked, but luckily his libido reaction was over; that was at least something. On the other hand, it was always nice to know that everything still worked properly down there. He hurried across the open courtyard and into the long house, then walked down the corridor and into his room. The washing beauty named Suva had not been in her room when he passed it. Probably best that way, he thought as he closed the door to his room. After another drink of water he lay down on the bed and fell asleep. He dreamed of Louise, naked, washing clothes.

CHAPTER 46

Thursday, 7 February, Evening
The longhouse of Lawrence, Borneo

Richard was awoken by Situ. "Hello, old chap. Ready to face the enemy?" Situ handed Richard his clothes, the ones he had lost on the landing. "I think you have a new admirer named Suva. She washed your clothes for you."

"Yes. I know. She seems nice," Richard replied.

"Yes…nice is the word. Maybe even a little bit better than nice" Situ said and gave Richard a tap on his shoulder. "Get dressed. It's time. I wait for you outside the house," Situ told Richard as he turned around and walked out the door.

Outside it was night, and a large campfire was burning. The long house occupants were sitting around the large campfire. Three Iban musicians in traditional tribal costumes were playing music. Another man was performing a fire dance with two lit pieces of wood in his hands. The musicians were playing on simple makeshift instruments. One musician was beating wooden sticks against a hollow log, another was playing a small wooden flute, and the third man was playing some sort of string instrument that Richard had never seen before. Although there were only three musicians, they sounded like a whole orchestra. Richard was shown a place to sit slightly away from the other people. Situ told him he would procure them some food. Richard watched the fire dancer perform to the music. It was a very surreal experience. The shadows of the fire seemed to dance against the nearby tree line of the jungle; there were no people with iPhones taking pictures here. There was no need for selfies; no picture in the world could capture this, Richard thought. Situ returned with some plates and cups. Richard picked up his cup and tasted the sweet-smelling liquid, and it nearly knocked him off the log he was sitting on. "Iban moonshine, old chap," Situ told him and patted Richard on the shoulder. "You like?" It was moonshine, sure enough, Richard thought. It tasted like it was at least eighty proof. They really have it all out here in the jungle, Richard thought, even their own distillery. An older lady came over just then and served them some fried vegetables and fried wild rice on a large leaf. The food was spicy and tasted better than it smelled. They watched the fire dancer perform and ate in silence.

Suddenly the music stopped and the people stopped talking. Richard saw a group of men approach from the shadows of the jungle, and then they stepped into the light. The group of Iban men was led by a tall figure dressed in white from head to toe; it was Lawrence. His face and white Arabic Bedouin outfit were smeared with blood and dirt. Another man from the group stepped forward into the light of the fire, carrying the head of a slain wild boar. A third man in the hunting party also stepped forward and threw the torso of the wild boar on the ground in front of the fire. All the people who had been watching the group of men approach stood up in unison. The music started again, and people started dancing around the open fire. Obviously it was party time in the long house.

"Iban roast, old chap," Situ whispered into Richard's ear. Richard saw how the trunk of the wild boar was placed on a table, cut open, and cleaned. A few minutes later large pieces of meat were placed on wooden skewers and placed over the fire. The smell of barbecued meat slowly spread around the campfire. Richard saw Lawrence disappear into the long house together with the beautiful young Suva. It did not take long before the barbecued meat, the Iban roast as Situ had called it, was served. They ate in silence again and watched the fire and the performance of the fire dancer.

Just as they had finished their meal, Lawrence came back. Richard was first aware of his presence when all the people around the campfire stopped talking and turned their heads toward the long house. Only the sound of the fire crackling could be heard, but even the flames of the fire seemed to lower themselves into submission at the presence of Lawrence.

Lawrence stood in the doorway of the long house, in silence, and looked down on his people. He was dressed in a new white Bedouin linen outfit, his long gray hair resting on his shoulders. He looked like a king, Richard thought. Hell, he was the king out here; there was no doubt anymore in Richard's mind.

"It's time, Richard. Go to him now," Situ whispered in Richard's ear.

Lawrence walked over to the Bedouin tent and disappeared inside it. Richard followed suit and went in after him. As Richard made his way into the tent, the people around the campfire watched in silence. Next to the tent opening there were two large ceramic pots with two waist-high cherry trees in full blossom.

After Richard entered the tent, he closed the tent opening behind him. It was like stepping into another world; Persian carpets were on the ground, and Moroccan candlelit glass lanterns hung from the tent's ceiling. Lawrence sat on some cushions, and he gestured to Richard to take a seat in front of him. If there was a song that could best describe the mood and setting as he sat down opposite Lawrence, it had to be the song performed and sung by David Bowie, "Secret Life of Arabia."

"So it is time you and I finally have a talk. I have lots to tell you, Richard, and I am sure you will have several questions for me as well," Lawrence said.

Richard nodded his head in agreement and remained silent.

"To be able to tell you why you are here, I need to start from the beginning. I know you know much of my story—Bitu told it to you at the house by the two rivers. Now I will fill you in on the missing pieces, OK?"

Again Richard nodded in agreement. His mouth was dry, and he felt tongue-tied; even if he wanted to, he could not speak a word. He had waited so long, but now when he was face-to-face to with the man his mind was empty.

"My story starts well over forty years ago. My wife had just passed away. Thomas was just a year or so old, and my life was shattered. I was at the command of Holzstam and Son Ltd., one of the most powerful trading and business empires in Southeast Asia. The death of my wife caused me to throw myself into my work; it was a way of handling my sorrow and grief. I became obsessed with the running of the business. I was the captain of the ship in total control of everything, my life became my work. I was in total control; no one dared question me, and the ones who did I destroyed. I needed to control everything—my family, my employees, my competitors, and my surroundings. There was no space for any unknowns in my life's equation. The urge to control was an escape of my sorrow and pain.

"Then I got sick. The signs had been there all along, and they had started as they often do. I started repeatedly checking doorknobs, windows, and light switches. Everything had to be done precisely the same way, every time. I had to raise a glass to my mouth several times in the exact same way—usually eight times, as this was my lucky number. My belief was, of course, that if I did not perform certain tasks in a special way, something terrible would happen to me. I became afraid of my own shadow. All objects around me had to be in the same place and in the same order as they always were. It was really a difficult time, Richard.

"You see, I realized that I was slowly losing my mind and took drastic measures. I saw a doctor who gave me the diagnosis of acute OCD, obsessive-compulsive disorder, along with paranoia and general anxiety disorder. Forty years ago not much was known about these conditions. Many sufferers were just believed to be insane and obsessed with fixed ideas. It could not get out that the head of the Holzstam business empire was a crazy lunatic. Nowadays there is therapy and even DBS, deep brain stimulation, available to cure the most serious cases of OCD. Imagine that, Richard, with today's technology they can implant electrodes into your brain that send out impulses causing your brain to concentrate on other things. Is that not marvelous?

"Anyways, treatment was not an option for me, so there was only one way open for me: escape. I isolated myself on the third floor of the estate in a controlled environment—my environment. It could not be known that I had gone crazy.

"My son was still young at the time, and there was no way the business could be handled by someone else. Also, there were thousands of employees counting on me and the business for their daily bread. You know just as well as I do that the social security net here is not what it is in Europe; one has to work or no bread."

"Could you not have some other family member run the business—your uncle, for example?"

"No, it could only be run by me."

Lawrence paused for a while and drank some water from a wooden cup.

"It was during this isolation that I became Lawrence of Arabia. I would watch movies, listen to music, read books, and do anything to pass my time in my self-proclaimed prison. I had always been fascinated by Lawrence of Arabia, even since my childhood as a boy. When watching the 1962 epic film something happened to me. I realized that this was who I wanted to be. I admired the man and his accomplishments—the way he had stepped out of his comfort zone and conquered his fears, and how he became a legend in our time; he was all that I could never be. After a while it was the only movie that was playing on my TV screen. I read all the books and articles—anything I could get my hands on that had to do with Lawrence of Arabia.

"During this immersion into the life of Lawrence of Arabia, I realized that my symptoms of OCD and anxiety had diminished. Why? Because I was concentrating on something that took my mind off my daily routines and worries. It did not take long for me to realize that if one believes and acts like they are someone else, they slowly become that other person. Call it alter ego, if you will. If one lives like a person who has already lived, there are no more unknowns in the equation; the path is already written. The fear that something awful would happen to me if I did not follow my routines exactly disappeared—of course it did—I was no longer Andreas. I was Lawrence of Arabia. My apartment on the third floor became a giant movie set from the making of Lawrence of Arabia, all for me to live my new life"

The old man paused for an instant, turned his head to the right, then to the left, and touched the small wooden table in between him and Richard eight times with his left index finger. He silently repeated something to himself, almost like a Buddhist mantra. Richard recognized the behavior; he knew it so well himself. Lawrence then looked at Richard and spoke again.

"I allowed no modern appliances or inventions into my reach that had been invented after 1916. No TV or telephone. It all had to be like it was back then; it had to be perfect! I soon realized that running the business was difficult without all the modern-day means of communication, but not impossible. In today's world, with twenty-four seven news coverage and the pressure on leaders to constantly be online—sometimes people make wrong decisions. Why? Because everything has to be done so quickly nowadays, and sometimes it's better to reflect before you make important decisions. I communicated via the telegraph and with handwritten coded messages to all my business entities during those years, and it worked fine. My messages would be coded into quotes from the movie *Lawrence of Arabia*, and only people with a healthy dose of imagination could understand them—this was not a bad thing.

"In 1995, on the sixtieth anniversary of the death of Lawrence of Arabia, my exile ended. I was sixty-five years old, and it was time to hand over the business to my son. I chose the jungle as my new home. You see, in order to overcome your fears in life, you have to go toward those fears, to confront them. I had always feared the jungle. Where does a man go who believes he is Lawrence of Arabia? What would be the opposite of the desert? I could think of no better alternative than the jungle, can you?"

"I don't know what to say, sir. No, I guess the jungle would be a good place to face one's fears," Richard said.

Lawrence started laughing and drank some more water.

"I like you, Richard. I know you understand me. You, too, have stepped out of your comfort zone many a time in your life. So let's go on with my story, shall we?"

"Please continue, sir."

"After days of wandering around in the jungle, a few Iban tribal men found me by a river, sick and dehydrated. They took me back to their long house, where they cared for me. I got better as time went by and soon started living like one of them in the long house. I started a new life and left my old life behind. I was born again. I wanted to help these people, to be one of them, and the rest you already know, Richard."

"You are truly a remarkable man, sir. You kept on being Lawrence, though?"

"Well, old habits die hard, and remember, never change something if it works." Lawrence reached for an old tape recorder on the ground next him. He pressed play, and the theme from the movie *Lawrence of Arabia* by Maurice Jarre filled the tent. "Wait. The story is not over, and this is where you come in. Would you not like to hear more?"

"Yes, please continue, sir," Richard responded.

"Very well. Here it comes. I first learned of your existence many years ago. I by chance read an Italian newspaper and came upon your article about Lawrence of Arabia. I made a note of your name, and soon thereafter another article followed, the one you wrote about the rain forest; maybe the universe was already communicating that our destinies would be entwined.

"When I consequently was informed of the fact that my bank, Rossi & von Horstenbrik Cie Bank, had hired a new private banker at their Zurich office, a banker named Richard Lardelli, I was convinced that it was destiny. My family is the single largest client that Rossi & von Horstenbrik Cie Bank has, and we command quite a bit of pull there, as you know. I got my hands on your personnel file and CV from one of my contacts at the bank, and the more I read, the more convinced I was that you could be the man who would finish the job. You were born and raised in Asia, spoke several languages, had the right education, worked in my bank, and were interested in Lawrence of Arabia and the preservation of the rain forest; it all fit so well. I arranged for you to be transferred to the Singapore office to handle my account at the bank. Yes, Richard, your path to where you are today is all my doing."

Richard thought back on his life in Singapore and his career at the bank. Of course it had all been too easy—the transfer to Singapore, the generous salary, the large black-and-white bungalow all to himself, and all the local Asian clients who had explicitly wanted him to handle their business. He had thought he was in demand because of his skills, but the truth was, of course, that he was just an average banker, nothing less, nothing more. He had immediately been assigned the two most important clients in the bank upon his arrival in Singapore, and now he understood that it had all been the work of Lawrence.

"The last few years we have had our eyes on you, Richard. I have people in the bank and outside the bank who have regularly reported back to me, telling me what you were up to. The more I heard, the more it convinced me that you were the right choice. Your biggest benefactor in the bank is someone with power and someone I trust, and no, it is not Maximillian von Horstenbrik. I also had some help from a certain person in Hong Kong; you also know her very well."

"You have been watching me? What does that mean? I don't understand," Richard questioned.

"Your best friends in Singapore are Prosper, Giorgio, and Matt. You are in love with a lovely young Singaporean girl named Louise. Your favorite hangout in Singapore is the Boat Quay bar named Midnight Oil—where you spend far too much time. You often talk to the night trader Eric at the bank, who, by the way, is a friend of mine. Your parents live in Rome. You recently went to Zurich, where you met my friend Ueli from the Zurich Border Police; he has a large, typical Swiss policeman–style moustache. I know every detail of your house and garden in Singapore. One of my men saved your life when you were about to go for a permanent deep dive off the shores of Singapore. This man saved your life! He has no name, because he chooses not to have one, but he knew exactly what you were going through at that moment, because he has been there in his own life several times. In fact, you and him have more in common than you will ever know. He was always afraid of the water, and at one time he decided to confront his fear—he nearly drowned and was about to let go, just like you. There is more, so much more to his story. I don't even know the whole story— he probably does not know it either. After nearly drowning, he taught himself how to swim. He took an oath that he would spend the rest of his life close to his fear, to remind him that life is worth living—he rarely ventures far away from the ocean. Now he is an old man who has conquered his fear; he chooses to live close to his fear, and that is his choice. He, too, kept an eye out for you. I know that you suffer from control issues and phobias. Yes, my dear Richard, like it or not, you have OCD and general anxiety disorder. How do I know? I know because we have followed and studied your behaviors all these years. I know that you touch and check your door lock at least eight times before you leave your house each day, that you always walk on the left side of the person you are walking next to, that you wash your hands at least several times after your bathroom visits, that you constantly check your body for signs of disease and signs of abnormalities, and that when you face difficult situations you often isolate yourself and procrastinate rather than confront your fears. You have periods of where you experience extreme energy and motivation, and other periods where you have difficulty facing everyday life. Sometimes you act rash and perhaps even careless, because you feel you are in danger—even when there is no imminent danger.

"Some fear is good, it keeps us alert, but to constantly live in fear—well nothing good comes out of that"

"If you conquer your fear, there is no limit to what you can achieve in life"

"Deep down, Richard, you know I'm right. I know because I see myself in you."

"I surrender; you know it all," Richard said. He felt like a small boy who had been caught in the act. There was nothing to say; he was at a loss for words.

"You see, over the past years, we have followed you and tested you."

"Tested me?" Richard asked.

"Well, do you think it was a coincidence that Youssef the gardener came up to you in a bar in Singapore asking you for a job?"

"You mean you know Youssef, my gardener and friend? You mean you set it up?"

"Youssef has been a friend of the cause for years. That lovely girl you met today, Suva—yes, Suva, Richard, is Youssef's cousin. See how small the world is and how everything in the world is tied together?

"You see, if we could get Youssef into your house, well, then we could watch you even more. Forget about how it happened. Let's just say I helped you improve your karma. You do good things in life, and good will come to you, Richard. You let a stranger in need into your life and house, and it was at that moment that I knew you were the one we wanted. Call it the ultimate test, call it destiny, call it whatever you want, it does not matter. You passed!

"Now we have arrived at the events that finally led you here. Oh, I almost forgot about the lovely, young Miss Suva. That's a story worth telling! We rescued Suva from a potentially dangerous future. Young Miss Suva had fallen into bad company and gotten on the wrong track in life. She is, as I said, Youssef's cousin. On a boat off the coast of Bali, one man wanted to do bad things to her, but she escaped, and Youssef asked me for help. That man, Richard, that man you know…His name is Maximilian von Horstenbrik ….He is still out there, and we will deal with him later, but for now he still has a part to play. We saved Suva from that life, and now you have seen her. She is twenty now and a beautiful young woman. All she dreams of is starting a family and showing her children to her parents to make them proud of her. Sadly, she can never go back to them. Why, you ask? Because for them she does not exist anymore. She got off to a bad start in life and kept the wrong company, but she changed her ways and started again, Richard. And look at her now. Is she not beautiful, and who are we to judge her? She actually was my joker up the sleeve, a card to be played at a later date, but then you met Louise."

Richard remembered now. Of course. Youssef had tried several times to set him up with her. All the pieces were starting to come together—all the pieces except his role. Why had he been chosen? An Iban woman stepped into the room with a bottle of water just then, which she placed next to Lawrence's feet. Then she silently left the tent just as quickly as she had entered. Lawrence lit up the *nargileh* water pipe next to the little wooden table next to him, and the smell of sweet tobacco soon filled the tent.

"The Strydsteen family are well known to me and my people," Lawrence said. "They have been running illegal lumber operations for years in this part of the world. Sarawak and the rest of Borneo are only part of their operation. They are responsible for much of the uncontrolled, illegal erasure of hundreds of acres of prime rain forest every day. They also run a shipping line together with other local business entities. They are present in the whole business chain, from the cutting down of trees to their transport and final sale. They are also active in the human trafficking sector. I have been trying for years to stop them. I cannot let them destroy the land and home of my people, Richard!

"When I found out the Strydsteen family maintained accounts with Rossi & von Horstenbrik Cie Bank, we made our move and set them up. The seizure of their ship in Marseilles and the capture of young Bernard Strydsteen were just parts of the plan; there is so much more. It took us several years to plot it all out. I have not been alone, however. My allies are powerful, and some of them you know well, Richard. The only problem was that Maximillian von Horstenbrik decided to use the setup to get rid of you, and this was not part of our plan. We knew that the news of the ship seizure and capture of young Bernard would bring attention and cause grief to the Strydsteen family; it would destroy them once and for all. However, we had not counted on Maximillian reacting the way he did. Before we had chance to make things right again, you resigned from the bank. So when I learned that you were back in Singapore, we decided it was time to bring you home, Richard."

"Home?"

"Yes, home. This could be part of your new life," Lawrence said. "Let me explain."

Lawrence stood up and started walking around Richard, who remained seated on the ground.

"Every day thousands of acres of rain forest are being depleted. It's happening all over the world, right under our noses. Why don't we hear about it? Because most of the media is controlled by powerful economic interests. People who raise their voices against these interests sometimes just disappear. You see, Richard, in many countries if you speak up about illegal logging, genetically engineered crops, human trafficking, and the depletion of the rain forest, or if you mention certain names of people—private, corporate, or in government—you may find yourself in a storm of trouble. Some of these forces are very powerful, and they sometimes, also have influence on some people who walk the corridors of power and government. If you speak up, you better be prepared, because mark my word, they will confront you. They will throw dirt at you and accuse you of all sorts of things; they might even invent your crime, charge you, and perhaps even put you in prison, all to silence you. We must tread very cautiously and carefully when going into combat for these ideals and causes. We must keep it quiet and secret for as long as possible.

"You of all people, with a past as a private banker, know the importance of keeping secrets, Richard. In fact, it's one of the reasons you are here. You think it's a coincidence you were sent back to Zurich shortly after you confronted Maximillian von Horstenbrik? I think you know what I mean when I speak of the importance of keeping a low profile and keeping your agenda and secrets close to your heart. I know you carry on your shoulders the secrets of countless people—perhaps more than any man should carry. Yes, Richard, you know that secrets are secret for a reason. In this very moment people all over the world are being forced to vacate their land, either by legal means or illegal means, land that they have lived on since the beginning of time. The rain forest is not only a forest; it is a treasure that might hold the answer to mankind's long-term survival. You see, when this great urbanization and immigration to the cities is over, when once the whole financial system collapses—what happens then? Why will it all eventually collapse? Because all these measures of wealth are backed up by what? Can you eat a piece of paper? Can you cure cancer with a piece of paper? What's the good of all paper and other forms of payment if there is nothing to back them up anymore, no food, no water, no natural resources, or oxygen anymore? This is why we must act now, when all my pieces of paper in the bank still have a value. This is why we must invest now in the future, and invest in something tangible. The rain forest is a treasure we cannot put a number on. It is life, and when it dies, we die. There is too much money spent on destroying the rain forest and its unique ecosystem and too little spent on saving it. The forces that advocate its destruction now are very powerful, but so am I. You see it is human nature, we destroy what we can and ask why later. The big problem will come when all governments and people realize that they need the rain forest to survive—when there is little of it left, not enough to sustain life for all and everything. Then an even bigger battle will begin. We must never, ever arrive at this point because it will be the end of us all. Not just you and me; it will be the end of everything. We must inform and teach people NOW of the value of the rainforest, before it is too late. Unfortunately, time waits for nobody or nothing. You agree?"

"Yes, I agree…with it all, sir."

"Now, do you want to help us? Are you in or not?"

"I'm in," Richard said.

"Good!"

"Tell me what to do, sir."

"First, you will go to Hong Kong as you planned and see the Tiger Lady," Lawrence said.

"How did you know that I was going to Hong Kong?" Richard asked.

Lawrence looked at Richard and their eyes met. The old man's bright blue eyes did not flinch for a moment as he looked into Richard's eyes. The old man's eyes were old, yet seemed young as well—a contrast and enigma, just like everything else about the old man. They were the eyes of someone that had seen a lot of pain and misery, the eyes of someone who carried more than one secret on his conscience—real secrets, the ones that weigh on your conscience, the ones that hurt. As Lawrence continued to look into Richard's eyes, a feeling of familiarity overwhelmed Richard. There was so much he understood, read and recognized in the old man's eyes. The old man said nothing, there was no need. At that moment, Richard knew why the feeling of familiarity had come over him—he was like Lawrence. There was no need for more questions, they understood each other. After several minutes of silence, Lawrence broke the silence.

"You do not need to know how or who or what anymore—it is insignificant. You know me now—and I know you!

"Go and see her, but don't mention anything about our meeting. She already knows and is one of us."

"I understand," Richard said. "And what about the people following me?"

"You will be given a phone number to call if you should have any problems, and a safe house can be provided quickly. If you should need to use the phone number, the code name is Aqaba. Go now and Godspeed."

Lawrence turned his back on Richard then, and started reading a book. The book was *The Seven Pillars of Wisdom* by T.E. Lawrence. Their meeting was over. Richard left the tent and Lawrence, and outside he was met by Situ.

"So are you one of us now?" he asked Richard.

"Yes, I am," Richard replied.

The following days were spent traveling down the river toward Santubong. They passed the long house by the two rivers, where Richard said good-bye to Bitu and Situ. Another two Ibans were to take him onward in a canoe on his journey back down the river. On the way they passed a large old wooden yacht that was traveling upstream, named *The Jolly Bachelor II*. Richard had no doubt in his mind who this yacht belonged to: Lawrence. *The Jolly Bachelor* had been the name of one of the ships of James Brooke, the first white rajah of Sarawak, and with this ship he had effectively fought pirates off the shores of Sarawak.

Along the journey down the river, Richard again thought of his past life—the bank, his friends, Louise—what would happen now?

He had had a plan himself: to start living a simple life, to do something different, to share a life with Louise. Would it still be possible? He still had the gift he had bought her at the airport in Zurich in his pocket, the surprise that he had never had the chance to give to her, which meant everything or nothing. He also wondered if Lawrence's plan would involve Maximillian von Horstenbrik. He hoped it would. For the first time in his life, Richard felt a part of something, something bigger, and something worth fighting for. He was not an outsider anymore.

CHAPTER 47

Friday, 8 February, Morning
Singapore

Massimo Rossi was sitting in a coffee shop in Tanglin Mall close to the Orchard Shopping District. His wife was on a shopping spree; she was an incurable shopaholic. Massimo and his wife had finally come to an agreement that if she was going to shop, then he would come along. He would wait for her in a coffee shop or restaurant while she shopped, and he only gave her cash, which was much easier to control than credit cards. Rosella's credit cards were no longer a powerful purchasing tool; they had been blocked. He had granted her this shopping day because today was a good day; things were working out just according to plan. What he had been working on so hard these past weeks seemed to finally be coming true. He had also granted the shopping day to Rosella to cheer her up. They had been going through a rough patch lately, and particularly over the last week or so Rosella had seemed very preoccupied and troubled, like she was carrying some sort of burden. She had also started to gain weight. Shopping usually did the trick for turning her mood around, so he had decided on this excursion.

Massimo had been traveling extensively over the last weeks to Borneo, Hong Kong, and Zurich. He was happy to be back in Singapore now. The trip to Borneo and the meeting with Lawrence had gone very well. They had discussed their ongoing plan in detail.

The setup of the Strydsteen family had worked out better than expected—the ship's seizure in Marseille, the capture of the young Bernard Strydsteen with bank and corporate documents and cash at the Italian-French border, the crash of the bank's share price, and the media's coverage of these events—it had all worked out as planned. The only thing that had gone wrong was Maximillian's unexpected move to try to pin the potential fallout on Richard and have him transferred back to Zurich. In the end, however, that seemed to have worked out OK too. Massimo had seen Richard on the canal when he was leaving Lawrence. Richard was then on his way to meet Lawrence, and he had since learned that Richard was on board with them as well now. It was all going according to plan. Lawrence had planned it well. Soon they would strike again and enter into the next stage of the plan, and they were ready.

Massimo opened his briefcase and took out a copy of the old document that was wrapped in a plastic folder—the document he had been given on his last trip to Hong Kong. The document was an old promissory note from 1939. It read that Maximillian's grandfather, Kurt von Horstenbrik, promised to pay Massimo's grandfather, Mario Rossi, $2 million. The note also guaranteed Mario Rossi a fixed controlling stake of the von Horstenbrik family's privately owned shares in the bank should the repayment agreement not be honored. The terms of repayment was ten years. The note was duly signed and witnessed by Otto Holzstam and a public notary in Macau.

Maximillian's grandfather had been a compulsive gambler and womanizer; it apparently ran in the family. On one of his trips to Hong Kong and Macau, he had finally pulled out all the stops and gambled it all, including a stake in the bank. Three weeks into his Asian tour, he was abducted by the Macau triads because he had run up gambling debts into the millions. The triads and gambling syndicates were not slow in claiming their money back; they never were. They had found him in some Macau opium den along with two prostitutes, stoned and broke. They threatened to kill him unless the debt was settled. Otto Holzstam had intervened and acted as mediator. A settlement had finally been arranged, and the debt was paid by Mario Rossi. The von Horstenbriks in Zurich claimed they did not have the necessary funds, but the real reason, most likely, was that they did not want Kurt von Horstenbrik back at all.

Upon payment of the debt and the release of the disgraced Kurt von Horstenbrik, the promissory note was signed between him and Mario Rossi. The note was signed in the offices of the public notary in Macau. The repayment in cash was to be done via the notary and Otto Holzstam in Macau, far away from Switzerland. If news got out that one of the heads of the renowned bank in Switzerland had gambled away a fortune and gotten himself mixed up with organized crime, it could have meant the end for the old family-run bank. At that time Rossi & von Horstenbrik was a purely privately owned bank, and the owners were the guarantors of the funds deposited in the bank. There was no way the news could be made public; it had to remain a well-kept secret. Two million US dollars was a very large sum back in 1939; nevertheless, Mario Rossi had been able to come up with the money to pay for Kurt von Horstenbrik's debt, but the loan was never repaid. In 1947, Mario Rossi was killed in a mysterious avalanche accident, and Kurt von Horstenbrik remained in command of the bank.

Massimo Rossi was now in possession of a copy of the recently discovered note, and he was going to use it. His grandfather would not go unavenged; it was payback time. It was time to turn up the heat on Maximillian. A little bit of pressure is always good; it was the only language the von Horstenbriks understood. Massimo finished his espresso with a smile on his face.

CHAPTER 48

Friday, 8 February, Afternoon
Rossi & von Horstenbrik Cie Bank, Singapore

Maximillian was sweating; the heat in his office was unbearable. The air conditioning was not working. He had put maintenance on it to fix the problem as soon as possible. Strangely, the air conditioning in the neighboring office of Massimo Rossi seemed to be working fine. Two hours had gone by since he had received the threatening phone call and the threatening e-mails to his personal e-mail account. An unknown voice had told him to pay $2 million—or he would be sorry. The voice had also told him, "A debt is a debt is a debt. It was true in old Rome, and it's true now." The voice had also said, "We know what you are up to and what you have done." Maximillian was confused. Who were these people? Some Roman-history-geek pranksters having a laugh? Shady business partners of the Strydsteen family who wanted to claim unpaid debts? The people he had hired to track down Richard who were maybe playing him for some more money? Could it be Richard? It could not be the people he had hired, Maximillian reasoned. They were professionals and had too much to lose should it get out that they had played a double game.

Maximillian's alternative mobile phone rang, and he picked it up and answered.

"Hello."

"Hello. Green bird here. We think we have found an alternative way of tracking down your bird. It's going to cost you a little extra. Interested?" the voice said.

"How much?"

"Double the usual fee. We have to bring in some extra help for the job, help from Japan."

"Go ahead," Maximillian instructed. "Just find the bird now. It's urgent. And the bird cannot be allowed to sing."

"Very well. We will keep in touch."

Maximillian sat back in his chair and thought of the past. He should never have gotten involved with Alain Strydsteen in the first place—all those parties with flown-in models from Hungary and Romania on Alain's yacht on Bali, all the "golf trips" to Indonesia and Cambodia. It had only been a matter of time before he had been asked to set up several offshore companies and bank accounts for them. He had been forced to do so; Alain Strydsteen had serious leverage on him. One time on Bali on Alain's yacht, Alain had flown in some prostitutes, and what had followed was a wild orgy on the yacht. One of the young girls, who was underage, had refused to perform certain sexual favors, and she had jumped overboard and swam to shore. Soon thereafter the police arrived, but the incident never went further than that; all the remaining underage prostitutes were paid off and as a result kept quiet. The only problem was that Alain had taken several compromising pictures of Maximillian and the young girl, pictures that became the leverage Alain would hold on Maximillian. Maximillian was sure that it had all been a setup. The sixteen-year-old girl had been in on it as well; he was sure of that. This was how it had all started, and it did not take long before he was asked by Alain to help him open up bank accounts and offshore companies for the Strydsteen family. This was the price he had to pay for Alain's silence. The risk of confronting Alain Strydsteen was too risky. Release of the pictures would be the end of Maximillian as the commander of Rossi & von Horstenbrik in Singapore. The young girl, whose name was Suva, was a Singaporean citizen. Release of the pictures to the media was an unthinkable alternative.

Now the bank accounts of Alain Strydsteen were frozen, including the ones at Rossi & von Horstenbrik Cie Bank in Singapore. The bank account of the son, Bernard Strydsteen, was frozen as well, and the name of the bank was all over the press. The bank's share prices had nosedived as a result, and it was a mess. Rossi & von Horstenbrik Cie Bank in Singapore was collaborating with the local financial authorities, and so far, the authorities had not found any wrongdoing on the bank's part. The bank had been the ones who had contacted the local authorities and had furnished the details of the suspected transactions and possible money laundering. However, Maximillian knew that as time went by, the deeper and deeper the investigators dug, they would make the connection between him and the Strydsteenes' offshore companies, and the friendship between him and Alain Strydsteen. It was only a matter of time.

Maximillian had the scapegoat, however. Yes, he would pin it all on Richard; he was the weak link. Richard had been responsible for the frozen accounts, and he had resigned from the bank in quite a hurry—it was almost perfect.

Now all that had to be done was to put the final spike in Richard's coffin: arranging for Richard to sign his confession. The documents that would seal Richard's fate were already prepared. Richard knew of the connection between Maximillian and the offshore companies, and he might even know of the friendship between Maximillian and Alain Strydsteen. Richard knew of the inconsistencies in the background of the account, and he had to be silenced; there was no other way. The only question was when and how. It had to be done *now*.

CHAPTER 49

One Week Later, Friday, 15 February
Joo Chiat Road, Singapore

Georgie "the Elvis" lay on his bed, listening to the King himself. It was one of his favorite afternoon activities. The volume was on maximum, and the walls of his small basement room were vibrating with the sounds of the song "Love Me Tender." Georgie "the Elvis" lived in a small basement room on Joo Chiat Road, a relatively quiet road, with mostly low-rise traditional shop houses lining it. A section of the road was home to several karaoke bars and nightclubs, and Georgie lived below one of the karaoke bars. He had once played a gig with his band there and had subsequently become friends with the owner, an older, attractive Singaporean woman. Their friendship had developed into a romance, and it did not take long before Georgie was living in the basement, conveniently close to his lover and landlord—when she called he came. The relationship had eventually ended, but Georgie had stayed on; not so many others were willing to live under a karaoke bar in a basement. The rent was cheap; he paid only SGD$400 a month for a room and en suite toilet. This small apartment was Georgie's kingdom, and on the door to his room there was a sign that read "Welcome to Graceland."

The entrance to his room was located at the back of the small shop house, and a small stairway from the backyard led down to the entrance of Georgie's kingdom. The dark stairway was sometimes used by customers of the upstairs establishment to take care of their natural toiletry needs, and every now and then there were some after-hours erotic encounters with some of the karaoke girls—used condoms on the stairway, was not an uncommon morning sight. Georgie did not mind all this, however, as long as the rent was cheap.

As Elvis Presley's "Love Me Tender" was finishing on his stereo, a sharp blow hit his face. It had come out of nowhere, and it nearly knocked him out. He opened his eyes, and there they were again, the two Boat Quay porno Rambo twins. Shit, they had found him, he thought.

"What do you want, man? This is my house, man," Georgie said. "Don't you guys knock where you come from?"

"We came to see you. We need some help," the first twin said.

"I told you all I know, man. This is my house, man."

"Where is Richard?"

"I have no clue, man. It's not like we are married, you know."

A forceful fist hit Georgie in the face just then, and his nose started bleeding. He could taste the blood in his mouth.

"You better tell us, or we will finish what we never started last time, remember? I promise you, we will not love you tender!"

"OK, OK. What do you want to know?"

"We want you to call Richard and find out where he is," the second man said.

"OK, OK. I'll do it. Just don't touch me, man," Georgie pleaded.

Georgie was given a mobile phone, and he dialed Richard's number. One of the twins pressed the button for the loudspeaker function. The phone rang twice before there was an answer on the other end.

"Hey, Richard. That you?" Georgie said.

"Georgie?" Richard responded.

"Yeah. Just wanted to see that you were OK, man. Where are you?"

"I'm just about to board a plane to Hong Kong. I'll be back in Singapore by Sunday. You OK?"

"Yeah. I'm doing great…I have to go now. Speak soon," Georgie said and quickly hung up.

"Good job, Mr. Elvis," the second twin said. "Now we want you to tell us if Richard has a girlfriend. We have heard he does."

"Sure he has a girlfriend, but why?"

"We want you to tell us where we can find her. We would like to talk to her a little."

Georgie had no choice. He told them all about Louise. Richard had often talked about her down at the pub. He told them she always went to church on Sundays. He also told them that she was really pretty, that he had seen a photo of her as well.

"Well done, Georgie," the first Rambo twin said, slapping him hard on the back.

Then they tied him to his bed and put Scotch tape on his mouth. Now what? Georgie thought as he struggled to release himself from the ropes, but it was impossible to get free.

CHAPTER 50

Friday, 15 February
Hong Kong

Richard sat comfortably in his seat on one of the Holzstam's private jets, on his way to Hong Kong. They were flying somewhere over the South China Sea. He could see all the lights from the many ships in the busy shipping lanes far below. He was alone in the cabin.

The trip back to Santubong after seeing Lawrence had taken several days. He had spent an additional couple of days at the Holzstam Estate resting and talking to Thomas Holzstam. He had been given new clothes and contact numbers in Hong Kong, to be used if he needed help. Richard was now clear in his mind: he had picked a side, he had committed himself to help Lawrence, and he was going to see this through as the master of his destiny. The only problem was he did not know yet what it was he was supposed to do. What role would he play? Lawrence was the great game master, the spider in the web. Lawrence was obviously playing all the pieces in this giant game of chess. Richard could not help thinking that maybe he was just a simple pawn, a pawn that would be offered in sacrifice for a bigger gain, just like in the game of chess. He now knew the enemy was the Strydsteen family, the destroyers of the rain forest, but what role did Rossi & von Horstenbrik Cie Bank and Maximillan von Horstenbrik play in the game? Was the bank a pawn as well? Then there was Massimo Rossi, the deputy CEO. And what about the

Tiger Lady? He would see her tomorrow, and she was also a part of the game—Lawrence had implied that—but what role did she play?

After arriving in Hong Kong, Richard said good-bye to the plane crew. He then went through customs and made his way the fast modern railway service that connected the airport to central Hong Kong in less than one hour.

On the way they passed the distinct green rolling hills on the right and the ocean on the left. Soon they reached the suburbs and more populated areas. It was 7:00 p.m. as the train made its way onto one of the bridges. Richard was now only a few minutes from arriving at Kowloon Station. He looked out over the bridge, over the water and bay, toward Hong Kong Island. There she was, Hong Kong, the city of trade and commerce, the Manhattan of the East. The hundreds of thousands of lights from the Hong Kong skyline lit up the sky around it. Victoria Peak rested like a large dark shadow behind all the skyscrapers and lights of the city below. It was one of the most competitive cities in the world, maybe the most competitive city of them all. It was a city of immense paradoxes—a bastion of capitalism, yet part of Communist China. It was a city of immense wealth, yet poverty was always around the corner. Every corner is made up of two angles, and you cannot have one without the other, Richard thought. Hong Kong was a SAR, a special administrative region of China. It had been allowed to keep its political and economic system for an additional fifty years after the departure of the former British colonial administration in 1997. This had been the agreement stipulated between China and England, and this was the way Hong Kong was today.

Richard knew several people from Hong Kong who had left Hong Kong before the handover to the Chinese, many of them going to Australia and Canada, among other nations. It had been a time of great uncertainty; no one knew if the Chinese would keep their promise. The date of the handover from the British administration to China took place at midnight on 30 June 1997. No one knew what would happen. Some feared that the Red Army's tanks would cross the border at one minute past midnight and that the agreement would not be honored. Many who had the economic means to do so hedged their bets and left. However, the vast masses did not have this luxury and stayed put—and why shouldn't they? This was their city, and they were Chinese. The agreement had been honored, and today the city of Hong Kong was more powerful and wealthy than ever before.

It was a city where dreams were built, and a city that could also eat you up and spit you out in one breath. It was also a city of immense cultural heritage, history, and charm. A friend of Richard's had once compared Singapore and Hong Kong to a pair of pretty twin sisters; the sister from Hong Kong would be the girl who entered the party with a bang, sparkly and talkative. The Singaporean sister would be more restrained and conservative, would sit in the corner and appraise the situation before making her move; but when she did make her move, there would be fireworks. They were both beautiful cities, and Richard loved them both in their own way.

He checked into the Mandarin Oriental Hotel. He would always stay there when he was visiting Hong Kong. It had beautiful, old, colonial-style rooms, with nice views of the Victoria Harbor below. He made some phone calls to Singapore. He called Prosper and Matt, and he also called Brian, his stock broker in Hong Kong. Brian and Richard were old friends and had worked together at a security broker in London many years ago. They agreed to meet up the following night for after-dinner drinks. They always did this when Richard was in Hong Kong, but unfortunately, they always forgot to eat dinner. It was late now, and tomorrow was another day. Richard went to sleep, and for the first time in a long time, he slept soundly, dreaming that Louise was with him in his hotel room.

CHAPTER 51

Friday, 15 February
Singapore

The man was dressed in an expensive custom-made dark suit. His facial features were distinctively Mediterranean, possibly Italian. He greeted the hotel entrance staff as he got out of the taxi at the Fullerton Bay Hotel in Singapore's financial district. The two hotel staff at the entrance waved at him. They knew him. He was one of the ang moh tipsters.

"Good day today, sir," the uniformed door staff greeted the foreigner.

"Rossi & von Horstenbrik Cie Bank Zurich Stock Exchange!" the foreigner replied. He repeated the name one more time then walked away. The hotel staff quickly gathered and spoke among themselves. Then they all picked up their mobile phones and dialed their brokers.

A few minutes later, not far away from the Fullerton Bay Hotel, Daniel Loh, a Singaporean securities broker at one of the local brokerage firms, picked up his phone. He noted the order to buy five thousand shares of Rossi & von Horstenbrik Cie Bank, to be executed at the Zurich Stock Exchange in Switzerland. Daniel Loh looked over his desk at his colleague, who sat on the other side of the banana-shaped trading desk. "Just received an order to buy some Swiss shares," he said.

His colleague looked at him and replied, "Rossi & von Horstenbrik Cie Bank?"

Daniel nodded his head in agreement.

"Me too," his colleague replied.

Daniel thought to himself for an instant that this was odd—these local boys never bought any foreign shares, especially not European ones. Daniel again looked at his colleague across the table. They smiled at each other with that smile that brokers have when they smell money: not the smile formed by the shape of the lips—no, that smile with sparkling dollar signs in their eyes, burning ever brightly.

They picked up their phones and started calling other brokers and colleagues in Singapore. Rossi & von Horstenbrik Cie Bank was in play. At the end of the Zurich trading day, Rossi & von Horstenbrik Cie Bank shares were up 15 percent.

CHAPTER 52

Saturday, 16 February
Hong Kong

At 5:00 p.m. the phone on Richard's night stand rang. It was the hotel lobby telling him that his chauffeur had arrived. Richard had been waiting for the call and was ready. He put on his custom made blue two-piece suit and a white shirt, no tie. He had picked up the suit that afternoon from his regular Hong Kong tailor, Singh & Singh & Singh & Singh Best Tailors Ltd. Kowloon. He had ordered it by phone from Borneo three days ago, and they had his measurements on file from previous orders. He hoped that the next generation of Singh tailors would not add their name to the company label as well; it was really getting too long, and pretty soon they would need a tailor just for the label. It was important that Richard look his best when meeting with the Tiger Lady. Luckily, she had not seen what he looked like a few days ago, traveling down the river in a canoe.

The driver was waiting for him outside the hotel. A chilly wind hit Richard's face as he stepped out of the hotel entrance. Hong Kong in January and February can be a bit chilly. The driver opened the back door of the black BMW, and Richard got into the back seat. Then they drove off into the heavy rush-hour traffic. The driver turned his head back and spoke to Richard. "I am taking you to the madame's new restaurant in Sai Kung," he said. Sai Kung was the old fishing village one-hour's drive from downtown central Hong

Kong and a popular weekend destination for many locals and expats. The small fishing village was located by a large bay and surrounded by green rolling hills—it was the perfect destination if one wanted to get away from the city for a while. The village was also famous for all its seafood restaurants. One hour later, Richard stepped out of the car as they had arrived in Sai Kung. The driver accompanied Richard during the five-minute walk down toward the bay and harbor front. Many fishing boats were out on the bay, and even some old *jonks* lay at anchor. It was like stepping into another time and dimension; the city seemed so far away from here.

The Tiger Lady was waiting for Richard outside her new restaurant, The Blue Dragon. She was, as usual, accompanied by her eldest daughter, Lynn. As the eldest daughter, Lynn would eventually take over the madame's business empire, as the madame had no sons, only two daughters. The Tiger lady was dressed in a traditional red Chinese silk dress with a large blue dragon embroidered on the front. The old madame was well into her sixties. She had long black hair, she was no tall, and she was very skinny. Despite her age, she could pass for forty-five any day. Some would say she was ageless. She reached out her hand to shake Richard's; she had the handshake of a strong man.

"Welcome to my restaurant. We just opened last week. Please come inside." She smiled as she spoke in broken English to Richard. The Tiger Lady quickly walked into the restaurant, with Richard and Lynn following behind.

"She is the boss," Lynn whispered in Richard's ear.

Upon stepping into the small restaurant, all the staff stopped what they were doing, and even the cooks in the kitchen seemed to stop cooking, upon seeing the Tiger Lady. She was truly the boss, Richard thought to himself as they sat down at a corner table. One of the walls in the restaurant was not really a wall: it was made up of at least fifty different aquariums all stacked one on top of another. The aquariums contained at least a hundred different species of live fish, lobsters, crabs, squid, clams, abalone, and oysters. Most of the fish and species Richard had never seen before. Had it not been a restaurant, one could mistake it for Sea World; unfortunately for the fish, however, it was a restaurant.

They sat down at a large round table, and a moment later the first dishes started to arrive. The Tiger Lady started speaking in Cantonese with Richard, and Richard listened attentively. He knew that Lynn would translate into English for him after her mother had finished speaking.

"My mother says she is sad that you left the bank. It would have been much better if you would have stayed. She wants to know why you resigned, Richard."

"I did not want to work in a bank anymore. I wanted to take a break and do something else," Richard explained.

The old lady looked at Richard, and then she spoke in Cantonese again.

Lynn translated. "She says it's not good not to work. Your hands will get fat. She thinks you should find a nice Hong Kong girl, get married and…make babies." Lynn started blushing as she finished translating this last statement to Richard.

The Tiger Lady then looked at Richard and spoke in perfect English. "OK, so my daughter did not translate all that I said. Why don't you marry my daughter Lynn. She is a good match, no?"

Richard nearly choked on his food, first at the revelation that the old lady spoke perfect English, and secondly at the fact that she wanted him to marry her daughter. Richard decided that it was best to come clean straightaway; this fiery old lady did not take prisoners.

"Thank you very much for the offer, but I already sort of have a girlfriend in Singapore," he said.

The Tiger Lady looked at Richard in disbelief and then replied, "Sort of girlfriends come and go, Richard. I tell you, Singaporean girls are only interested in the man's money. My daughter is much better. She already has money, so the only interest is to make babies."

There was playfulness in her voice, but no glimpse of humor in her eyes. She was serious, and come to think of it, he had never heard her make a joke. Lawrence was straight to the point, but the Tiger Lady took it to a new level. No wonder they were friends. Richard again thanked her for the offer and did his best to explain diplomatically that he was flattered that she had considered him as a candidate for her lovely daughter Lynn. "But, well, I really like this other girl. She could be the one for me," he said.

"Could be the one? Sort of girlfriend? Sounds like you have some thinking to do," she replied. "You and my daughter make baby in the cubicle. You see all, no one see you—very exciting," she said. She was relentless. Richard knew about the cubicle. He had heard the rumors. He had never been invited—he was too old for the Tiger Lady—men under thirty were her game.

The Tiger Lady finally accepted Richard's explanation with a sigh. "OK, your loss."

Richard saw out of the corner of his eye that Lynn also seemed to be pleased with the fact that she would not have to marry Richard. The madame was constantly on the lookout for a husband for her daughter; Lynn was the eldest, and at thirty-five years of age she was still unmarried. Richard decided it was best to change the subject as quickly as possible. Lynn also seemed keen to move on to another subject as well.

"I did not know you speak such good English," Richard quickly countered to break the ice and the uncomfortable silence that had set over the table.

"Of course you did not. A wise man once said, 'Keep your neighbor close, drink a beer with him, and try to learn his secrets and weaknesses, but never let him know the ingredients of your daily soup.'"

Richard had heard this expression before; it was the motto of old Otto Holzstam. The Tiger Lady looked straight at Richard. "I see you have heard this expression before. That's good," she said. She continued. “My father and Otto Holzstam were close friends. It was Otto who organized my family’s escape from Hong Kong before the Japanese came with the onset of World War II. He got my father and mother a place on one of the last boats that left Hong Kong. They spent the remaining years of the war in Portugal.”

Some waiters arrived then and cleared the table, and then more food arrived. The Tiger Lady continued her story. “My father was a public notary in Macau and worked closely with the Holzstam family. Otto Holzstam was the closest friend my father had. They had been through a lot together. Otto’s son, Andreas, was also a friend of my father’s. He was with my father when he passed away in Macau twenty years ago.”

Richard did not know how to react. Should he act surprised, like he did not know that Andreas, alias Lawrence, knew the family of the Tiger Lady, or should he just keep quiet and listen? He decided to keep quiet.

“You see, Richard, all our destinies were entwined a long time ago. It was meant to be.” The Tiger Lady then spoke a few words in Cantonese with her daughter Lynn. Then she again looked at Richard. She suddenly pulled out an old envelope and opened it. Inside was an old document that she passed to Richard. Richard took the old document in his hand and quickly read it. It was a promissory note for $2 million. Kurt von Horstenbrik had pledged to pay Mario Rossi this amount, and the repayment was to be made in cash at the offices of a designated notary in Macau. The note was dated 1 July 1939. Otto Holzstam and Alfonso de Silva, the father of the Tiger lady, had signed the note as witnesses. The note also stated the terms of the repayment: the amount had to be settled in cash and at least the Tiger Lady’s father, Alfonso, or Otto Holzstam had to be present as witnesses upon repayment.

“Have you seen this note before, Richard?” the Tiger Lady asked.

Richard answered that he had never seen this note, nor had he known of its existence.

"Very well. Now you might start to understand more of how my family and the Holzstam family's destinies were decided."

Richard looked at the Tiger Lady then. "Please tell me more," he said.

The Tiger Lady continued her story. "My father was murdered. He was shot by a lone gunman in a Macau restaurant. The killer escaped and was never found. My father was Alfonso de Silva, the notary." The Tiger Lady pulled out a handkerchief from her purse and dried her eyes as she had started crying while speaking about her father.

"Andreas, alias Lawrence, was with him when he was shot, and it was then, in those last moments of his life, that he told Andreas Holzstam of the existence of the note and that it had never been repaid. My father's last words were 'The von Horstenbrik family did this to me. I am the last witness.' Many years later, Thomas Holzstam found his father's copy of the document. It was then that we decided to put our heads together—to join forces and strike back."

The Tiger Lady had stopped weeping, and her facial expression had now changed from sorrow to anger. She spoke again, and Richard could see that she was clearly upset.

"My father was an honorable man, and he did not deserve that end. By the time we got hold of the note, Kurt von Horstenbrik was already long gone and buried. When my father died, Kurt von Horstenbrik had already been dead for over twenty years, so someone else ordered the killing of my father. We started our own investigation, and after a while we realized that all indications pointed in the same direction: Maximillian von Horstenbrik. He had been in Macau that same day, and he had been seen with a person who looked very much like the killer, a young, bald Caucasian man. Our evidence was all circumstantial, however, and could never be used in court. So we decided to get back at him and his family in another way; we would hurt them where they hurt the most: their power and money. Oh, yes. The von Horstenbriks all knew of the existence of the note; Maximillian surely did not act alone. Now we have waited many years, and now we will act!" The Tiger Lady took the old document from Richard's hands. "It's payback time." She paused and took a deep breath. "Don't worry. We are not going to hurt anybody. Just rattle the cage a little."

The rest of the dinner, the Tiger Lady told stories of her childhood in Macau, Hong Kong, and Portugal. She had married an older man from Portugal in Macau, but he had passed away soon after the birth of their second daughter and she had never remarried. She told Richard of her business ventures in China, of the restaurants and casinos in Macau. Her daughter Lynn told Richard about the family's business in the casino industry and how they were planning to expand; they just needed to find some more investors and maybe a friendlier bank. She explained that they wanted to be less reliant on the traditional *junket* operators who provided loans to their clients, and by clients, she meant, of course, gamblers. Junket companies were the companies that provided the casinos with clients—they did everything from sourcing and transporting clients to the casino to providing loans to the clients. The Tiger Lady was now interested in finding a bank to provide the loans to her customers so that they could be less reliant on the junket operators. However, it was a fine line to walk. Most banks shunned the idea of having anything to do with the gambling sector, especially providing loans to gamblers. The banks had been happy to take the Tiger Lady's money and proceeds from the casino business as long as they did not have to ask questions. Then it all changed. New banking rules were introduced, and the banks were less inclined to take the Tiger Lady's money unless she could show documentation of where the money had come from. Casino proceeds were seen as risky and a sector to scrutinize in detail.

"Do you know how many banks and fortunes have been created with casino money, Richard?" the Tiger Lady asked.

"No, I have no idea, Madame," Richard answered.

"Well, more than you can count!" she answered angrily.

Another concern was that the junket operators would, of course, not easily give up this lucrative market.

"If all goes well, we will soon have our little business in place," Lynn interrupted and closed the conversation.

It was past 9:00 p.m. when they finally got up from the table to leave the restaurant. When they said good-bye outside, the Tiger Lady's last words to Richard were, "A debt is a debt is a debt. The time has come to pay up. Take care of yourself, Richard, and we will see each other again soon. As a wise man once said, "It is written.'"

Five minutes later Richard was in the car again, being driven back toward Hong Kong Central. He looked out the car window. What a lady, what a story, he thought. What had he gotten himself into?

Richard met Brian, his stockbroker friend, at 11:00 p.m. at one of the bars in LKF, Lan Kwai Fong, the bar and entertainment district. Richard needed some alcohol in his system; it had been too long since he had had a real drink. They met at a small bar and sat by the window, watching all the drunk tourists, expats, and locals outside. LKF was like it always was on "a night out ": fun, loud, and drunk.

Brian and Richard talked about their old times in London, their old friends, and the places they used to go when they were a lot younger. Ten years ago they would have been standing outside with all the fun people; now they sat in the window seats and talked about the meaning of life—yes, they were definitely getting old. Brian asked Richard what was going on with Rossi & von Horstenbrik Cie Bank. He had heard that Richard was no longer working for them. He was also particularly interested to find out if Richard had any ideas why the shares of Rossi & von Horstenbrik had been so volatile lately, first down over 30 percent a few weeks ago and now back up. It looked like they would reach an all-time high next week. He wanted to know what was going on. Richard knew that Brian would ask him; after all, once a broker, always a broker. He told Brian that he had no clue, but that he believed the bank was a good long-term investment. Brian interpreted this as if it was a signal to buy. They left the bar and moved on to another club, the Dragon Eye. This was followed by a visit to the private club, the Chee Club, where Brian was a member. When they finally staggered out of the Chee Club, it was past 4:00 a.m., and neither of them could talk or walk like two older, responsible adults should be able to.

The morning after, Richard woke up with a splitting headache. Never again, he thought as he made his way to the shower. It was early Sunday morning, and he still had some time left in Hong Kong before his morning flight back to Singapore. He checked out of the hotel and decided to spend the rest of the morning out and about.

Later in the morning, when he was sitting on the Cathay Pacific flight back to Singapore, he started writing down a schedule of things to do when he got back. He would first find another place to stay. Maybe he would call Georgie again to let him help. He could not return to Madame Tsui's castle. He would arrange to have his things picked up from there. He had to get in touch with Louise, but he did not want to put her in danger. He had no clue what Lawrence and the Tiger Lady were planning, but whatever it was, it was big, and most likely not without danger. Neither of them had survived this long and built their fortunes and business empires on being nice. Lawrence seemed like a god—a man who was not capable of doing harm—but Richard had heard the stories and rumors about what had happened to the people who had crossed him. He reached down into his pocket just then and touched little Mary's special rock. Then he reached into his other pocket to check if the little box that contained Louise's surprise gift was still there, and it was. He had to wait, though. It was too dangerous for them to be involved with him right now.

He had called Prosper the night before, who said Richard could stay with his family for a few days, no problem. Richard landed in Singapore early Sunday afternoon and arrived at Prosper's place just before 2:00 p.m. They talked for a while and then decided to go for a late lunch. Richard had not eaten since the meeting with the Tiger lady the previous evening.

Chapter 53

Sunday, 17 February
Fort Canning Road, Singapore

Louise had participated in the 11:00 a.m. church service. She had been alone with her daughter Mary today; her father and uncle were on some sort of secret mission. They had been very hush-hush the last few days, and she had not been able to get a word out of them. They were up to something—she was sure of it. The church had been particularly busy this morning. People had even been standing up along the church walls and aisles as all the seats had been taken. Richard was, of course, nowhere to be seen. At one time she had seen someone who looked like him, but it was not him. Her mind had been playing tricks with her again. He was gone. She just needed to face the music and get on with her life.

After the service, Louise had left little Mary with one of her friends at the church. The friend was an older woman who would often teach some of the youngest children about the Bible. They would sit on one of the grass lawns close to the church, and the lesson would usually last for an hour or so. After leaving Mary, Louise decided to go for a walk in the nearby Fort Canning Park. She needed some time to herself, time to think and reflect.

She walked along the foot trails in Fort Canning Park, under the shadows of the trees. It was quite cool, and the midday sun and heat seemed far away. After a while she started walking back toward the church again; it was more or less time to pick up Mary. She decided to take the way back around the Singapore National Museum. It was a bit farther of a walk, but she wanted to look and see if there were any interesting exhibitions taking place. After having passed the museum, she headed back to the church, and as she was walking up Fort Canning Road, only a few meters from the church gate, it happened. Suddenly, a white van stopped alongside her, and a Japanese-looking man, who was driving the car, spoke to her from the open window. "Miss Louise?"

Louise responded instantly and by default, "Yes?"

The sliding side door of the van suddenly opened, and another Japanese-looking character with a strange-looking haircut reached out and pulled her into the van. She managed to scream "Help!" before the door closed behind her and the van drove off.

She was being held down on the floor by the very strong Japanese man. Then she saw that another person was lying next to her, tied up and gagged. He was dressed like Elvis Presley and seemed to be crying. The Japanese man put a wet cloth over her mouth and nose, and she felt the strong smell sting her nostrils. The last thing she heard was a voice saying, "The love bird is in the cage," and then she passed out.

Outside the church, a group of Louise's friends had seen the whole incident. One man tried to stop the van from driving away, and he almost got run over. It was all over in a matter of a few seconds; the van drove around a corner and was gone. The police arrived within minutes and started asking all the witnesses for information, and the security cameras were checked as well. It did not take long before all nearby police units had the registration number and make of the van, along with Louise's particulars. The hunt was on.

The white van stopped by the river, less than five minutes after the abduction of Louise. The badly bruised and beaten-up Georgie "the Elvis" and the sleeping Louise were carried from the van and put into the trunk of an awaiting red Toyota car that quickly drove off. The Japanese man who had pulled Louise into the van took off the Afro wig he had been wearing, along with his clothes, and threw them in the river. He put on a pair of running shoes, shorts, and a T-shirt and set off at a relaxed jogging pace. Moments later he was gone.

CHAPTER 54

Sunday, 17 February
Singapore

Maximillian had just gotten the call: the love bird was in the cage, finally. Now it would not take long for Richard to fall into the trap. Maximillian felt good. Finally, some things were going his way again, he thought.

During the past week he had completed the final touches to the documents, the ones that would seal Richard's fate, one of which was the letter to young Bernard Strydsteen. The letter would be sent from Richard's personal e-mail along with a signed letter in the normal mail. Better to be safe than sorry, Maximillian thought with a smile on his face. Yes, today was a good day.

Richard would type the e-mail and paper letter himself; they would make him do it. The text had been worded in such a way that any reader would understand that he had been helping the Strydsteen family in their business ventures for years, that he was their man in the bank. Maximillian had also prepared a funds transfer instruction addressed to Rossi & von Horstenbrik Cie Bank in Singapore, where Bernard Strydsteen requested his account be closed, stating that all the assets be transferred to a Swiss bank account in the name of Richard Lardelli. Maximillian had Richard's banking details, his account number and bank name at hand. He had gotten the information from the bank's human resources department.

He also had several blank A4 sheets of paper with Bernard's original signature. It was easy. He would just print the prepared text on the blank paper with Bernard's signature on it; it was much more credible to have the signatures in original. Also, he had given instructions to make sure that some of Richard's saliva and maybe a few pieces of his hair be found on the letter he signed—no blood—that would not be credible and would only raise suspicions.

The fund transfer instruction along with the e-mail and letter would prove that Richard was guilty—as guilty as one could be. Sure, there might be doubts raised by the Police. They could wonder all they wanted to; the e-mail, letter, and transfer instruction all linked Richard to the Strydsteen family.

And anyway, neither Richard nor that Elvis character would ever be found, so they would never be questioned. Lastly, the kidnapping of Richard's little goody-goody girlfriend from the church would be blamed on Richard. This would blow away any credible defense for Richard.

"Is it not wonderful with what you can do with a pen and paper?" Maximillian said out loud and smiled as he closed the door to his office and left.

He was happy again. It was Sunday afternoon, and the sun was shining—shining for him, of course. What was he going to do now? He decided to go down and get a massage. He had recently discovered a new massage parlor, where the masseuse was young and pretty and a happy ending was always guaranteed.

CHAPTER 55

Sunday, 17 February
Singapore

Detective Arvin Singh met Edwin in a small coffee shop on Upper Changi Road. Detective Singh reported the results of his investigative efforts and all that had happened since the disappearance of Richard Lardelli almost two weeks ago. Arvin had put three of his best people on the job. They had followed the two bald ang mohs, the ones who had chased Richard. They had also watched the house where Richard was supposedly staying, but without any sign of Richard. They had concentrated their efforts on the two bald ang mohs and had gathered many interesting facts about them. They had been able to learn their identities from the hotel staff. They had kept tabs on the hotel and had been able to follow the men around without blowing their cover. The two men had had several meetings with three Japanese gangster-looking fellows, all in the same bar in China Town. They had taken several photos of the group of men. The men had looked as if they were studying maps, and one of Arvin's staff had also been able to get so close to them that he had overheard some words. They had heard the Japanese men several times mention the names Richard-san and Elvis-san. Another name the Japanese had also mentioned was the name Maximillian-san. The two bald white men had never mentioned any names; they had just nodded their heads in agreement. It had been hard to pick up any parts of the conversation because everyone in the group spoke in Japanese.

At a later stage the group of men had met with an older banker-type man at a Starbucks coffee shop in the financial district. Arvin's men had taken several photos of the motley crew and their banker friend. Through detailed and hard investigative work, they had been able to gather that the banker was Mr. Maximillian von Horstenbrik, a renowned banker and chief executive officer of a Swiss bank in Singapore.

Arvin showed all the photos to Edwin and continued telling him the additional details about the identities of the Japanese men. Two of them were suspected to be affiliated with the *yakuza*, the Japanese mafia. Edwin studied the photographs. During his career in the police force he had been faced a few times with cases that involved the yakuza. One look at the pictures of the Japanese men and he was convinced that they were indeed yakuza. They all sported white suits, sunglasses, and permed hair. Lastly, he noted that two of the Japanese men were sporting another sign that could not be mistaken; both had one finger that was only half a finger, the end severed in a clean cut from the finger joint. Edwin knew, of course, that looks often deceive, but one look at these Japanese fellows together with the two giant bald Caucasian men with that distinct tattoo on their arm—the tattoo that said it all—and there could be no doubt. These guys were not the types he would want to meet on a dark street.

Arvin had done some investigative work on the Swiss man as well. He was in his late fifties, divorced, and had been in Singapore since the 1990s. His sources told him that he was a regular at many of the brothels and massage parlors down in the red-light district of Geylang.

"What a jolly bunch we have here, Arvin!"

Arvin looked at Edwin." Yes, you have to look for more troublesome company to keep. Really quite extraordinary, really."

Edwin gave instructions to continue the investigative work and to let him know as soon as there was any sign of Richard again. He also told Arvin that he wanted to take part in the investigation personally from now on. They both agreed that these people were probably planning something of a no-good nature. However, they knew it wasn't a crime to look at maps, sport a perm, or meet in a coffee shop.

Lastly on the agenda, Arvin told Edwin that he believed that Richard had left the country. A distant relative who worked at the Seletar Airport was sure he had seen someone who looked like Richard board a private plane there. The relative could not remember the exact date, but it had been at least ten days ago. The man had been shown a picture of Richard by Arvin himself, and the relative was quite sure that he had seen that man at Seletar Airport. So Richard was most likely not in Singapore anymore, Edwin and Arvin agreed.

"This gets stranger and stranger by the minute," Edwin told Arvin.

CHAPTER 56

Sunday, 17 February
Singapore

Richard and Prosper walked down Orange Grove Road toward Orchard Road. They walked past the Shangri-La Hotel, and Prosper almost got run over by a taxi that crossed their path as they passed the taxi exit of the hotel. Once on Orchard Road they walked down toward the Tanglin Shopping Mall. They had decided that they would have lunch in one of the restaurants there. It was just past 3:00 p.m. on this very hot Sunday afternoon.

They found a little lunch restaurant and ordered their food. Prosper was eager to find out what the hell Richard had been up to; after all, he had been impossible to reach for the last two weeks. Richard told him that he had been on a little trip to Borneo and Hong Kong, saying, "Just some little sight-seeing excursions, that's all."

"My dear Swiss friend, you are not telling me all there is to tell. I can see it in your eyes. That's OK, though. I am sure you had a good reason to go," Prosper said.

Richard did tell Prosper about the chase at the Mustafa Center and about the two bald giants who had followed him.

"Wow! Sounds exciting—just like a movie."

They had just finished their meal when Richard's mobile phone rang. It was Louise. She spoke in a terrified voice, and she was crying.

"Richard, please come at once. I am scared. They are going to hurt me unless you come now."

"Louise, where are you? Who is going to hurt you?"

He got no answer. Instead, a man's voice came on the phone, a voice that spoke English with a Japanese accent. In the background, he could hear Louise crying and screaming.

"If you want to see Louise again, you better come now," the voice said. "Do not tell anyone or contact the police. We will know if you do, *daijoubu*?"

The voice spelled out an address on Joo Chiat Road. Richard wrote down the address on a piece of paper.

"I am coming right now," Richard said. "Don't you dare do anything to Louise!"

Richard shouted to Prosper, "I have to go. Louise needs me, man."

"If you have to go, you have to go, my friend," Prosper replied.

Richard rushed out of the restaurant, leaving Prosper alone by the table drinking his coffee. This man definitely lives an interesting life, he thought as the waiter came over with the bill.

"Thank God I'm not single anymore," he said to himself as he stood up and left the money for the bill on the table.

Chapter 57

Sunday, 17 February
Singapore

Edwin had come home to his apartment just after 4:00 p.m. Arvin Singh was still with him. They had decided to continue talking and decide what to do next, and Edwin's home seemed a perfect place where they could talk undisturbed.

The doorbell rang, and Edwin made his way to the door to open it. In front of him stood two police officers in uniform and two officers in civilian clothing. Edwin knew the two civilian-dressed men well; they had been his colleagues for many years. The officers asked if they could come inside. In the minutes that followed, Edwin was told that his daughter was believed to have been kidnapped. The shock of the news caused Edwin almost to faint. Louise was all he had.

The officers started asking Edwin questions about Louise's habits, friends, ex-husband, lovers, enemies, and financial difficulties. Edwin had difficulty answering, but he did his best. So many times before he had been in the same situation, only he was on the other side of the table asking the questions. Edwin asked Arvin to stay with him; he needed the support of his friend, and also he thought that Arvin's work these past weeks might have something to do with the disappearance of his daughter. On the standard questions Edwin replied that, as far as he knew, Louise had no enemies, financial difficulties, or any other problems whatsoever. He told the officers about Richard and the private investigation they had conducted as well. It was at this time that Arvin got a phone call; it was one of his detectives.

The young Sikh named Raswinder was Arvin's nephew, and he was calling from an address on Joo Chiat Road. He had followed the target, the two bald Caucasian men, there that morning. The men had remained at the address for an hour or so and then left. The young Raswinder had been unable to follow them; his motorbike had failed to start. He had decided to remain at the address to wait and see if the men came back. After a while he had seen a man who was dressed like Elvis Presley exit the address, accompanied by three Japanese-looking men. He was fairly sure it was the same men he had seen before in the coffee shop in China Town with the two bald Caucasians. Arvin, who, at this point, had already turned on the loudspeaker function on his phone so the police officers could listen in, told Raswinder to continue his report. Raswinder continued and told his listeners that the group of the men had left in a white van. He described the van; he had taken the registration information, and it matched the van the police were currently looking for. Raswinder's bike had again failed to start, so he had decided to remain where he was. Raswinder continued his story and said that an hour or so later two of the Japanese men had come back driving a red Toyota car. They had unloaded two large cardboard boxes from the trunk; the boxes were marked Sony and looked to be heavy, and the two Japanese men seemed to struggle carrying them down the stairs and into the house. Raswinder then dropped the bomb, telling them that Richard had just appeared and had entered through the same door the Japanese had entered.

The elder of the two civilian-clothed police officers, experienced and effective, acted immediately. "That's them," he said. "We got them now!"

Within a few minutes, a special operations unit, together with the closest Police units, were on their way to the house on Joo Chiat Road.

CHAPTER 58

Sunday, 17 February, 4.18 p.m.
Singapore

Richard was sitting on a kitchen chair with his hands tied behind his back. He had been beaten several times in the face. The yakuza-looking man in front of him had been very violent; Richard had lost one tooth already. Louise and Georgie "the Elvis" were lying on the floor; they seemed to be sleeping, or, most likely, they had been drugged. Louise seemed to show no physical signs of being beaten; she was also fully dressed, so at least they had not laid their hands on her, Richard thought. Georgie, on the other hand, looked like he had been run over by a bulldozer; his face was all bruised, and his pants and shirt were all dirty.

When Richard entered the small apartment, he had immediately been punched in the face, and it had put him out stone cold. When he had awoken, he was tied to a chair and had a taste of blood in his mouth. The Japanese man in front of him was small in stature but punched like a boxer, not that he knew how it would feel to be punched by a boxer, but this was surely not far from it, he thought. The small man continued to scream at him in Japanese, "*Gaijin baka*," calling him a stupid foreigner in Japanese.

Richard again looked at the document that lay on the table in front of him. The other Japanese man untied Richards's hands. He then grabbed one of Richard's hands and rubbed it several times over the document. The other man then cut off some of Richard's hair, which was placed in an envelope. Richard again read the letter. So this was it? They were going to pin it all on him. It was a funds transfer instruction, signed by Bernard Strydsteen, instructing Rossi & von Horstenbrik Cie Bank in Singapore to close his account and transfer all assets in favor to a bank account in Switzerland, a bank account in the name of Richard Lardelli. This was the final spike in his coffin. Richard had no doubt about what they would do to him next. He just hoped they would spare Louise and Georgie, but he doubted it. Earlier they had forced him to send an e-mail from his personal e-mail account, and type a letter that he had then been forced to sign. In the letter he asked Bernard Strydsteen what he wanted to do with the money once it had been deposited in Richard's account in Switzerland. Richard realized that by smearing his hand on the letters and by having pieces of his hair, they wanted to try to be able to prove that he had sent the letter. Even if that did not work, the funds were being wired to him, and the e-mail tied him to the letter. Another blow struck his face just then, and he felt another tooth come out in the back of his mouth.

Suddenly, the door blasted open, and the room filled with smoke. Before he knew it, Richard was on the floor with his hands tied behind his back. He felt like a snail—no legs, no arms, and helpless. In the tumult that followed, he could make out police officers wrestling down the two Japanese gangsters; it was done in seconds. He saw them being led out of the room. He saw ambulance personnel tending to Louise and Georgie, and they were both placed on stretchers and taken away. A police officer spoke to him, but Richard could only see the man's mouth moving; he could not hear him. It must have been the noise from the blast that had knocked his hearing out, he thought. His mouth did not seem to listen to his brain, and he felt numb and short of breath. Suddenly, he felt a sharp pain in his chest. He gasped for air, but there was none. Then it all went black.

CHAPTER 59

Sunday, 17 February, 5.18 p.m.
Joo Chiat Road, Singapore

PR-One and PR-Two sat in the back seat of a taxi, and the taxi turned into Joo Chiat Road. The taxi stopped as there was traffic ahead of them. PR-One looked ahead and saw that there was a motorcycle police officer halting the traffic; the road was blocked. PR-One and PR-Two both saw the special operations police buses parked outside the house that kept the "merchandise". They looked at each other, paid the taxi driver the fare, and stepped out into the confusion on Joo Chiat Road. Several police officers were blocking the entrance to the house; PR-One and PR-Two saw ambulance personnel carrying out two stretchers, one with Louise and one with that Elvis character.

"Son of a bitch. That Elvis has more lives than a cat!" PR-Two told his partner. Their Japanese brothers-in-arms were handcuffed and sitting on the ground, surrounded by police. PR-One and PR-Two quickly made their way onto a side street and walked away from the scene. It was game over, and they knew it; they were professionals, and professionals know when it's over and how to take a loss. PR-One picked up a mobile phone from his pocket and called a number, a number he was only to use for emergencies.

Maximillian had just stepped out from the massage parlor. He felt relieved and relaxed; the ending had been happy, as always. It was late Sunday afternoon. Soon he would make his way down to Chancery Lane to the house of his ex-wife and see his daughters, as he always did on Sundays. Then the phone rang.

"Hello, Asian bird of prey?"

"Yes. Who is this?" Maximillian asked.

"Hunting Bird here."

"How did you get this number?"

"Shut up and listen!" the voice told him.

"So tell me the good news."

"You're screwed. Your bird, love bird, and singing bird are with the men in blue now. Game over."

"I do not understand."

"Game over. Operation over. Mr. Blue has them, and they will come after *you* now, get it? *Kaputt*, *schluss*, *finito*, *fine*, *fertig*, finished—get it?"

"What do we do now?" Maximillian asked.

"If I were you, I would leave now."

"Leave?"

"Yes, leave. Immigrate to an island where Mr. Blue cannot reach you. They will come for you, be sure, and they will come quickly."

PR-One ended the conversation, threw the phone in a garbage can, and joined PR-Two in an awaiting taxi. The taxi drove off in a hurry, destined for Tuas checkpoint and the Malaysian border. Maximillian took a taxi home, grabbed his special suitcase—the one he had reserved for emergencies. In it he had sufficient clothes for a few days, some cash, and a few passports. Money would not be a problem; he had enough to last him a lifetime, all deposited in several bank accounts all over the world, some in the country where he was going. He also brought with him his detailed book of other people's secrets, the journal he had kept and updated so meticulously over the years. He looked out the window one last time and looked at the Singapore skyline. The sun was setting, and time had run out. He left his penthouse apartment and hailed a cab outside his condominium. The taxi driver pulled away and drove toward the causeway and the Malaysian border.

CHAPTER 60

Wednesday, 20 February
Singapore

When Richard opened his eyes the first thing he saw was a man dressed in white looking down at him. Richard looked around and saw that he was in a hospital room. He was connected to several wires and tubes that led to a machine by his bedside, a machine that went beep, beep-beep.

The man introduced himself as Dr. Chan, and the pretty nurse introduced herself as Cindy. She had large breasts, and Richard could not help himself in looking at her cleavage.

Feeling better today, Mr. Richard, are we? Nothing wrong with your eyes, that's for sure," Dr. Chan said with a smile. He explained to Richard that he was in a hospital and that he was safe now. The doctor went on to tell him that he had suffered a severe heart attack and heart failure, and that he had been in and out of a coma for the past three days. "You are fine now, and your condition is stable. Had it not been for the quick intervention of the ambulance staff at the scene, you would not be here today, Richard. They saved your life."

Richard tried to think back. He remembered the house on Joo Chiat Road and how he had felt pains in his chest. "I remember seeing police officers talk to me, but then it all went black."

"You remember? That is good. It means you have probably not suffered any permanent brain damage," Dr. Chan replied.

"Great! That is a relief, doctor," Richard said.

"You must rest now Richard," the doctor said, and the nurse gave him an injection. Richard started feeling very pleasant, and then he fell asleep again.

When he awoke again it was nighttime, and he saw that it was dark outside. Dr. Chan again came over to his bed; Richard was the only patient in the room.

"How do you feel?" Dr. Chan asked as he looked at the funny machine that went beep-beep.

"Confused, but happy to be alive, doctor," Richard replied with a smile.

"Good. A smile is always the first sign of recovery." The doctor then went on to explain that they had run several tests. Richard's blood pressure was high, his liver values were bad, and his cholesterol levels were through the roof. "It's really a miracle that you made it so long, Richard." The doctor was no longer smiling. "From now on you will go on a strict diet. We need to get your cholesterol values down, and you will need to start taking medication for your blood pressure. You will also need to control your alcohol intake." The doctor gave Richard a friendly tap on the shoulder. "It's not forever, and it's not the end of the world, Richard. Think of it this way. Maybe this is a chance for you to start all over again, a new and healthier life. We will keep you here for a week or so, just to make sure that you will be OK," and with those words Dr. Chan left Richard to his own devices and thoughts, and think he did.

The next day two police officers in civilian clothing arrived at Richard's bedside. They introduced themselves as Inspector Koh and Inspector Sanjay. For the next two days Richard spoke to the two detectives. He answered all their questions as best he could. They never asked about Lawrence or the Tiger lady—their main interest was Maximillian and the hired abductors. After two days they left him alone. He did ask them at one time if he was a suspect and what had happened to Louise and Georgie. The detectives replied that it was an ongoing investigation—that was all they were at liberty to say. They did tell him however, that Louise and Georgie were fine; they had both been released from the hospital and were recovering at their respective homes. The inspectors also told him that he was not allowed to have any contact with the outside world; he would be confined to the hospital ward. Because the investigation was ongoing, it was for his own safety. It was best that he remain where he was without any contact with the outside world. The two detectives did allow, at Richard's request, for him to have a TV moved into his room, and he was allowed to read the newspapers.

The following days he spent in his bed, watching TV and reading newspapers. He had heard nothing from Louise or any of his friends. Dr. Chan told him that the Swiss Embassy had been contacted and had been informed of his whereabouts; the embassy had also notified his parents in Rome. The days passed by slowly, and time seemed to stand still in Richard's hospital room. He felt alone, and he wondered if Louise would ever want to see him after all of this. There were times when he thought he heard a knock on the door, and he imagined Lawrence entering his room and taking him away and saving him. It was ridiculous, he realized. Only a few weeks ago he had considered the man a social outcast and heretic, just like everyone else did, and now he thought Lawrence would save him, like a second father, a protector. At one time Richard contemplated that they had pumped him full of drugs and that he had imagined it all—the jungle, the long house, Lawrence, Louise—it all sounded like a pipe dream. If it was a dream, why did he remember it all? Maybe he would soon wake up on SQ348 back to Zurich and not remember a thing, just like in a dream.

CHAPTER 61

One Week Later, Wednesday, 27 February
Zurich, Switzerland

The shares of Rossi & von Horstenbrik Cie Bank had rallied on heavy trading volume the last few days. The share price had now reached a new all-time high. The buying of the shares had been particularly heavy the preceding week. On the previous Friday, during late-afternoon trade, something peculiar had happened. At around 2:00 p.m. someone had placed an astronomical-sized bid, an offer to buy Rossi & von Horstenbrik Cie Bank shares at a price 10 percent over the last traded price. The size of the buy order was huge; someone was willing to buy over 90 percent of the outstanding shares traded on the Zurich Stock Exchange at a premium to the market. At first, many had thought that it had been a computer error; nobody with a right, sound mind would offer to buy practically the whole stock offering of a traded share at a price above the market. Who had that kind of money? It was surely a mistake of some bank or broker, or some poor bank clerk with fat fingers had just added way too many zeros.

The bid stayed in the market, however, and eager shareholders started to sell, to hit the bid. It had not taken long; money moves fast, and everybody wanted to sell and take advantage of the outstanding price. Who doesn't want to sell to someone who was paying 10 percent more than the market? Sell they did, and in large volumes; the order was finally completed. Almost all stockholders, who had either held the shares for a long time or those who had only bought the shares in the recent run-up of the price, jumped at the chance to get out; there were still too many unknowns regarding Rossi & von Horstenbrik Cie Bank. Some of the novice shareholders had jumped at the possibility to sell; after all, it had been strange that the price of the shares had gone up so much recently, and the bank seemed to be heading for an imminent disaster. The head of the R & H Shareholders Club was one of the few that knew something the market did not know. He knew the reason why the shares had gone up—he also knew that the large bid in the market was no mistake. When the large offer to buy shares appeared in the market, the club directors called all its members and convinced them to sell their shares at the offered price; it was all according to plan. And sell they did.

At the end of trading that fateful Friday, only then did it occur to the financial press that someone had bought 90 percent of the outstanding common shares. Rumor had it that the large single order had come from one bank in Asia. Had someone in Asia just laid their hands on one of the oldest Swiss private banks? How was it possible?

Reinhardt Santorian, the bank's communications officer, called to the waiting press members to take their seats. The press conference took place at Rossi & von Horstenbrik Cie Bank headquarters in Zurich. The sudden press conference had been called that same morning. Some journalists, with their obligatory cup of coffee in hand, were still making their way into the room as Santorian began the press conference. He presented the chairman of the bank, Heinz von Horstenbrik, and passed the microphone to him. Flashes from reporters' cameras, along with the lights from all the TV crews that were broadcasting live worldwide, were all concentrated on the old chairman of the bank. The old man looked down on his feet and adjusted his tie, and then he looked out over the large crowd; it was time.

"We have called this press conference to announce to you some important information regarding Rossi & von Horstenbrik Cie

Bank and its ownership. As you well know, there has been speculation in the press for the last week that the ownership status of the bank has changed. Therefore, without further delay, we would like to communicate to you that this is true. The current ownership structure of the bank has changed. As you well know, well over 90 percent of the outstanding common shares of Rossi & von Horstenbrik Cie Bank were bought last week on the open market by two Asian entities. Holzstam and Son Ltd. bought 70 percent of the outstanding common shares, and 20 percent were bought by Blue Dragon Sai Kung Holding Enterprises Ltd. I also wish to communicate to you that this morning the von Horstenbrik family, in a separate and private sale, has sold 70 percent of their privately held shares to the same buyer, Holzstam and Son Ltd. A configuration chart of the new ownership will be handed out to you shortly. Holzstam and Son Ltd. is, effective this morning, the single largest shareholder with a majority of the voting rights.

"The new structure of ownership will lead to some major changes in the board and management of the bank, including myself, as I resigned from the bank this morning. The von Horstenbrik family will take a step back from the active management of the bank, and several of my family members resigned from the board of directors of the bank with me this morning as well."

The old man seemed to have tears in his eyes as he handed over the microphone to the communications officer, Reinhardt Santorian. A young TV reporter from an American news channel who was sitting in the first row saw her chance; she was not going to let this opportunity go. This was her day; she had been there since the morning to make sure she got a good seat. Her cameraman was in a strategic position so he could get both the young reporter's face and the chairman in the same camera shot; it was perfect. She stood up. "Mr. Chairman, this is Judith Smith from—" That was all she had time to say before the old chairman interrupted her.

"Miss Smith, I won't take any questions today. I am sure that you and your viewers will appreciate the fact that this is a very difficult time for me and my family. We will answer all questions at another time, and this press conference is now over."

The communications officer and the old chairman stood up and left the room. For the old chairman and the von Horstenbrik family, it was all over.

"Did you get it all OK? Could you hear me and then him saying my name? Did you get my name?" the young Miss Smith asked her cameraman.

"Yeah, I got it, babe. You looked great!"

Miss Smith smiled. Getting her name on global TV news meant everything for her. Who cared about some old Swiss gnome and his bank?

She positioned herself close to the stage, earpiece and microphone in place, waiting for the questions from the news anchor in their studio in the United States, all live, all in real time. While answering the questions, she made sure to mention her name at least two times in the two-minute segment: "This is Judith Smith reporting live from…" And, "This has been Judith Smith reporting…" The anchorman mentioned her name twice as well, and he even complimented her on her "excellent reporting." Judy knew that the anchorman's compliment on her live reporting came with a price. Oh, well, she thought. Everything in life has a price. She was on her way—look out, world!—a new name in intercontinental cable news had been born today, an expert in banking and European affairs.

The sensation was a fact. The new world was moving in on the old world. The renowned old Swiss bank had been bought by an Asian entity. Rossi & von Horstenbrik was the first, but surely not the last. The new paradigm was here and now.

CHAPTER 62

Thursday, 28 February
Singapore

Massimo Rossi turned off his laptop. He had watched the live broadcast of the press conference from his home in Singapore yesterday. The circle was complete: Rossi two, von Horstenbrik zero—game over. The von Horstenbriks had lost control of the bank, and it was only a matter of time before the remaining family members would sell their private shares—they would be left with no other choice. The presentation of the old promissory note to the von Horstenbrik family, along with the exile of Maximillian von Horstenbrik from Singapore, had finally sealed the deal. If news got out regarding the old debt and the already tarnished von Horstenbrik family name, the renowned banking family would be done for good. They had sold their shares. What else were they going to do? They had realized that it was game over and that it was better to get out while they still could.

The plan had worked almost to perfection—the setup of the Strydsteen family, the tip-off to the authorities regarding the seized ship in Marseille, the tip-off to the police regarding young Bernard Strydsteen's movements over borders, the successful highly discreet deal with the R & H Shareholders Club that they would sell their shares when the time was right, the tip-off to small speculators in Singapore and Hong Kong to start buying the shares. Lawrence and the Tiger Lady had started buying small blocks of the shares on the open market several weeks ago. However, the R & H Shareholders Club had wanted to sell at a premium, at least 40 percent over the then traded market price; only then would they sell their shares, they said. It would not have been credible if Lawrence and the Tiger Lady had placed a bid to buy 90 percent of the outstanding shares at a 40 percent premium over the market price; the markets would sense that something was up. To get the price closer to the agreed price, they had created a buzz in the market by tipping off some local Asian speculators. The news had spread fast—money moves fast—and it did not take much buying in the thinly traded stock to get the price up. The offer and agreement with the R & H Shareholders Club directors had been that if they sold their shares, they held the majority of the publicly traded shares, they not only would get a premium to the market price, but they would also be able to keep their jobs, and it was all for a worthy cause as well. The R & H Shareholders Club would be part of a project involving saving the rain forest—how could they refuse? Redundancy was the new norm in global financial institutions, so the offer that they would be able to keep their jobs was a sweet one that could not be refused, and they would make a profit as well—and bankers will be bankers. The plan had worked. Lawrence had created the crisis, gained control of the bank, and gotten the von Horstenbriks out of the picture. Massimo was pleased. It was a good day.

Maximillian von Horstenbrik was a mere memory. The Singaporean press reported that he was believed to have fled to Cambodia. Massimo did not care where he was as long as he was out of the picture. Massimo had avenged his grandfather and had reinstated the honor in the Rossi name. Soon things would be different in the bank. The Rossis were back in the game after having been gone for over a half a century. With Lawrence in command, they would grow and become a force to be reckoned with in the global financial market.

"*Oggi giustizia, domani il mondo*," (Justice today, tomorrow the world), Massimo shouted out in Italian as he slammed his fist on a table and smiled at his wife, Rosella.

Rosella looked at him then. She had seen the press conference as well and knew what it meant for her world. She looked at her husband and smiled. "Shopping?"

CHAPTER 63

Saturday, 2 March
Singapore

Richard had spent his time in the hospital reading the papers every day. He had learned of the Rossi & von Horstenbrik takeover. Lawrence and the Tiger Lady had stepped in and bought the whole thing. Somehow he was not surprised; the idea had been there in the back of his mind all the time. There was always something bigger to go after, a bigger goal to strive for, and he had been only a pawn in the larger game Lawrence had been playing. Lawrence had played them all: Richard, Maximillian, Massimo Rossi, the von Horstenbrik family, the Tiger Lady, the stock market, the speculators, the Rossi & von Horstenbrik shareholders, the media. They had all had different motivations for their actions, and he had capitalized on that and had steered them all his way. The end result had been, of course, to gain control of the bank.

Richard read in the papers that Massimo Rossi had been elected the new chairman and CEO of the bank globally, and that he would be based in Singapore. Little was mentioned in the papers about Lawrence and Holzstam and Sons Ltd., besides them being the new owners with every intention to expand the bank's business globally, especially in Southeast Asia.

The two detectives had visited Richard again and told him that the investigation was finished. Maximillian von Horstenbrik had effectively fled the country and was suspected of being in Cambodia. Interpol was collaborating with the Singaporean police force in the investigation, and they were hopeful that they would soon locate and apprehend Maximillian, along with the two bald-headed European hit men he had hired; they were also believed to have fled to Cambodia. The two Japanese men who had been arrested for the abduction of Louise and Georgie "the Elvis" were in custody and would be charged with a multitude of counts against them, including kidnapping, causing harm, etc. They also informed him that he was not a suspect, they had kept him in isolation only for his own protection.

Maximillian von Horstenbrik and his involvement in the case had been mentioned at length in the local press. He was suspected of being the mastermind behind the kidnapping plot, and he was also suspected of falsifying documents and criminal breach of trust. One of the newspapers had dedicated several pages to describing the lifestyle of the once high-flying ang moh banker in Singapore, including pictures of his penthouse, the names of the jet-setters he used to spend time with, and his supposed interests in the red-light district. Richard was not surprised to see in one tabloid that an Asian investor having bought a Swiss bank carried little weight among the headlines, nor was he surprised that the life and sexual exploits of Maximillian von Horstenbrik had created major headlines—sex and gossip sell tabloids, after all.

There was also little mention of Louise and her father's role in the whole story. Richard had learned from the two investigators that had it not been for Edwin, Louise's father, and a certain private investigator, Richard would most likely not have been here today. It had been Edwin who had tipped off the police on Richard's location, and he had provided the facts and details that led to the arrests and intervention at Joo Chiat Road. Georgie "the Elvis" Fernandes had been featured in a lengthy article in one of the local evening papers, with a photo of himself dressed as Elvis. Same old Georgie, Richard thought. Georgie Fernandes was reported to be promoting his new band, called "Not Just Elvis".

Later that day he was able to leave the hospital. He checked into a serviced apartment hotel, not far from Orchard Road. He had tried several times to call Louise, but she was not taking his calls or answering his e-mails. Why would she after all that she had gone through, and all because of him.

CHAPTER 64

Thursday, 7 March
Singapore

On the fifth day of Richard's stay in the apartment hotel, Prosper visited him, and they sat by the pool and talked for hours. Richard was happy to see that at least he still had one friend in the world. After some small talk, Prosper proposed that they should go for a drink. "You need to get out of here. A change of scenery is what you need, my crazy friend from the jungle."

Five minutes later they sat in a taxi.

The taxi stopped on Circular Road just behind Boat Quay. "Are you taking me to Midnight Oil?" Richard asked Prosper.

"Maybe, maybe not," was his reply.

They walked down Boat Quay Lane, a walk Richard knew so well. They walked past Harry's Bar, past Texas Longhorn, past BQ Bar, and finally arrived at Midnight Oil.

They were all there; the beer garden was full of people. Richard saw Matt, Giorgio, Georgie "the Elvis," Jonas, the Ghandi twins, the taxi boys from Fullerton Bay Hotel, Youssef, Eric the night trader from the bank, the Gurkha man from the Mustafa Center, Louise's father, Edwin, with Louise's uncle, Arnold, a Sikh with a red turban who Richard knew by now, and last but not least, Louise. Georgie "the Elvis" saw Richard and Prosper first and yelled out, "Tarzan is here!"

Louise stood up and walked toward Richard to greet him. She looked more beautiful than ever, and Richard did not know what to do, or what to say. Maybe she was mad at him, he thought. But he did not have to wait long to find out. She smiled and kissed him on the mouth quickly, and they hugged each other in a long, warm hug. Matt and Giorgio started yelling, "Kiss, kiss, kiss," and there was nothing else to do, so they kissed again, and this time properly.

"I am so glad you are here and safe. I have missed you a lot," she said to Richard. Those words were the best words he had heard in weeks, maybe the best so far in his life.

It all made sense now; it was right—no regrets—and it was happening now. It was this moment he had wanted to be in ever since he had made his mind up to leave it all and come back to Singapore, back to her.

They walked hand in hand and sat down at the table with Louise's father, her uncle, and the Sikh in the red turban. Richard remembered the tall Sikh man.

"Hello, I am Arvin Singh. Remember me from the Mustafa Center?" The Sikh spoke with a strong Indian accent.

"Yes, of course," Richard replied. "I should have stopped when you tried to help me that day."

Edwin then explained that it was he who had hired Arvin Singh to follow Richard, and it was thanks to Arvin that they had all been saved that fateful day on Joo Chiat Road.

"I cannot thank you enough. There are no words that could express the gratitude that I owe you," Richard said to Louise's father and Arvin.

"Shut up and drink!" Louise's uncle shouted out. He was already red-nosed and raised his glass with a smile. "Today is Thursday, not Sunday, and my brother Edwin here can say nothing lah! Cheers!"

They all toasted their glasses, and Louise's uncle left the table and went to the bar to get more beers.

"You have to excuse my brother. He does not get out that much," Louise's father remarked.

"He is a good man," Richard replied.

Richard then asked Edwin why he had gotten the idea to hire a private detective and follow him. Edwin explained that the main objective had been to help Louise get over Richard.

"I wanted to be able to tell her that you had moved on and that you were seeing some other woman. When we realized that you were really in some sort of trouble, we increased the surveillance." Edwin gestured toward Arvin.

"When we lost you that day at the Mustafa Center, we concentrated our efforts on the men who were following you instead, and it was a blessing that we did so," Arvin filled in. "When Louise was kidnapped and brought to the house on Joo Chiat Road in a box, our man who was watching that address contacted us, and the rest you know."

During the conversation, Louise held Richard's hand tightly under the table.

"I hold no grudges against you, Richard. On the contrary, the reason you were followed was merely because I was concerned about my daughter. She is all I have, and you understand that." Edwin looked Richard straight in the eye. "I just want my daughter to be happy. Is that so strange?"

They all saw tears form in Edwin's eyes, and he quickly wiped them away.

The jolly uncle, Arnold, who was getting jollier by the minute, tried to lighten the mood a bit. "See, old cop he is lah. Inside he big softie lah."

Richard looked Edwin straight in the eyes and told him," Sir, for what you have done for me, there are not words enough to express my gratitude. You saved my life, and a mere thank you is not enough. How could I ever repay you?"

Edwin, who had recovered from his momentary lapse of emotional weakness, smiled at Richard, raised his glass, and put it against Richard's pint glass. "I'm sure we can think of something. I always wanted to go to Borneo, you know," and they all laughed together.

The head of the Fullerton Bay Hotel door staff came over just then and handed Richard a key to one of the hotel suites. As he handed Richard the key, he smiled and said, "A little something from all of us at the door…Rossi & von Horstenbrik—that was a good one. What a run-up in price. We all sold at the top. Great pick. Great pick indeed." After shaking Richard's hand several times, he excused himself saying, "Have to get back to the hotel now. Hope you enjoy your stay."

"Is that for you and me, Richard?" Louise whispered into Richard's ear as she looked down at the hotel key.

"Yes, it is, "Richard replied, smiling.

"So what will you do now, Richard? I assume you will stay in Singapore?" Edwin asked. "Do you have a new job yet?"

Richard could not tell him that he was going to work for Lawrence—at least that was what he hoped. "I have a very interesting lead that I am following now, sir," Richard replied as diplomatically as he could.

Arvin Singh, who had been quiet most of the time, now made his voice heard. "Just make sure you let us know where you are. It makes it so much easier for us to follow you, you know."

Richard and Louise laughed. Edwin and Arvin did not; maybe they were still planning to follow him. After a moment of silence Edwin and Arvin started laughing, and they looked at Richard. "We had you there for a moment, did we not?" Arvin said as he continued laughing.

"Yes, you got me," Richard replied. He was not all convinced, though, that they were joking. Maybe it was not such a bad thing to have someone be concerned about you after all, he thought, and who better to look after you than an ex-police officer and a private detective, who are also friends.

The hours passed by, and the happy gathering got louder and merrier as night slowly set in; it was now dark outside. Richard at one time switched tables to join his friends, Matt, Prosper, Giorgio, and Georgie "the Elvis." Matt was extremely happy to see Richard again and suggested that they should all do tequila shots. Richard knew that he could not deny his friends, so tequila it was. Richard had one shot, then turned his attention to Georgie "the Elvis."

"How are you, Georgie? I am so sorry for all that happened," Richard said.

"Don't be sorry, man. Be happy. Thanks to you, my career is alive again. I was in the newspapers, you know," and Georgie pulled out a newspaper clipping and showed it to Richard. "I'm back," he said and tapped Richard on the shoulder. He had that spark in his eye that only Georgie "the Elvis" had, a glimpse of hope and victory. He had been down and out so many times in life, but Georgie "the Elvis" had always come back.

"Yeah, you are back, Georgie!" Richard said.

He did not get much of chance to speak to Giorgio; he was busy chatting up some barmaid from one of the neighboring bars. All he heard was Giorgio telling her about the fabric his shirt was made of. "Italian silk from the town of Alba. Look. Feel it. It's so soft. It's very exclusive, you know. My family has been friends with the owner of the factory for many generations. Look. See the initials GDM here? Those are my initials; it stands for Giorgio de Matti. It's a very old noble name. My father is a duke—do you know what a duke is?" The girl touched his shirt, smiled, and giggled, all while playing with her hair. Richard left Giorgio to what he did best: pick up girls.

Prosper was sitting at the same table and was involved in a heated conversation with the Ghandi twins over the topic of Indian independence from the British. One of the Ghandi twins was pointing his umbrella at Prosper. Come rain or shine, the Ghandi twins were famous for their multiple and innovative uses of the umbrella. One of the twins did not share Prosper's view that colonialism had been good for India. Prosper had irritated the twins with a comment on the "Save the Rain Forest" jackets, which had been given to them by Eric, the night trader. Prosper had really irritated the more hot-blooded of the two twins with the comment, "Ghandi never wore rain jackets, did he?" and "Does it rain in India?" Luckily, the other Ghandi twin was not so hot-blooded, and soon they would all laugh together again; it was always like this.

Matt had continued doing tequila shots with Jonas, and by the looks of the empty glasses on the table, Matt would surely fall asleep soon under the table.

Georgie "the Elvis" suddenly stood up and proposed a toast. "To Tarzan and Jane, to Richard and Louise!" Georgie had started calling Richard Tarzan after hearing about Richard's adventure in the jungles of Borneo.

"To Tarzan and Jane…To Richard and Louise," the crowd joined in.

Only Louise's father kept quiet during the toast. It was probably a bit too much for him to handle that his daughter was being compared to Jane, the bride of Tarzan, the ape-man.

Suddenly a small boat appeared out of the darkness on the Singapore River. It steered toward the quay by Midnight Oil. Richard saw that it was Massimo Rossi, accompanied by Situ the Iban standing on the front of the boat. Massimo called out, "*Ciao*, Richard! Ready to face the real enemy?"

The boat pulled up alongside the quay, and Massimo gestured to Richard to get on board. "Miss Louise, can I borrow Richard for a while? Not to worry. It's completely safe. I will bring him back within the hour," Massimo said.

"You better!" Louise answered. She approached Richard then and whispered in his ear and squeezed his hand. "Give me the keys to the hotel. I'll wait for you there."

Richard jumped aboard the boat, and the boat pulled away. Richard saw his friends waving at him.

"You better come back. There are plenty more drinks here. Prosper promised me that you guys would be here all night!" Jonas shouted at him.

Massimo showed Richard to a seat on the back of the boat, and they both sat down next to each other. "We have much to talk about, you and me, in the following days, Richard. Now sit back and enjoy the ride. We will soon be there."

The boat chugged up slowly toward the river inlet by the large Fullerton Hotel, and it picked up speed as they raced toward Marina Bay Sands Casino. They passed the giant casino and hotel structure on their right, which had become one of Singapore's landmarks. Soon they were out on the open water, a fresh, hot, salty breeze blowing in their faces; the boat was going very fast now.

Then he saw her. The boat was, at first, just a distant shadow, but then, as they came ever closer, he recognized it: *The Jolly Bachelor II*. Lawrence was here. He had to be here. If his boat was here, he was here too. The old wooden yacht laid at anchor, and the crew on deck signaled them to approach slowly. Two minutes later their small speedboat had pulled up alongside the old yacht, and a wooden ladder was lowered from the deck.

"You first," Massimo said to Richard as he secured the ladder on the deck of the small boat.

"Look Richard, your friend from the water, over there! " Massimo called out. Sure enough, a few meters away, in the water, treading water, was the old fisherman that a few weeks ago had saved his life. The man gave a thumbs up to Richard, Richard responded with the same gesture. The circle of events was nearing completion.

A few moments later Richard stood on the deck of the old yacht, where Jones, the old butler, greeted him. "Hello, Mr, Richard. So good of you to drop in on us. He is waiting for you in the tent."

There, ahead of him, the Bedouin tent had been erected on the foredeck of the yacht. It was not enough that Lawrence had come all the way here from Borneo on a boat, but he had brought the tent as well—of course he had; he was Lawrence of Arabia. Richard walked toward the tent and entered into it. Just like the tent in the jungle on Borneo, two small cherry blossom trees in large ceramic pots stood on each side of the tent opening, in full bloom.

The inside was dimly lit by lanterns and candles, and Lawrence sat on a cushion in the middle of the tent. He gestured to Richard to take a seat in front of him. Richard sat down in silence and waited for Lawrence to speak; he was the master. Lawrence removed his Bedouin head-cloth, poured himself a glass of water, and looked straight at Richard. Those bright-blue eyes of his seemed to enter Richard's soul. After looking at Richard in silence for a while, he spoke.

"Welcome, my dear Richard. Good to have you here."

"It's good to be here, sir. You are truly an amazing man, sir."

Richard tried to act calm and in control with a cool, steady voice and straight posture. It was all to no avail, however. The man who sat on the cushions in front of him saw right through him, like a father to a son, a son to a father. All the fears, all the thoughts, all the mysteries, they would all be solved now, for good or bad. Richard felt naked like a newborn. Maybe this is how we feel when we are born, he thought. We just don't remember it. Maybe we don't remember for a reason, or maybe we do remember, but we have chosen not to recollect those precious moments of destiny.

"I just do what…I can do. Now sit down, Richard. You are shaking like a leaf."

It was true. He was shaking, but not from cold. It was probably his body that was starting to send him signals, "Attention, attention! Fear and uncertainty ahead." He knew his body and how it worked; it was all part of his anxiety disorder.

"Yes, you truly did, sir. You had planned all along to buy Rossi & von Horstenbrik, had you not, sir?"

"Yes, that was one of my goals, but not the only one. You see, Rossi & von Horstenbrik was merely a part of my plan, and certainly not the end game. It is, as you say, a means to arrive at my goal, or, as Machiavelli said, the end justify the means. You see, you, Massimo Rossi, our charming common friend in Hong Kong—the one you call the Tiger Lady—the shareholders, the Strydsteen family, Maximillian von Horstenbrik , and countless others all played a part, some knowingly, others unknowingly. You see, if you want change, you must know the players in the game—if you want to win, that is. You must play them against each other; this is how you win in any game. All players have their own agendas and motivations in playing any game, and if you know what those are, you are in a much better position to win the end game. You let them play against each other and do the job for you. By knowing all my opponents and allies—their motivations, their aspirations, their fears, their friends, their families, their lovers, their spouses, and their enemies—the advantage was mine. It's not that hard to master the game, and that was my game plan. By setting up the Strydsteen family, one thing led to another. The ball was in motion, and people are so predictable. A wise man or woman will go for the end game—a donkey will always go for a carrot. Now that the von Horstenbriks are gone, the Rossi family is back in power. I bought myself a bank, and you got your freedom back. And they all lived happily ever after, right?"

"I don't know what you mean, sir. I don't understand, what is the end game then? What about your people and the rain forest?"

Lawrence started laughing.

"Aha, you are a little wise…and definitely not a donkey. Let's not get caught up in the details on how the plan was achieved. In fact, the less you know, is probably better and safer for you. Let's concentrate on what's going to happen now, shall we?"

"By all means. You are the master, and I am listening."

The man was truly a master. Every move of all the players in the game had been anticipated in advance. How? Because he had planned it all. Lawrence knew how each one of them would react and act, given certain circumstances, often ones that he had orchestrated.

"As we speak, a trust foundation is being formed, a trust foundation to secure the safety and future of my people on Borneo and in the other areas. Yes, I never told you that we have areas in Africa and South America as well. The foundation will be so powerful that anyone who chooses to oppose us will think twice. It will have vast economic means, and the first deposit into the foundation's account will surpass $10 billion. It is a mere fraction of my wealth. More will be deposited as need arises. Money needs a home. Enter Rossi & von Horstenbrik Cie Bank; this is why I needed the bank. Massimo Rossi wanted to avenge his grandfather and reclaim the power the Rossis once had. The Tiger Lady wanted to avenge her father and needed a bank for her business ventures in Macau and Hong Kong. You see it all ties in. We all had our motivations."

"That's great. Where do I come in?" Richard asked.

"I want you to work for the foundation. To be stationed here in Singapore—my eyes to the world, so to speak. Or would you prefer the jungle? All bodies of movement have a heart. I have chosen a little red dot on the map to be the center of my activities, a red dot on the map called Singapore. How do you feel about that?"

"I say yes. But you knew the answer already. Of course I want to help you and work for you, and yes this city is home for me…at least for now"

"Good. Then it is settled. Now, I want you to go back to that lovely young lady waiting for you. Love waits for no one. Don't miss the boat, Richard. In fact, there is a boat waiting for you outside right now. Go now!"

The old man lit two white candles on an old wooden chandelier next to him.

"Two candles, Richard, one for me and one for you. Soon there will be three, then four, then more and more. The chant has just begun, dear Richard. The path is long. Have no doubt, we will prevail."

"Thank you, sir. I will not let you down. Good-bye then."

"See you soon, and remember, nothing is written in the stars until you write it, Richard!"

"I'm writing now, sir. This is my book of life, and no one else can write it for me!"

"Truly, you are learning fast. Go now and write your book of life!"

As Richard was leaving the tent, Lawrence pressed play on his old tape recorder, and the sound of a military march filled the tent.

"*Marcia Carolus Rex*, the march of Charles XII of Sweden."

"What about the theme from *Lawrence of Arabia*? What happened?" Richard asked.

"Well, nobody is perfect." Lawrence responded.

CHAPTER 65

Friday, 8 March, 1.18 a.m.
Singapore

Richard left Midnight Oil. Things were getting messy, and it was best to leave before Jonas put the "Sorry, we're closed" sign up in time for the real party to start.

He had a life now. It was time to go home. Someone was waiting for him at home now. It was time to grow up, time for Richard to be himself. He walked back toward the hotel. The streets were empty now, and Boat Quay was going to sleep. He thought about how far he had come in these past weeks. He had accomplished something; he was a part of something now. He was not alone anymore, and he was in love. He had started therapy for his anxiety and OCD issues as well. It was all coming together—the past, him, Louise, his friends, his health, Lawrence—and it was all real. He was home now, and he knew it, and when you know, you know.

Richard opened the door to the hotel room, and he called out to Louise, who responded, "I'm here in the bathroom taking a bath. Want to join me?"

Richard sat down on the large double bed for a moment. He reached into his pocket and took out little Mary's special rock along with the small gift box, the one he had carried with him since he had left Zurich airport, the one that meant everything. He put both under one of the pillows. A soft package lay on the bed next to him, and there was an envelope on top with his name on it. He opened it and read the note inside:

Dear Richard,

I enjoyed our talk tonight. Please accept this gift. It will help you concentrate on what's important and on what lies ahead. This will help you understand. It will help you clear out any doubts and distortions in your mind. It will help you in curing your anxiety and obsessive-compulsive disorders. It will help you concentrate on the future, and it will help you perform tonight. It will help you be who you were meant to be. I know you will understand.

Kind regards,
"Lawrence"

Richard opened the package, undid the paper wrapping, and pulled out the contents: a white Arabic desert Bedouin linen with a head-cloth. If it was good enough for Lawrence, it was good enough for him, he thought. He got undressed, put it on, and looked in the mirror on the wall. "So is this what I have become? The story repeats itself. *No*, this is my story, my book of life, and only I write it!" he said aloud to the mirror. The mirror did not reply in agreement. Just like in real life, we can ask all we want, but the answers to the important questions we have to find ourselves, and we truly never know what lies ahead; all we can do is to do well and wish for the best. We will make mistakes and fall down along the way, but we must learn to always get up again and to learn from our mistakes; that's what's important. Some of us will have the fortune or misfortune in life to once look into the abyss, that bottomless pit, to face our fears, to choose between losing it all or gaining it all, to taste the real spice of life, to taste the price, to perhaps have to choose between two evils, and to make a choice, however terrible it seems. Sometimes it takes the end of a life to create a new life, a new set of circumstances, a new start. Those who have been there all know that their lives will never be the same again. In the end, we are the result of not just our victories, but also our shortcomings, our mistakes, and our failures. Some of the greatest leaders, movements, nations, and inventions have been born out of mistakes or failures. The greatness is creating something good out of it, something that helps more than just yourself, and never looking back—this is the game and the life of giants. At the end of the day, week, month, year, and lifetime, what makes a great person is not what he or she did right; it is what the person did when faced with danger, fear, failure, mistakes, and adversity—why he or she did it and whose life they touched along the way. This is why we remember people.

Richard opened the door to the bathroom just then, and Louise was lying in the hot, steaming water, covered in white foam.

"Oh, kinky. I did not know you were like that...I like your outfit!" Louise said.

Richard was about to say something, but he was interrupted by Louise.

"Nobody is perfect. I have secrets too. If it works for you, it works for me...Now, my man of the desert, get in the tub!"

THE END

EPILOGUE

Two Months Later

The two Singaporean technicians removed the Rossi & von Horstenbrik Cie Bank sign outside the bank entrance and replaced it with a new sign that read Rossi & Holzstam Cie Bank (Singapore) Ltd.

Thousands of miles away on a large boat out at sea, Joseph Salwa and Mustafa al Taqwa stood on the deck of the large ship. The fresh sea breeze blew in their faces. The sun was shining, and they had just eaten a big lunch in one of the restaurants on board. They were two of the 101 survivors from the SS *Botaki Star*—the human cargo that had been seized in the harbor of Marseille almost one year ago. Now, along with their families, they were on their way to a new future and a new beginning. An anonymous benefactor had organized and paid for their trip to a new country far away, and this time they traveled not as cattle below deck but as human beings. They had been offered jobs working in the construction industry, more precisely to build villages in the jungle. The benefactor had said that they would help build a new country, a country not defined by borders or government, but a country where they would be free to choose their own destinies. They had also been allowed to bring their families. They had heard that the land was called Lawrenceland, but they had not found it on the map. But then again they did not care for maps; besides, it was a new country. Upon arrival on the ship, the wise old white man in Bedouin clothes had spoken to them on a large video screen, "Come and live your lives, prosper, and create your own destinies. Bring your families; people make people, not borders or governments. Help me save something that is worth living for: it's called life. Together we will build a place where the unfree are free and the misunderstood are understood."

Youssef, the ex-gardener, sat on a motorcycle behind Detective Arvin Singh, who was driving. The motorcycle was traveling on a busy road somewhere in the center of Singapore. The pair kept a safe distance from the car they were following. Arvin Singh communicated to Youssef via the radio set that was installed in their helmets: "Now that you are a detective, watch and learn. Always keep your distance from the objective. Got it?"

"You mean like you kept your distance from me and Richard?" Youssef asked wittily.

"You were always a smart and eloquent one, now you can use that knowledge!"

In Lugano, Switzerland, Rosella, the wife of Massimo Rossi, opened the entrance door to the discreet clinic that had been recommended to her. She had made up her mind. It was now or never. Time was running out, and her stomach seemed to be getting bigger by the day. The seed had been sown; the only problem was that it was not Massimo's seed that grew inside her.

Young Yann von Horstenbrik closed the door to Massimo Rossi's office behind him. He could not understand it. He had been asked to stay with the bank in Singapore, but why? He was the only von Horstenbrik family member left in the bank worldwide. Mr. Rossi, as the new CEO, had advised him that Lawrence wanted him to stay on, that he still had a part to play—that was, if he wanted to. He had of course said yes, but now that he closed the door behind him, he wondered what the old man had in mind for him—what did "a role to play" mean? On top of this, Richard had invited him for drinks down at Boat Quay later that day. Yann went to his office, closed the door behind him. He tried to make sense of it all, he found few answers, the world as he knew it had been turned upside down.

The older woman in the blue dragon silk dress watched the young dealer at the baccarat table hand over to the older dealer. The young, handsome man had finished his shift. She studied the young man as he walked away from the table, like a tiger studying its prey. She had a perfect view of the casino floor from her vantage point inside the large tinted glass cubicle that hung from the ceiling high above the casino floor. "I want him tonight," she said, and she sat down on the bed and removed her dress. "I see everything, and no one sees me," she said as she removed her shoes.

The two discreet security guards on the casino floor heard the voice of the madame in their earpieces. It took them only five seconds to stop the young dealer. "She wants you tonight. Time to step up," they told him. The young dealer understood the meaning. He was new, and it was his turn to be broken in. And it was her casino, her money, her profit.

It was the middle of the night in Singapore, and the city was asleep. The elevator in the high-rise skyscraper in the financial district stopped on the sixty-second floor. Jones, the old butler, walked into the new, large, empty office, the headquarters of Lawrence's Singapore operations. He approached the large window and looked out over the city. He lit the two candles in the old wooden chandelier on the window ledge—two candles only.

The two watchmen on the boat that laid at anchor in the Singapore Straits saw the signal from the sixty-second floor. The younger of the two men approached the tent on the foredeck of the boat and entered. "The signal has been sighted, sir," he said to the old man seated on the cushions.

"Very well. So this is how it starts. *Les jeux sont faits*," (the bets are placed) he answered in French.

"Would you like me to send a reply, sir?" the young man asked.

"Three candles. Three candles only—anchors away!" the old man answered.

"Destination?"

"Home—home to where the story began" the old man answered.

The plan was moving ahead; this was only the beginning.

The old fisherman on the little boat saw the signal from the distant yacht. Three candles, three lights, three stories, one beginning, and one end. He took out the boat-axe, and with a powerful blow, struck a hole in the old wooden hull of the little boat. He took out a little porcelain container that contained the ashes of his departed father—he opened the container, put it in the water and let go. He painted his face red and blue in colored tribal facial paint. He painted one side of his face red, the other side blue. He threw his old Motorola mobile phone into the water, along with all his life belonging's. As water started entering through the hole in the hull of the small boat, he got undressed naked. He jumped into the water as the boat started sinking. He started swimming, not towards the Singapore shoreline, but in the opposite direction, towards the open sea and his island. He was free now, he was going home—home to where his story began. One last journey with his faithful friend—he was not alone. A friend who was old like himself, and who also saw everything in two colors.

Many miles away in a different country, an elderly Caucasian gentleman was sitting poolside, sipping on a Singapore Sling cocktail. He was accompanied by two young topless girls who spoke little

English, but they knew how to use their mouths in other ways, and in ways the elder man preferred. The man's mobile phone rang.

"Hello."

"Hello, Asian bird of prey?"

"Yes."

"We are ready to go. Your bird and love bird have been located again."

"Do it…Go for it!"

He let the girls continue. He looked at the mirror that was positioned close to the sun bed, positioned so he could see himself and the girls and what they were doing. His mind took a mental picture of their work on his body—arousal complete, he entered bliss. He smiled at the mirror, and his reflection smiled back.

"I'm back," he said and laughed.

AUTHOR BIOGRAPHY

Cristian A.E. Guler grew up in Europe and Asia. He holds a BS in business administration; is fluent in English, Swedish, German, and Italian; he also possesses additional knowledge of several Asian languages. He worked for twenty years in the banking and financial industry. After ten years as a foreign exchange trader and investment specialist for several leading financial institutions in various global financial centers, as well as ten years as a private banker in Switzerland and Singapore, Cristian decided it was time to step out of the comfort zone and pursue his passion for writing and art. In 2014, he founded his own company dedicated to publishing, multimedia, and the arts. *The Quiet Ang Moh* is Cristian's debut novel.

46928601R00191

Made in the USA
Charleston, SC
24 September 2015